Nicholas Dickson

The Bible in Waverley

Sir Walter Scott's use of the Sacred Scriptures

Nicholas Dickson

The Bible in Waverley
Sir Walter Scott's use of the Sacred Scriptures

ISBN/EAN: 9783337094171

Printed in Europe, USA, Canada, Australia, Japan

Cover: Foto ©Andreas Hilbeck / pixelio.de

More available books at **www.hansebooks.com**

THE BIBLE IN WAVERLEY

THE

BIBLE IN WAVERLEY

OR

SIR WALTER SCOTT'S USE OF THE

SACRED SCRIPTURES

BY

NICHOLAS DICKSON

EDINBURGH

ADAM AND CHARLES BLACK

1884

CONTENTS.

Contents.

INTRODUCTION.

DURING the last illness of Sir Walter Scott at Abbotsford, we are told by his biographer and son-in-law, Mr. Lockhart, that the great novelist, feeling a little brighter and better one morning, desired to be placed by the central window of the library that he might be able to look down upon the Tweed. Pleased with the sight of the river which he loved so well, and soothed by the murmur of its waters, the invalid next expressed a wish to have something read to him. On being asked what book he would like, "Need you ask?" he replied, "there is but one." The Bible was accordingly brought, and the fourteenth chapter of St. John's Gospel was read. "Well, this is a great comfort," Sir Walter remarked, as Lockhart closed the book, "I have followed you distinctly, and feel as if I were yet to be myself again."

In the room where this incident occurred there were nearly twenty thousand volumes, all carefully classified and regularly arranged in cases round the walls—choice and costly works, in the richest bindings, and many of them gifts from the most illustrious men and authors of the time. Surrounded by such a great collection of books, repre-

B

senting all that was most interesting in literature, Sir
Walter felt that, for him at least, there was "but one."
As the days went slowly past, and as his weakness increased, the Bible was the only book through the reading
of which he derived either inward strength or consolation.
In the best sense of the expression, it was indeed the
means of helping him to feel himself again by freeing his
thoughts from all distracting cares, and preparing him
for the great change which he calmly and resignedly
set himself to face.

We shall be much mistaken if we associate Sir Walter
Scott's love and veneration for the Bible only with his
last illness at Abbotsford. From childhood he had
known the Holy Scriptures. Their divine truths had
been taught him by his affectionate parents, whose upright and virtuous conduct was ever in unison with the
religious principles they sought to instil into the minds
of all their children. When a boy at the High School of
Edinburgh, the rector on one occasion happened to ask
the dux of Scott's class if he could give an instance where
the word *with* is used as a noun and not as a preposition.
All were silent till the query reached the future novelist,
who at once replied by correctly quoting from memory
a verse from Judges sixteenth and seventh. "And
Samson said unto Delilah, If they bind me with seven
green withs that were never dried, then shall I be weak,
and be as another man." Thus early had the sacred
narrative made a deep impression on his memory. As
a youth, his imagination was kindled into poetic fervour
by the sublime passages in the Book of Job and the

prophecies of Isaiah. The precepts, promises, and prayers of God's Word were the guide and the stay of Sir Walter's manhood; and so, when age and adversity came upon him, it need excite no surprise that, though surrounded by his magnificent library, the author of *Waverley* should say in reply to Lockhart's question, "What book would you like?" "Need you ask? there is but one."

Having indicated how much the Bible was to Sir Walter Scott from his childhood all through a long and eventful lifetime, on to his declining days and death, it is natural to inquire if its influence can be traced in any of his writings, or if the Sacred History was of any literary assistance to him. It will not, we believe, be a difficult matter to answer either or both questions in the affirmative. If there be any difficulty in the matter at all, it lies, not in pointing out how much the author of *Waverley* owes to the Bible, but in bringing together into one readable whole the extraordinary mass of Scriptural allusions, references, and illustrations which are scattered in the richest profusion through every one of the Waverley Novels. Bishop Wordsworth in his interesting work, *Shakespeare's Knowledge and Use of the Bible,* remarks that the great dramatic poet was, "in a more than ordinary degree, a diligent and devout reader of the Word of God, and that he has turned this reading to far more and far better account than any of his critics would seem to have suspected, or at all events has yet attempted to point out." This is equally true of Sir Walter Scott. It is rather a matter of surprise that while almost every other characteristic of his writings has been fully criticised and commented upon, his knowledge and extensive use of the Bible should have been forgotten or overlooked.

No one who reads the Waverley Novels carefully and attentively, or reads them in any fashion indeed, can fail to be struck by the frequency with which Scriptural expressions and turns of thought are to be found in nearly every chapter. These expressions and suggested thoughts, however, form but a small part of Sir Walter's literary use of the Bible. Many of its truths and narratives, as we shall see further on, are illustrated in a way that is at once delightfully fresh, new, and clear. It is possible, without any straining whatever, to apply to almost every novel of the series some particular Scriptural lesson or truth which receives a new and interesting exposition in the course of the story. Who can read the tragic tale of *The Bride of Lammermoor*, for instance, without being reminded of the sacred text, "Vengeance is mine; I will repay, saith the Lord." The Master of Ravenswood witnesses the dying agonies of his father, and hears the terrible curses breathed against the Lord Keeper. These curses seem left as a legacy of vengeance; and afterwards at his father's funeral we hear the Master swear that he will requite the ruin and disgrace that have been brought upon him. As the story proceeds, however, we feel that it is not to the unfortunate young man that vengeance belongs, but to God, who claims it as specially and peculiarly His own.

Ivanhoe is, we affirm with all reverence, a fine illustration of the inward strength and peace that are to be got from a strong and implicit trust in the divine promise, "Call upon me in the day of trouble; I will deliver thee." Readers of the romance will readily grant this as they recollect the many dangers and trials which beset the lovely heroine, her fervent prayers and devotions, and her final deliverance.

Waverley reminds us of the text, "Put not your trust in princes." *The Pirate* is an interesting illustration of the apostolic injunction, "Use hospitality one toward another without grudging." And so on through the rest of the series.

While each novel may thus be considered as forming an interesting illustration of some leading Scriptural statement, injunction, or promise, there is not, we think, the slightest evidence to show that Sir Walter had any special text in view when he began to write a new book. The story he has to tell flows forth as fast as pen or secretary can record it; but it takes colour and shape from the great wealth of sacred imagery and illustration with which his heart, his head, and his memory are all abundantly stored. He inverts the order of the preacher who specially announces the text or subject of his discourse before beginning the discourse itself. Scott keeps his to the last, and then, in effect, he says to his readers, "Now I have told you a story, but if you can get anything out of it more than mere amusement, it will be the source of much gratification to me." We recollect of only one instance in which Sir Walter mentions the Scriptural truth which has unconsciously been illustrated in the course of the story. It is at the close of *The Heart of Midlothian* where, before parting with his readers, he thus addresses them :—"This tale will not be told in vain, if it shall be found to illustrate the great truth, that guilt, though it may attain temporal splendour, can never confer real happiness ; that the evil consequences of our crimes long survive their commission, and, like the ghosts of the murdered, for ever haunt the steps of the male-factor ; and that the paths of virtue, though seldom those of worldly greatness, are always those of pleasantness and peace." It would be difficult, we believe, to find a more impressive illustration of the truth of the royal preacher's text, "Wisdom's ways are ways of pleasant-ness, and all her paths are peace," than the story of *The Heart of Midlothian.*

From a vast mass of material, the accumulated notes of many careful readings of the Waverley Novels, we now proceed to select as much as will let our readers see how frequently, and in what a variety of ways, Sir Walter enriches these charming works by his references and illustrations brought from the sacred narrative.[1]

---

[1] It may be opportune here to note that Scott was the author of two sermons, written with the kind intention of serving a young friend who was pursuing his theological studies. They were after-wards published, under the title of *Religious Discourses by a Lay-man,* and form part of vol. 30 of *Scott's Miscellaneous Prose Works.*

THE BOOK OF GENESIS.

AN incident in the story of *The Highland Widow* takes us back to the very beginning of the Sacred History. The Rev. Michael Tyrie, a kind and faithful minister, meets the widow in the glen, and in the conversation which follows, with reference to her unfortunate son, the name of God is incidentally introduced by the clergyman as the great Creator "who formed the earth and spread out the heavens." Then we pass on to a scene in *The Fair Maid of Perth* where, at the trial by bier-right in the church of St. John, Eviot, the young page of Sir John Ramorny, "swore by all that was created in seven days and seven nights . . . by the God and Author of all," that he was innocent of the murder of Oliver Proudfute the bonnet-maker.

It is true that through these two quotations we get only a mere glimpse of the sacred narrative, as recorded in the first chapter of Genesis; but we have to remind our readers at the outset that the object of our present study is not to seek and search for extracts in illustration of a continuous and unbroken narrative, but simply to point out the various ways in which the author of *Waverley* uses the Bible in the construction of his tales and romances. It may be that at times we come across only a simple reference; but, as we shall presently see, it may also be some great truth which necessarily arrests the novelist's attention, *as a novelist,* and which in his hands receives something new and fresh in the way of illustration.

The creation of man in the image of God is the first point at which Sir Walter pauses. In describing duels, battles, sieges, and assaults, he always lets us feel how sacred a thing, above every other consideration, is human life; and how dreadful it is to destroy, or attempt to destroy, the temple in which is enshrined the image of God. Duellists are frequently interrupted in their murderous work by some one who arrives on the scene, and stops the fight by appealing to their better feelings, and urging them to remember that it is the image of God they are doing their best to deface or destroy. In *The Abbot* there is a graphic account of the battle of Langside. When the two opposing parties come into close quarters, with their war-cries of "God and the Queen," and "God and the King" respectively, all political and military considerations are forgotten, and the feeling uppermost in Sir Walter's mind seems to be one of horror at the dreadful slaughter that is going on, as fellow-subjects shed each other's blood "and in the name of their Creator defaced His image." The wounded Ivanhoe is lying on a couch listening to Rebecca, who is describing to him the storming of Torquilstone Castle, which she witnesses from a latticed window. As the besieged hurl back their assailants, and as one after another falls in the assault, the terrified girl exclaims, "Great God! hast Thou given men Thine own image that it should thus be cruelly defaced by the hands of their brethren?"

There are other circumstances, however, than sieges and battles in which Sir Walter illustrates the sacredness of human life. The creation of man in the image of God is a fact which appeals to our common humanity and sympathy, when any of our fellow-creatures may happen to be placed in positions of imminent danger. Reuben Butler, in *The Heart of Midlothian*, on his way to visit Effie Deans in prison, meets an excited mob dragging Porteous off to execution. Being a clergyman, Butler is laid hold of and compelled to walk beside the unfortunate captive, in order to prepare him for instant death. He does all he can to turn the infuriated crowd from such a desperate design. "For God's sake," he exclaims, "remember it is the image of your Creator which you are about to deface in the person of this unfortunate man. Wretched as he is, and wicked as he may be, he has a share in every promise of Scripture, and you cannot destroy him in impenitence without blotting his name from the Book of Life. Do not destroy soul and body. Give time for preparation." Arnold Biederman, the worthy chief magistrate of Unterwalden, learns that his friend, the elder Philipson, is in great danger, and a prisoner in the dungeon at Brisach; he pleads with his fellow-travellers to hurry forward with him to the Englishman's relief, but one of them wishes to keep clear of the quarrels of strangers and look after Swiss interests only. Biederman humanely reminds him in reply, "This man is not of our country, doubtless; but he is of our blood, a copy of the common Creator's image, and the more worthy of being called so, as he is a man of integrity and worth."

The novel from which the above quotation is made, *Anne of Geierstein*, opens with the appearance of two travellers, Philipson and his son, who, with their guide, are overtaken by a bewildering snowstorm on the Alps. To extricate themselves from their dangerous position, the son attempts to scale a broken path so as to reach the castle of Geierstein and obtain assistance. The description of the scene is one of the most vivid passages ever penned by Scott. While writing it he seems to have had in his thoughts not only the dignity of humanity in man's being created after God's own likeness, but also the "dominion over the creatures" with which man was invested, as recorded in Genesis first and twenty-eighth. As Arthur Philipson goes forward on his perilous journey his weight displaces a tremendous mass of rock, which crashes down the mountain-side into the valley below with the noise of thunder. Fortunately he seizes hold of a projecting tree, to which he clings in the extremity of his terror. Sick and giddy, his position is rendered yet more dreadful by the appearance of an Alpine vulture which hovers round him, and at length alights on a crag not four yards from the tree to which he is still clinging. What a position for a human being to be in! And then, as Sir Walter depicts the unhappy traveller's feelings, he asks, "Was he doomed to feel the vulture's beak and talons before his heart's blood should cease to beat? Had he already lost the dignity of humanity, the awe which the being formed in the image of his Maker inspires in all the inferior creatures?" The vulture did not get its expected victim, however, and in the escape of Arthur Philipson, the reader is made to feel what a tremendous depth of meaning there is in the intimation that God made man after His own image, and that "man's lordship of the creation is a part of his original constitution."

The account of man's creation is followed by a fuller statement in the sacred narrative with reference to the outward form of the human body. "The Lord God formed man of the dust of the ground," Genesis second and seventh. Sir Walter's allusions to this subject always help us to distinguish clearly the great difference which exists between the mere framework of man, and the God-made image, or soul, therein placed by the Creator himself. Reference has already been made to the murder of Oliver Proudfute at Perth. Addressing the assembled citizens in connection therewith, the senior Magistrate gives the following directions—"Let the chirurgeon, Dwining, examine *that poor piece of clay*, that he may tell us how poor Proudfute came by his fatal death." The corpse was then to be swathed in a clean shroud, and placed before the high altar in the church of St. John. Sir Walter thus describes the scene—" On the bier placed before the altar were stretched the mortal remains of the wounded man, his arms folded on his breast, and his palms joined together, with the fingers pointed upward, as if *the senseless clay* were itself appealing to heaven against those who had violently divorced the immortal spirit from its mangled tenement." This common physical origin of ours reduces us all to the same physical level. The Bishop of Tyre, however, does not seem to be sure of this, for when he asks the physician in *The Talisman* if he will undertake to cure King Richard with " that simple-seeming draught," the sage replies in astonishment, "I have just cured a, beggar, as you may behold ; are the Kings of Frangistan made of *other clay* than the meanest of their subjects ?"

In *The Abbot* Henry Seyton boasts of his ancient ancestry, and plainly intimates that his sister can never be aught to Roland Græme beyond what she is to every churl's blood in Scotland. Roland's grandmother overhears the offensive remark, and sternly asks, "Of what clay are they moulded, these Seytons, that the blood of the Græmes may not aspire to mingle with theirs ?" And in *Kenilworth*, when Tressilian tells Lambourne to keep company with his own associates, the latter replies ironically, "How these gentles, that are made, questionless, of the porcelain clay of the earth, look down upon poor Michael Lambourne ! "

Before leaving the subject of the special creation of man, there is one other text in connection with it which is frequently referred to in the Waverley Novels. We allude to the statement in Genesis second and seventh, where we are told that God breathed into man's " nostrils the breath of life, and man became a living soul." This breath of heaven, or " breath of his nostrils," is used by Sir Walter generally to express all that is sacred, true, honourable, and dear as life itself. Thus the Countess Amy advises the Earl of Leicester, in *Kenilworth*, to shake himself free of all the entanglements that he has allowed to gather round him in connection with his secret marriage : "Be like a true-born English gentleman, knight, and earl, who holds that truth is the foundation of honour, and that honour is dear to him as the breath of his nostrils."

In *The Talisman* De Vaux speaks of military renown as "the breath of his nostrils." Ivanhoe tells Rebecca that the love of battle is the food on which he and his order live : "the dust of the melee is the breath of our nostrils." And Geoffrey Hudson, the dwarf in *Peveril of the Peak*, considers honour to be the breath of his nostrils, for he adds that "in no case can we be said to live if we permit ourselves to be deprived of it."

Following the Scriptural narrative we come to the abode or home which was intended for man after his creation. The natural beauty of the primitive Eden suggests to Sir Walter many fair landscapes and pleasant places of retreat. In *The Talisman* there is the "Diamond of the Desert," with its refreshing shade and living waters, which "rendered the fountain and its neighbourhood a little Paradise." The romantic beauty of Flora M'Ivor's retreat, as seen by Waverley, seemed "an Eden in the wilderness." In the English lake district, as described in *Guy Mannering*, we have the "Paradise of romance" at Mervyn Hall ; and on the western Scottish Border, there is the "little Eden of beauty, comfort, and peace" around Mount Sharon, the home of Joshua

Geddes and his gentle sister Rachel, in the novel of *Red-gauntlet.*

But Sir Walter does not confine his pictures of Paradise to out-door scenery only. When Frank Osbaldistone, in *Rob Roy*, was in Die Vernon's own apartment at the Hall, she remarked to him, "You think this place somewhat disconsolate, . . . but to me it seems a little Paradise, for I call it all my own, and fear no intrusion."

Into the garden of Eden God put the man whom He had formed " to dress it and keep it." In allusion to this occupation of our original parent, Andrew Fairservice, in *Rob Roy*, speaks of Adam as "the first gardener." When Waverley arrived at Tully Veolan on a visit to the Baron Bradwardine he found no one to welcome or even to admit him into the house. Going in search of some of the domestics, he found, on a parterre of flowers, an old man at work, whose appearance seemed to indicate

"Old Adam's likeness set to dress this garden."[1]

In *Castle Dangerous* there is an allusion to Adam naming the living creatures ; but the allusion is so slight that it need not detain us here. Much the same may be said of the deep sleep into which Adam was cast, when God took from him a rib with which He formed Eve. Andrew Fairservice speaks of womankind in general as "slices o' the spare rib." To Eve's connection with the temptation and the fall, however, there are so many references throughout the Waverley Novels that we can trace almost every incident in the sacred narrative from the intimation of the serpent's craft and cunning in Genesis

[1] Shakespeare, *King Richard II.*, Act III., Scene 4.

third and first, down to the expulsion of our first parents from Paradise. In four lines placed as a motto to the twelfth chapter of *Quentin Durward*, Sir Walter introduces the subtle character of Satan as a preface to his portrait of Oliver Dain, the crafty favourite of Louis XI.

> " This is a lecturer, so skilled in policy,
>   That (no disparagement to Satan's cunning)
>   He well might read a lesson to the Devil,
>   And teach the old seducer new temptations."

The "old seducer" enters Eden in the form of a serpent for the purpose of tempting Eve. Giles Gosling, the honest host of the Black Bear, in *Kenilworth*, is speaking of his daughter to his nephew, Michael Lambourne, a dissolute, drunken fellow, who thus replies. "Why, uncle, thinkest thou that I am an infidel, and would harm those of mine own house?" "It is for no harm that I speak, Mike," answered his uncle, "but a simple humour of precaution which I have taken. True, thou art as well gilded as a snake when he casts his old slough in the spring-time; but for all that, thou creepest not into my Eden. I will look after mine Eve, Mike, and so content thee."

Eve listens to the voice of the tempter, and her curiosity is awakened, an incident which the author of *Waverley* uses for illustration in a great variety of ways. "Since the days of our grandmother Eve," he says in *Waverley*, "the gratification of inordinate curiosity has generally borne its penalty in disappointment." And so we find throughout the Novels numerous instances of this "inordinate curiosity" in almost every rank of life.

We see waiting-maids curious to know the secrets, when there are secrets going, of their mistresses ; landladies anxious to know more than they do know of their guests ; post-mistresses prying into the letters passing through their hands ; and many more such-like incidents.

The curiosity of Eve ripens into gratification, as we learn in Genesis third and sixth. Dame Glendinning, in *The Monastery*, is extremely anxious to know something of the secret volume which belongs to her guest, the homeless Lady of Avenel. " Good father," she says to the monk who has asked for the book, and in whose hands she reluctantly places it, "you must instruct mine ignorance better ; but lack of wit cannot be a deadly sin, and truly, to my poor thinking, I should be glad to read the Holy Scripture." " I daresay thou wouldest," said the monk, " and thus did our mother Eve seek to have knowledge of good and evil. And thus sin came into the world, and death by sin."

But matters did not end here, for Eve "gave also unto her husband with her, and he did eat." Mordaunt Mertoun gives the following admonition to his son, who is preparing to visit Magnus Troil and his daughters. Referring to the latter he says : "I bid you beware of them ; for, as sure as that sin and death came into the world by woman, so sure are their soft words and softer looks, the utter destruction and ruin of all who put faith in them." The beautiful but capricious Queen of Richard I. in *The Talisman*, in mere frolic lures Kenneth the Scot away from his post of guarding the English flag by means of a supposed message from Edith Plantagenet. During his absence the flag is stolen, and for this breach of military discipline the young Scot is condemned to death. His friend, the physician, comforts him with this reflection, that his offence of being tempted away from the post of duty by a woman is one which has been only too common "since the days of Sultan Adam." But this same physician, El Hakim, who is no other than Saladin in disguise, afterwards intercedes with King Richard to spare the life of the young Scot. "Great King," said El Hakim, . . . "I would remind thee that thou owest . . . a life . . . even the life of this good knight who is doomed to die, and but for such a fault as was committed by the Sultan Adam . . . the father of all men."

After the fall came sin and shame. In *The Pirate* there is a description of a fair at Kirkwall, and on one of the booths there was a small sign, on which was painted an emblematic device representing our first parents in "their vegetable garments," with this legend—

> "Poor sinners whom the snake deceives
> Are fain to cover them with leaves."

The lines proceed to intimate that though even leaves are scarce and few in Shetland, there is clothing in abundance of other kinds to be had within the booth.

In *The Surgeon's Daughter* there is only a passing allusion to the special sentence pronounced on Eve for her share in "the great transgression;" but to that pronounced on Adam there are several references throughout the Waverley Novels. The tenants on the

Dumbiedyke estates were so poor as to require an extra allowance with which to provide themselves bread and other articles of food, and these they ate "under the full force of the original maledictiom." Triptolemus Yellowley, in the novel of *The Pirate*, was educated for the Church, but his tastes lay in the direction of agriculture, to which he afterwards devoted himself. His theological learning amounted to his being able only to state the fact that "to labour the earth and win his bread with the toil of his body and sweat of his brow, was the lot imposed upon fallen man."

In many various ways we can trace through the pages of the Waverley Novels the sad effects of the fall of man. In the motto prefixed to the thirteenth chapter of *The Talisman* Sir Walter says—

> "You talk of Gaiety and Innocence !
> The moment when the fatal fruit was eaten
> They parted ne'er to meet again ; and Malice
> Has ever since been playmate to light Gaiety."

In *The Abbot*, Henry Warden, the chaplain at Avenel Castle, in his sermon to the assembled household, pours out upon the head of Roland Græme the full vials of his wrath, as he considers the young and handsome page wanting in respect for the preacher and his sacred office. Among other effects of the fall he singles out pride, and declares that it "and self-opinion kindled the flaming sword which waves us off from Paradise. Pride made Adam mortal and a weary wanderer on the face of the earth, which he had else been at this day the immortal lord of." The preacher proceeds -to point out the further effects of pride, and finally exhorts his hearers to rend from their bosom "this accursed shoot of the fatal apple."

Before leaving the subject of Adam and Eve, it may interest our readers if we point out one or two of Sir Walter's references to them as the common parents of our race. In *Redgauntlet* the Provost says to Alan Fairford: "They are flesh and blood like ourselves, these poor Jacobite bodies—sons of Adam and Eve after all." In the story of *The Two Drovers*, Robin Oig is preparing to leave the north for the English markets with his cattle, when his aunt appears and entreats him not to go. "There is blood on your hand, and it is English blood," said she, looking in alarm and horror at him. "Prutt, trutt," answered Robin, "that will never do, neither: . . . you cannot tell by the colour the difference between the blood of a black bullock and a white one. And you speak of knowing Saxon from Gaelic blood! All men have their blood from Adam." Quentin Durward is speaking to Count Crèvecœur about the ancestry of the former, when the Count replies that it is not birth he refers to, but rank, fortune, and high station. "As for birth," he continues, "all men are descended from Adam and Eve." "My Lord Count," repeated Quentin, "my ancestors, the Durwards of Glen Houlakin——" "Nay," said the Count, "if you claim a further descent for them than from Adam, I have done. Good even to you."

The sad and sorrowful associations which cluster round the names of Cain and Abel seem to be much in the mind and thoughts of the author of *Waverley*

when he has occasion, and that is pretty often, to por-
tray the fierce and terrible human passions which too
frequently end in the dreadful crime of murder. In the
pleasant and hospitable home of Dame Glendinning at
the Tower of Glendearg there are two brothers, the
delight and the joy of their widowed mother. The
homeless Lady of Avenel and her daughter Mary accept
with much gratitude the shelter of the Tower, as narrated
in *The Monastery*. Mary soon becomes the object of *both*
brothers' affections; and while she chooses Edward as her
companion in books and studies, she gives her heart to the
more adventurous Halbert. Then the demon of jealousy
enters the household, and the brother-hating begins. There
is a report that Halbert has been killed by Sir Piercie
Shafton, and Edward is actually glad to hear of it, though
outwardly he conceals his feelings. When he learns, however, that Halbert is safe and well, and when he sees the
joy of Mary Avenel at the welcome news, he is driven to
desperation, and hastens to Father Eustace, to whom he
confesses the passion that had been devouring him.

"May God be gracious to thee, my son; even in such
evil mood did the first murderer rise up against his
brother, because Abel's was the more acceptable sacrifice."
Edward then declared his intention of embracing the
monastic state which the father had so often recommended, and his desire to return at once with him to the
monastery of St. Mary's. He could not endure again to
see Mary Avenel's eyes flash with joy at the restoration
of her lover, his own brother. "It were a sight," he
says, "to make indeed a second Cain of me."

In *The Antiquary* Lovel accepts the challenge from Hector MacIntyre, and after he does so, his reflections on the probable consequence of the duel are thus described by Sir Walter :—"In a few hours he might be in another world to answer for an action which his calmer thoughts told him was unjustifiable in a religious point of view ; or he might be wandering about in the present, like Cain, with the blood of his brother on his head. And all this might be saved by speaking a single word." But pride would not allow him to speak that word.

Reuben Butler, in *The Heart of Midlothian*, meets a stranger in the Park near Edinburgh. Thinking that he has come to settle "some affair of honour," Reuben approaches and gives him this advice :—"Think," he said, "what an awful alternative you voluntarily choose for yourself, to kill or to be killed. Think what it is to rush uncalled into the presence of an offended Deity. . . . Or suppose yourself the scarce less wretched survivor, with the guilt of Cain, the first murderer, in your heart, with his stamp upon your brow—that stamp which struck all who gazed on him with unutterable horror, and by which the murderer is made manifest to all who look upon him."

Among the antediluvian patriarchs Methuselah, the son of Enoch, is distinguished as the man who attained the greatest recorded length of human life. Sir Walter refers to him at least twice in the Waverley Novels : but as the references are simply comparisons, or illustrations of great age, we need not detain our readers by giving the quotations.

There is an interesting incident in the personal history

of Sir Walter Scott which is brought to our recollection by that portion of the sacred narrative which now comes under our consideration—Noah and the flood. On the thirty-first day of January 1831 Sir Walter went to Edinburgh for the purpose of executing his last will, and arranging some other private matters. For the first time in his life he took up his quarters at a hotel in his native city; but disliking the noise and bustle of the place he was easily persuaded to accept of the hospitality of Mr. Cadell. There came on, during his stay in Edinburgh, a storm of such severity that he' had to remain under the friendly roof of his bookseller until the ninth day of February. In the mornings he usually wrote for several hours at *Count Robert of Paris*, and Mr. Cadell remembered that on one occasion Mr. Ballantyne reminded Sir Walter that a motto or heading was wanted for one of the chapters already finished. Looking out at the gloomy weather for a moment, the author of *Waverley* sat down and penned the following lines :—

> "The storm increases—'tis no sunny shower
> Foster'd in the moist breast of March or April,
> Or such as parched summer cools his lips with ;
> Heaven's windows are flung wide ; the inmost deeps
> Calls in hoarse greeting one upon another ;
> On comes the flood in all its foaming horrors,
> And where's the dike shall stop it ?"

These lines are prefixed to the fifth chapter of *Count Robert*, and as we read them they forcibly remind us of the expressive words of Scripture, " the fountains of the great deep (were) broken up, and the windows of heaven were opened."

The references to the deluge are so numerous in the Waverley Novels that we can trace the causes which led to the flood being sent upon the earth, the ark that was prepared by Noah, the entering in of the animals, the incident of the raven, the dove, and the olive branch, the ark resting on Mount Ararat, Noah planting a vineyard, the curse pronounced on Ham, and the rainbow in the cloud. In describing the remarkable Standing Stones of Stennis, Sir Walter, in the novel of *The Pirate*, introduces a striking reference to the sinful and gigantic race of the antediluvians. "These remarkable blocks of stone, all of them twelve feet, and several being even fourteen or fifteen feet in height, stood around the pirate in the gray light of the dawning like the phantom forms of antediluvian giants who, shrouded in the habiliments of the dead, came to revisit, by the pale light, the earth which they had plagued by their oppression, and polluted by their sins, till they brought down upon it the vengeance of long-suffering heaven."

Along with the patriarch and his family, there went into the ark "of clean beasts and of beasts that were not clean, the male and the female, as God commanded Noah." When Philipson, in *Anne of Geierstein*, arrived at the German inn, he received anything but a hospitable reception from its surly host, John Mengs. "The guest was suffered to enter, rather than admitted into, the general . . . room of entertainment which, like the ark of the patriarch, received all classes without distinction, whether clean or unclean."

In *Old Mortality* Henry Morton suggests to Lord Evandale that the latter might act the part of mediator. " Hear me, my lord," said Morton; "I believe you may not be unwilling to bear the olive branch between our master, the king, and that part of his subjects which is now in arms."

Roland Græme, in *The Abbot*, returns from the mainland to the island in Loch Leven, where, in the Castle, Queen Mary was detained a prisoner. Entering her apartment, the page is thus received, "Roland, you are welcome home to us—you have proved the true dove and not the raven. Yet I am sure I could have forgiven you if, once dismissed from this water-circled ark of ours, you had never again returned to us. I trust you have brought back an olive branch, for our kind and worthy hostess has chafed herself much on account of your long absence, and we never needed more some symbol of peace and reconciliation." At the assault on Tillietudlem Castle, in *Old Mortality*, Edith sent out her maid to ascertain the cause of the attack; but Jenny, once engaged in the bustle and confusion, found so much to engage her attention that she quite forgot the state of uncertainty and anxiety in which she left her mistress. Edith, therefore, "having no dove to dismiss in pursuit of information, when her raven messenger failed to return, was herself obliged to venture in quest of it out of the ark of her own chamber into the deluge of confusion which overflowed the rest of the castle."

The following reference to the bow in the cloud is in *Quentin Durward*. Philip de Comines, in reply to Count Crèvecœur's question regarding the complexion of the news he has brought, "They were," he said, "like the colours of the rainbow, varied in hue as they might be viewed from different points, and placed against the black cloud or the fair sky. Such a rainbow was never seen in France or Flanders since that of Noah's Ark."

Settling down to the affairs of every-day life after the flood, "Noah began to be an husbandman, and he planted a vineyard; and he drank of the wine, and was drunken." Arnold Biederman, in *Anne of Geierstein*, is entertaining Philipson in the hall, while the young people and the domestics are enjoying their sports on the lawn. Resuming the wine-flask, he fills the cup of his guest, and pours the remainder into his own. "At an age, worthy stranger," he said, "when the blood grows colder and the feelings heavier, a moderate cup of wine brings back light thoughts and makes the limbs supple. Yet I almost wish that Noah had never planted the grape, when of late years I have seen, with my own eyes, my countrymen swill wine like very Germans, till they were like gorged swine incapable of sense, thought, or motion."

Count Robert of Paris and the Countess are shown a black slave by Agelastes, who, in introducing him to them, observes, "This poor being is of the race of Ham, the undutiful son of Noah; for his transgressions against his parent he was banished to the sands of Africa, and was condemned to be the father of a race doomed to be the slaves of the issue of his more dutiful brethren."

Here and there in the Waverley Novels the references to the incidents in Noah's life appear to indicate a new starting-point in human history. We need only quote one instance, and it is found in the lines prefixed to the twentieth chapter of *The Fortunes of Nigel :*—

" Credit me, friend, it hath been ever thus,
Since the ark rested on Mount Ararat.
False man hath sworn, and woman hath believed,
Repented, and reproached, and then believed once more."

Among the names of the descendants or " generations of Noah," recorded in the tenth chapter of Genesis, there is one which is specially singled out and introduced to the notice of the reader " as a mighty hunter before the Lord." This is Nimrod, whose name and associations are not likely to be left out of the Waverley Novels, which contain so much that is descriptive of country life, rural sports, and military adventures. Frank Osbaldistone, in the novel of *Rob Roy*, is on his way to his uncle's in Northumberland. On approaching the neighbourhood of the Hall, his horse pricks up its ears at the enlivening notes of a pack of hounds in full cry. Frank soon after sees the fox pursued by the huntsman and three or four riders. The sight of the latter, as they sweep past, leads him to think that they may probably be his cousins, and then he begins to reflect upon what kind of a reception he, knowing so little of country sports and country life, is likely to meet with from " these worthy successors of Nimrod." In the following quotation from the same novel Sir Walter catches up the true character of Nimrod, who was not a mere hunter of wild beasts, but a leader and commander of men, and the founder of the great Babylonian Empire. As Frank and Diana Vernon ride out to see another fox-hunt later on in the story, the former observes that he does not see his cousin Rashleigh in the field. "Oh, no," Die replies, "he's a mighty hunter, but it's after the fashion of Nimrod, and his game is man." The Sub-Prior, in *The Monastery*, on his arrival at Glendearg, misses one of Dame Glendinning's sons. He inquires where "that naughty Nimrod, Halbert," is, and expresses the hope that he has not turned, like his great prototype, his hunting spear against man. The Dame explains that her son has gone up the glen to get venison, on hearing which the Sub-Prior muttered something about savoury meat such as his soul loved, referring, no doubt, to the venison which Isaac, when old and blind, sent Esau to get, but which was brought by Jacob instead.

Ruler of men, or hunter of animals, the Antiquary, in the novel of that name, "detested the whole race of Nimrods."

The next outstanding point in the sacred narrative after the flood is the attempted building of the Tower of Babel, with the subsequent confusion of speech and the dispersion of the "builders vain." Biblical commentators have done much to give their readers some idea of the noise and commotion which must have been the result of a multitude of people, engaged in one common enterprise, having their speech suddenly confounded, and unable to understand each other. To the novelist, the associations of the story of Babel furnish abundant material for intensifying his descriptions of noise, confusion, and uproar in battles, sieges, public gatherings, and convivial parties. At the Highland feast given by

Fergus MacIvor in honour of his friend Waverley, the
bagpipers, three in number, screamed, during the whole
time of dinner, a tremendous war-tune; while the echoing
of the vaulted roof and clang of the Celtic tongue produced such a Babel of noise, that Waverley feared he
would lose the sense of hearing and never be able again
to recover it.   Here, in a few lines, is a finished picture
of the uproar caused by a crowd of revellers who, headed
by the Abbot of Unreason, are making their way to the
Monastery, in *The Abbot*, for the purpose of ridiculing the
church and its services.   "The winding of horns, blown
with no regard to harmony or concert; the jangling of
bells, the thumping of drums, the squeaking of bagpipes,
and the clash of cymbals—the shouts of a multitude, now
as in laughter, now as in anger—the shrill tones of female
voices, and of those of children, mingling with the deeper
clamours of men, formed a Babel of sounds which first
drowned and then awed into utter silence the official
hymns of the convent."   When Touchwood hears Mrs.
Dods suggesting that he has been down at the spa well,
he exclaims, "Spaw do you call it, madam? If you mean
the new establishment that has been spawned down yonder at St. Ronan's, it is the very fountainhead of folly
and coxcombry—a Babel for noise, and a Vanity-Fair
for nonsense."

We find many interesting references to Abraham in
the Waverley Novels.   In *The Heart of Midlothian* David
Deans thus writes to his affectionate daughter, Jeanie,
in the prospect of leaving St. Leonard's Crags to settle
in the west of Scotland.   "I-receive this dispensation,"

ho says, "as a call to depart out of Haran, as righteous Abraham of old, and leave my father's kindred and my mother's house, and the ashes and mould of them who have gone to sleep before me, and which wait to be mingled with these auld crazed bones of mine own."

The novel of *Kenilworth* contains several references to the patriarchal custom of having more wives than one. Varney, the Earl of Leicester's Master of the Horse, is an accomplished courtier, but a subtle and heartless villain. From faithfully carrying out his master's dark designs and advancing his interests in various directions, he has come to exercise great influence over the Earl. He hopes to see him, at no distant date, the husband of Queen Elizabeth, notwithstanding the Earl's secret marriage with Amy Robsart. Here is Varney's argument with his master while proposing a way out of the difficulty. "Have we not known, in other countries, how a left-handed marriage might subsist betwixt persons of differing degree? Ay, and, be no hindrance to prevent the husband from conjoining himself with a more suitable partner."

"I have heard of such things in Germany," said Leicester.

"Ay, and the most learned doctors in foreign universities justify the practice from the Old Testament," said Varney, whose argument we need not at present follow any further. At Kenilworth the Queen listens to the Earl's addresses, but when she afterwards learns of his secret marriage, her indignation knows no bounds at the outrage she has sustained as a guest and as a woman.

"What, ho, my Lords, come all and hear the news—my Lord of Leicester's stolen marriage has cost me a husband and England a king. His Lordship is patriarchal in his tastes—one wife at a time was insufficient, and he designed us the honour of his left hand."

The mention of patriarchal tastes reminds us of some other matters peculiar to the patriarchs. The wealth of David Deans consisted in his flocks and herds. Dominie Sampson speaks of Dandie Dinmont as one "like the patriarchs of old, cunning in that which belongeth to flocks and herds." And before Waverley entered the banqueting hall of the chief, at the feast already mentioned, he was offered the patriarchal refreshment of a bath for his feet.

When Abraham went to Egypt with Sarah, he made an arrangement by which he thought to protect her from the license of a despotic king and court—she was to pass as his sister. This incident suggests a remarkable scene to Sir Walter while writing *Kenilworth*. The Master of the Horse arrived at Cumnor Hall with a letter from the Earl of Leicester to the Countess, entreating her to bear the name of Varney during her approaching visit to Kenilworth Castle. As might be expected, such a request throws the unhappy lady into a state of great excitement. Matters are made worse when Foster, under whose charge the Countess was kept at Cumnor, attempts to interfere with the show of authority. "Nay, lady, I must needs say you are over hasty in this—such deceit is not utterly to be condemned when practised for a righteous end; and thus even the patriarch Abraham feigned Sarah to be his sister when they went down to Egypt."

"Ay, sir," answered the Countess, "but God rebuked that deceit even in the father of His chosen people, by the mouth of the heathen Pharaoh. Out upon you, that will read Scripture only to copy those things which are held out to us as warnings, not as examples."

"But Sarah disputed not the will of her husband, an' it be your pleasure," said Foster in reply; "but did as Abraham commanded, calling herself his sister, that it might be well with her husband for her sake, and that his soul might live because of her beauty."

"Now, so heaven pardon me my useless anger," answered the Countess, "thou art as daring a hypocrite as yonder fellow (pointing to Varney) is an impudent deceiver! Never will I believe that the noble Dudley gave countenance to so dastardly, so dishonourable a plan."

In his wild and excited address to the insurgents before the battle of Bothwell Bridge, Mucklewrath, as described in *Old Mortality*, incited them to take Henry Morton and "stone him with stones, and thereafter burn him with fire, that the wrath may depart from the children of the Covenant." In the tumult and excitement caused by the delivery of such an address Poundtext, one of the moderate party, rose up and endeavoured to calm the increasing fury of the factions by exclaiming, in the words of Abraham when he and Lot were about to separate, "Let there be no strife, I pray thee, between me and thee, and between my herdmen and thy herdmen, for we be brethren."

, as

After the battle of the four kings agains¹ are
recorded in 'the fourteenth chapter of Genesis the
told that Abraham refused to take anything had
King of Sodom in return for the good servi.rs of
rendered by rescuing Lot and all the other p²d by
war. The words he used in his refusal are qu{ *of*
Master Solsgrace in the following scene from *Pls-*
the Peak. Sir Geoffrey Peveril summarily dismissie
grace from the vicarage and conveys him to Mothe
Hall. In their absence much damage is donese-
clergyman's property, and when Sir Geoffrey or
quently offers compensation and full satisfacbm
everything damaged or lost, the divine replies, at
a thread to a shoe-latchet I will not take anyth·
is thine."   *ck,*

That stern old Royalist Sir Henry Lee, in *Ih*m-
resolutely refuses to make any compromise with,"
well's party. "I will take nothing from the usəm
he says to Colonel Everard; "I will not take fro:o-
an old cap to cover my gray hairs, a cast cloak ay
tect my frail limbs from the cold. They shall ɪm
they have, by their unwilling bounty, made A
rich; I will live, as I will die, the Loyal Lee."   ɪe

In describing the ancient cross which stood ɪe
market-place of Kennaquhair, Sir Walter states, n
Monastery, that close beside it there at one time grd
immensely large oak tree which had perhaps wit-
the worship of the Druids, long before the stately ɪ-
tery near it had reared its spires in honour of the ɪ
tian faith. The tree was used by the villagers·

common meeting-place, and regarded by them with peculiar veneration : a feeling common to most nations, and which may perhaps be traced back to the remote period when the patriarch Abraham entertained the angels under the oak at Mamre.

Lot's wife is mentioned now and again in the Waverley Novels, but the references to her are generally employed in the way of simple illustrations or comparisons. Thus Mysie Happer, in *The Monastery*, explains to the landlord of the inn at which she arrived on horseback behind Sir Piercie Shafton, that her own palfrey had to be left behind in the Tasker's Park, where he had "stood still as Lot's wife with very weariness;" and when Goldthred's bride, in *Kenilworth*, finds no palfrey waiting for her at the prearranged spot, she stands in astonishment and disappointment, "like a picture of Lot's wife."

In *The Abbot*, Magdalen Græme, a Catholic enthusiast, takes her grandson Roland to the nunnery of St. Catherine's, and introduces him to the Abbess, in whose presence she consecrates the boy to the service of Queen Mary. "Thou art a happy woman, Sister Magdalen," said the Abbess, "that, lifted so high above human affection and human feeling, thou canst bind such a victim to the horns of the altar. Had I been called to make such a sacrifice —to plunge a youth so young and fair into the plots and blood-thirsty dealings of the time—not the patriarch Abraham, when he led Isaac up the mountain, would have rendered more melancholy obedience." With all her enthusiasm for the Queen, the grandmother of the consecrated boy yet hopes that "there will be a ram

caught in the thicket," and that "the hand of our re-
volted brethren shall not be on the youthful Joseph.
Heaven can defend its own rights, even by means of
babes and sucklings, of women, and beardless boys."

The incident of Esau selling his birthright to his
brother is one which, we might almost say with certainty, will come before us in the course of our present
study. It points many a moral elsewhere, and adorns
more than one of the Waverley tales. The first instance
in which it comes under our notice is in connection with
a matter which looks not unlike a page of modern Irish
history. When our old friend the Baron Bradwardine, in
Waverley, had to go into hiding for his share in the troubles
of 1745, his estate passed into the hands of his unworthy
and selfish kinsman, Malcolm Bradwardine. When this
new laird went to collect his rents he was fired at by one
of the tenants in the gloaming! Alarmed at such a
reception he fled to Stirling, where he advertised the
estate for sale, and eventually disposed of it at a sum
utterly disproportioned to its real value. Later on in
the story we learn that when the Baron was made acquainted with the welcome news of the estate being,
through the kindness of his friends, once more his own,
his first thought turned to his unworthy kinsman who,
he said, "had sold his birthright, like Esau, for a mess
of pottage." The Duke of Burgundy, in *Anne of Geierstein,* asks the Chancellor what the terms are on which the
English army under Edward IV. had agreed to evacuate
France. "By fair words," was the reply, "by liberal
presents, and by five hundred tuns of wine." "Wine!'

exclaimed the Duke; "Heardest thou ever the like, Signor Philipson? Why, your countrymen are little better than Esau, who sold his birthright for a mess of pottage."

Roland Græme, in *The Abbot*, relates to Catherine Seyton that he has made up his mind to enter the service of Queen Mary. Delighted at his decision, Catherine assures him that if he will be as firm in mind as he is bold in deed and quick in resolution, future ages will honour him as the saviour of Scotland. While seeking to advance his own interests after faithfully attending to those of the Queen, Roland, in his reply, is thinking of a well-known incident in the life of Jacob. "When I have," said he, "toiled successfully to win that Leah, Honour, thou wilt not . . . condemn me to a new term for that Rachel, Love?" "Of that," said Catherine, "we shall have full time to speak; but Honour is the elder sister, and must be won the first." Bridgenorth, in *Peveril of the Peak*, draws Julian into the Gothic recess of an old-fashioned apartment, and reminds him that he has not yet told the cause of his present visit. Julian was about to explain when Bridgenorth interrupted him, "Nay, never vindicate thyself, but mark me further. The patriarch bought his beloved by fourteen years' hard service to her father Laban, and they seemed to him but as a few days. But he that would wed my daughter must serve, in comparison, but a few days; though in matters of such mighty import, that they shall seem as the service of many years."

In the novel of *The Surgeon's Daughter* we have several family sketches which remind us of the home-life of

Jacob and the wife he loved so tenderly. In Dr. Gray's
"anxious longing for posterity," for example, we hear
the passionate cry of Rachel, "Give me children else I
die." As in Jacob's home so was it in the village
doctor's; for when children came, death entered and the
mothers were taken.

This passionate longing for children is also much in
the thoughts of the lonely Lady of Avenel, in *The
Abbot;* and when death carried off the infant heir of
Colonel and Lady Talbot, in *Waverley*, the bereavement
was all the more difficult to bear, for, "long without a
family, they had fondly exulted in the hopes which were
now blasted."

Some of the incidents in the life of Joseph come
before us in the Waverley Novels. There is the coat
of many colours in *The Pirate.* Barbara Yellowley was
encased in a garment called a Joseph. It had once been
green, but latterly, betwixt stains and patches, it had
become like the vesture of the patriarch whose name it
bore—the coat of many colours. In *The Talisman* there
is an interesting reference to Joseph being sold as a slave
by his brothers. Kenneth the Scot has been bestowed
upon the Arabian physician by King Richard more as a
slave than a servant. Exiled also from the camp of the
Crusaders, the young soldier feels downcast and dis-
heartened. The physician sits down beside him, and
administers comfort in the following kind and en-
couraging words—"My friend," he said, "be of good
comfort—for what saith the poet—'It is better that a
man should be the servant of a kind master, than be the

slave of his own wild passions.' Again, be of good courage; because, whereas Ysouf Ben Yagoubo was sold to a king by his brethren, even to Pharaoh, king of Egypt, thy king hath, on the other hand, bestowed thee on one who will be to thee as a brother." To Joseph's dreams and to his temptation we have an allusion in *Nigel* and *Woodstock* respectively; but as they are merely by the way we need not here detach them from their context.

As the last days of Jacob drew near, he called his sons around his bed that he might bestow upon each of them his blessing, and tell them in prophetic vision what should befall them in the latter days. Sir Walter frequently quotes some of the similes used by the aged patriarch on that occasion, especially the "unstable as water," descriptive of the character of Reuben. Simon Glover, in *The Fair Maid of Perth*, describes his apprentice thus—"He is hot as fire, but he is also unstable as water." In *Redgauntlet*, old Mr. Fairford and his son Alan are speaking of Darsie Latimer, whom the former regards as "an arch lad and somewhat light in the upper story—I wish him well through the world, but he has little solidity, Alan, little solidity." Alan does his best to defend the character of his absent friend, but with little success, apparently, as the old gentleman retorts "unstable as water, he shall not excel. . . . He goeth to dancing-houses, and readeth novels—*sat est.*" In *St. Ronan's Well* Touchwood, who has travelled much, is fond of relating his adventures and praising the customs of other countries at the expense of his own.

The banker remarks to him that he does not seem to be much pleased with the changes and improvements that have been made at St. Ronan's. "Pleased!" replied Touchwood, "you have got an idea that everything must be changed—unstable as water ye shall not excel. I tell ye, there have been more changes in this poor nook of yours within the last forty years, than in the great empires of the East for the space of four thousand, for what I know."

Another of the similes which Sir Walter quotes very often is that which describes Issachar as "a strong ass couching down between two burdens." Before leaving England, Rebecca called upon the Princess Rowena to thank her for all the kindness she and her father had received from Ivanhoe, the husband of the latter. With much gentleness Rowena urges the Jewess to remain with them, adding, "My husband has favour with the king. The king himself is just and generous." "Lady," said Rebecca, "I doubt it not—but the people of England are a fierce race, quarrelling ever with their neighbours or among themselves, and ready to plunge the sword into the bowels of each other. Such is no safe abode for the children of my people. Ephraim is an heartless dove—Issachar an over-burdened drudge, which stoops between two burdens. Not in the land of war and blood, surrounded by hostile neighbours and distracted by internal factions, can Israel hope to rest during her wanderings." King James, in *The Fortunes of Nigel*, applies this text to himself in the pedantic way which characterised him, and which Sir Walter in the novel has caught up very cleverly. His Majesty and the Prince were entering the gate of the palace when a female bowed and presented a paper, which the King received, and, with a groan, thrust it into a side pocket. The Prince expressed a wish to know the contents of the paper, but James replied, "D'ye think, Baby, that I can read all that is thrust into my hands? See to me, man,"—he pointed to the pockets of his great trunk breeches, which were stuffed with papers—"We are like an ass, that we should so speak, stooping between two burdens. . . . Ay, ay, . . . I saw this land of England, and became an over-burdened King thereof."

THROUGH the pages of the Waverley Novels we can trace most of the outstanding points in the history of Israel in Egypt, the life and legislation of Moses, and the wanderings of the chosen people in the Wilderness. Some of these traces are but as faint impressions in the sand, and might be broken up by our trying to set them here; but they exist, nevertheless, and the frequency with which we meet them is indeed remarkable.

The first mention of the name of Moses in the Waverley Novels is, if we mistake not, in *The Monastery*, and it occurs in connection with his killing the Egyptian and hiding the body in the sand. In the interview which Halbert Glendinning has with the Regent Murray and Lord Morton, the young man makes a frank confession of his duel with Sir Piercie Shafton, and states further that he believes the Englishman to be dead. Turning to Morton, the Regent asks, "What shall we do with this young homicide? What will our preachers say?" "Tell them of Moses and of Benaiah," said Morton, "it is but the smiting of an Egyptian when all is said out." "Let it be so,"-said Murray laughing, "but we will bury the tale as the prophet did the body in the sand."

In describing the scene where the Hermit of Engaddi, in *The Talisman*, takes Sir Kenneth into the subterranean chapel, Sir Walter had evidently in mind the command given by God to Moses as the latter approached the burning bush in the desert of Midian. "Put off thy shoes," said the Hermit, "the ground on which thou standest is holy. Banish from thy innermost heart each profane and carnal thought, for to harbour such while in this place were a deadly impiety." And when the old Royalist, Sir Henry Lee, hears that there are three of Cromwell's regiments at Oxford, he exclaims: "Seat of learning and loyalty! These rude soldiers are unfit inmates for thy learned halls and poetical bowers; but thy pure and brilliant lamp shall defy the foul breath of a thousand churls were they to blow at it like Boreas. The burning bush shall not be consumed, even by the heat of this persecution."

When Moses and Aaron received the divine command to go before the King of Egypt and demand the freedom of the oppressed Israelites, a series of signs and miracles was to follow for the purpose of attesting the authority of their mission. In the heading prefixed to the fifteenth chapter of *Quentin Durward*, we are introduced to the magicians whom Pharaoh brought with the view of counteracting the effect of these miracles.

"He was a son of Egypt, as he told me,
    And one descended from those dread magicians,
    Who waged rash war, when Israel dwelt in Goshen,

With Israel and her Prophet—matching rod
With his the sons of Levi's—and encountering
Jehovah's miracles with incantations,
Till upon Egypt came the avenging Angel,
And those proud sages wept for their first-born,
As wept the unletter'd peasant."

In these few lines we have a brief and rapid sketch of
Sacred History, from the time when Moses and Aaron
stood before Pharaoh, down through the ten plagues till
the destroying angel came on his awful errand of slaying
the first-born of every family in Egypt.

While the bright and sunny land of Egypt was for
three days enveloped in darkness so thick that it might
be felt, there was light in the dwellings of Israel in Goshen.
There is an interesting reference to this in *The Heart of
Midlothian*, when Jeanie Deans goes to London to plead
her sister's cause before the Queen in person.   Though
successful in her mission, there was attached to the
pardon a condition which greatly distressed the affectionate Jeanie : Effie was to leave Scotland.   On this point,
however, her mind was much relieved by a letter which
she received from her father in reply to one she had
written to him.   "Do not let your heart be disquieted
within you," he writes, "that the victim who is rescued
from the horns of the altar where she was bound by the
chain of human law is now to be driven beyond the
bounds of our land.   Scotland is a blessed land to those
who love the ordinances of Christianity. . . . But we
are to hold in remembrance that Scotland, though it be
our native land, and the land of our fathers, is not like
Goshen in Egypt, on which the sun of the heavens and

of the gospel shineth allenarly, and leaveth the rest of the world in utter darkness." In *The Monastery* also, the land of Goshen furnishes Sir Walter with an illustration descriptive of the rest and peace which the Abbeys of the Scottish Border at one time enjoyed, even during the ravages of a frontier war. "For several ages the possessions of these Abbeys were each a sort of Goshen enjoying the calm light of peace and immunity while the rest of the country, occupied by wild clans and marauding barons, was one dark scene of confusion, blood, and unremitted outrage."

Preparatory to leaving the land of their oppression, the people of Israel were instructed through Moses to borrow of the Egyptians jewels and raiment. This is not the place to explain that the common objection to the morality of this proceeding, borrowing what the Israelites had no intention of repaying, is founded on the word *borrow*, which should be translated *ask.* It may be pointed out that, after all, the articles asked for formed only a very slight recompense for what the Egyptians had robbed the Israelites of during a century of bondage. This "spoiling of the Egyptians" comes frequently under our notice in the Waverley novels. On the way to Glasgow, Frank Osbaldistone, in *Rob Roy*, is accompanied by Andrew Fairservice, who entertains him with reminiscences of the many times he had formerly crossed the English border into Scotland with "whiles twa bits o' ankers o' brandy on ilk side of me." Frank asks him how he could reconcile himself to such conduct as cheating the revenue. "It's a mere spoiling of the Egyptians," replied Andrew;

"puir auld Scotland suffers eneuch by thae blackguard loons o' excisemen and gaugers, that hae come doon on her like locusts since the sad and sorrowfu' Union ; it's the part o' a kind son to bring her a soup o' something that will keep up her auld heart." The Antiquary considered that even if old Edie Ochiltree had robbed the German adventurer in the ruins of St. Ruth, he "would only have plundered an Egyptian." And when the pedlar in *The Pirate* was discovered rifling Cleveland, who had been washed ashore from the shipwreck, he justified his conduct by saying that he was only "taking the lawful spoil of the Egyptians."

The Israelites at length leave Egypt, and by the route they take Pharaoh is tempted to pursue and overtake them. We are reminded of this by an incident in the romance of *Ivanhoe.* Disguised as a palmer, Ivanhoe kindly guides Isaac the Jew away from Rotherwood, so as to place him out of the reach of the templar who had secretly arranged that Isaac should be seized and conveyed to the castles of either Front-de-Bœuf or Malvoisin. After pushing rapidly through the forest, and by devious paths, the palmer broke the silence by directing Isaac's attention to a large decayed oak tree, which, said he, "marks the boundaries over which Front-de-Bœuf claims authority—we are long since far from those of Malvoisin. There is now no fear of pursuit." "May the wheels of their chariot be taken off," said the Jew, "like those of the host of Pharaoh, that they may drive heavily."

From a feeling of deep and profound gratitude for so kindly guiding him out of a great danger, Isaac offers to give Ivanhoe a letter or scroll, which is to be taken to the town of Leicester and there delivered to a wealthy Jew, who will provide the disguised palmer with a horse and armour that he may enter the lists at Ashby during the approaching passage of arms. Ivanhoe suggests that possibly he may prove unfortunate in the encounter, and so run the risk of losing what he could neither replace nor pay. "No—no—no—It is impossible," replied the Jew. "I will not think so. The blessing of our Father will be upon thee. Thy lance will be as powerful as the rod of Moses." There is much significance in naming the rod of the prophet along with the lance of Ivanhoe. The former was the outward or visible symbol of the power of God on several memorable occasions, as, for example, when it was thrown down and became a serpent; when it was lifted up and turned once more into a rod ; when Moses lifted it over the Red Sea ; and when he smote the rock with it in the desert. And as we afterwards read of the wonderful valour of Ivanhoe at Ashby, there is, we think, no irreverence in stating that Isaac was sincere and right when he expressed his assurance that God would be with him, and that his lance would be like the rod of Moses.

In the romance of *Ivanhoe* we meet with much that reminds us of some of the more memorable events in the desert life of the Israelites. On the evening of the day of her trial Rebecca sought consolation and resignation in prayer from the dangers and sorrows which seemed to be closing in upon her. In the hymn which concluded her devotions, we have a finely-wrought poetic setting of

the history of her forefathers when they left Egypt, and
the lessons which that history is designed to teach.

> When Israel, of the Lord beloved,
>   Out of the land of bondage came,
> Her father's God before her moved,
>   An awful guide, in smoke and flame.
> By day, along the astonish'd lands
>   The cloudy pillar glided slow ;
> By night, Arabia's crimson'd sands
>   Return'd the fiery column's glow.
>
> There rose the choral hymn of praise,
>   And trump and timbrel answer'd keen,
> And Zion's daughters pour'd their lays,
>   With priest's and warrior's voice between.
> No portents now our foes amaze,
>   Forsaken Israel wanders lone ;
> Our fathers would not know THY ways,
>   And THOU hast left them to their own.
>
> But, present still, though now unseen ;
>   When brightly shines the prosperous day,
> Be thoughts of THEE a cloudy screen
>   To temper the deceitful ray.
> And oh, when stoops on Judah's path
>   In shade and storm the frequent night,
> Be THOU, long-suffering, slow to wrath,
>   A burning, and a shining light !
>
> Our harps we left by Babel's streams,
>   The tyrant's jest, the Gentile's scorn ;
> No censer round our altar beams,
>   And mute our timbrel, trump, and horn.
> But THOU hast said, the blood of goat,
>   The flesh of rams, I will not prize ;
> A contrite heart, an humble thought,
>   Are mine accepted sacrifice.

Following the people of Israel into the wilderness, we arrive with them at Marah, where their trials, their wants, and their murmurings began.

A quiet domestic scene in *The Heart of Midlothian* reminds us of the Waters of Marah which the Israelites found so bitter and so distasteful. David Deans and his daughter Jeanie are about to partake of their mid-day meal during the time when a great sorrow has filled their hearts and overshadowed their home. To his petition for a blessing on their simple repast, the old man adds the supplication "that the bread eaten in sadness of heart, and the bitter waters of Marah, might be made as nourishing as those which had been poured forth from a full cup and a plentiful basket and store."

After the Waters of Marah had been sweetened, the people of Israel took to murmuring for want of bread and flesh. They also openly expressed the wish that they had died in Egypt, where they sat by the flesh-pots and ate bread to the full. For at least once in her life-time Barbara Yellowley, in *The Pirate*, resolved to offer hospitality on a scale hitherto unexampled in her experience. Her brother, much puzzled to account for the liberal way in which she was preparing to entertain young Mordaunt Mertoun, made his way to the kitchen and found Barbara consigning to the pot a smoked goose which, with others of the same tribe, had long hung in the large chimney. "What is this of it, sister?" said Triptolemus. "You have on the girdle and the pot at ance. What day is this wi' you?"

"E'en such a day as the Israelites had beside the flesh-pots of Egypt," was his sister's reply.

In answer to the desire for bread and flesh, God sent the manna and the quails. The son-in-law of the Emperor, in *Count Robert of Paris*, is speaking of the Crusaders and their progress eastward. "It was reported," he said, "that the western hosts expected miracles to be wrought in their favour, as when Israel was guided through the wilderness by a pillar of flame and a cloud. But no showers of manna or of quails relieved their necessities, or proclaimed them the chosen people of God."

At Rephidim the Israelites fought their first great battle. Amalek opposed their progress, and while the chosen men of war fought under Joshua, Moses stood on an overlooking height with the rod of God outstretched in his hand. He was attended by his brother Aaron, and by Hur, the husband of Miriam, both of whom supported the hands of Moses till sunset, and the battle was ended. After the skirmish at Drumclog, as related in *Old Mortality*, the Cameronian preacher, Kettledrummle, claimed no small share of the merit of the victory. He appealed to Morton and Headrigg, who had been beside him, "whether the tide of battle had not turned while he prayed on the Mount of Jehovah-nissi, like Moses, that Israel might prevail over Amalek; but granting them, at the same time, the credit of holding up his hands when they waxed heavy, as those of the prophet were supported by Aaron and Hur."

We have already stated that there is much in *Ivanhoe*

which reminds us of the history of Israel while in the desert. Perhaps the most interesting passage in this connection is the one which refers to the giving of the law from Mount Sinai. At the trial of Rebecca, the presiding Grand Master of the Templars recommends her to confess the crime of witchcraft with which she is charged, implores her to turn from the faith of her fathers, and save her life by embracing the Christian faith. Then, finally, he asks, "What has the law of Moses done for thee that thou shouldest die for it?"

"It was the law of my fathers," said Rebecca; "it was delivered in thunders and in storms upon the mountain of Sinai, in cloud and in fire. This, if ye are Christians, ye believe—it is, you say, recalled; but so my teachers have not taught me. . . . I am a maiden, unskilled to dispute for my religion, but I can die for it, if it be God's will."

Wide and deep as the gulf was which separated the Jews from the English people in the time of Ivanhoe, there were yet two points in the human history of both where that gulf was narrowed and bridged over. Rebecca names these in the singularly touching appeal which she makes to the Lady Rowena for permission, on behalf of her father and herself, to travel through the forest under the protection of the Saxon retinue. Making a way through the attendants of Athelstane to the palfrey of Rowena, Rebecca knelt down, after the Oriental fashion in addressing superiors, and kissed the Saxon lady's garments. "Then rising and throwing back her veil, she implored her, in the great name of

E

tho God whom they both worshipped, and by that
revelation of the law upon Mount Sinai in which they
both believed, that she would have compassion upon
them, and suffer them to go forward under their safe-
guard."

Throughout the Waverley Novels there are numerous
interesting illustrations of the moral law, as briefly contained and summarised in the Ten Commandments.
Instead, however, of placing these before the reader
now, we prefer to retain them until our study brings
us down to the New Testament, where we shall find the
precepts of the moral law, and Sir Walter's illustrations
of them, broadened out, and considered in the light of
the Christian dispensation.

The incident of Moses striking the rock is one which
Sir Walter frequently employs in illustration of the
effect produced on a landscape by the presence of
water. Frequently, too, he uses it to illustrate the
influence of kindness and human sympathy in filling
the heart with gratitude, or in relieving the feelings
by a flood of tears. What a pleasant and refreshing
picture we have in the following extract from *Count
Robert of Paris*, descriptive of the place selected by the
Emperor for the halt of his army near the town of
Laodicea :—

"A mountain torrent, which found its source at the
foot of a huge rock, that yawned to give it birth, as if
struck by the rod of the prophet Moses, poured its
liquid treasure down to the more level country, nourishing herbage and even large-trees in its descent, until

at the distance of some four or five miles, the stream
. . . was lost amid heaps of sand and stone."

When it became known that the unfortunate Mr.
Bertram, in *Guy Mannering*, had broken his heart in the
effort to leave Ellangowan, the mansion of his fathers,
there poured forth, on the part of the country people,
his neighbours, "a torrent of sympathy like the waters
from the rock when struck by the wand of the prophet."

In *The Betrothed* the Abbess, usually so cold and
reticent to her niece, on one occasion went so far out
of her way as actually to kiss her. "Slight as the
mark of kindness was, it was unexpected, and, like the
rod of Moses, opened the hidden fountains of waters.
Eveline wept, a resource which had been that day
denied to her—she prayed—and finally sobbed herself
to sleep, like an infant, with a mind somewhat tran-
quillised by having given way to this tide of natural
emotion." And speaking of the bounty of King Richard,
the physician, in *The Talisman*, says of it that it has
" filled my cup to the brim ; yea, it hath been abundant
as the fountain which sprung up amid the camp of the
descendants of Israel, when the rock was stricken by the
rod of Moussa Ben Amran."

In *The Monastery*, with its supernatural machinery of
the White Lady of Avenel, we have several incidents
which were no doubt suggested to Sir Walter by the
story of Balaam and his ass. Notably, there is the
adventure of the Sub-Prior when he finds that he is
followed by Christie of the Clinthill. Anxious to get
forward to the monastery before him, the Churchman

struck his mule with a riding-wand, but instead of mending her pace, the animal suddenly started from the path, and the rider's utmost efforts could not force her forward. The White Lady, unseen by the Sub-Prior, was in the way, and it was not till she vanished that the terrified animal would resume the journey.

As the Master of Ravenswood, in *The Bride of Lammermoor*, approached the Mermaiden's Well his horse, which was moving slowly forward, suddenly stopped and refused to proceed farther. Apparently the animal saw something which his rider did not. Dismounting, and making fast the bridle to a tree, Ravenswood went on to the fountain, where he saw what his horse had seen before him—the apparition of old Alice. Returning to the animal, he found it "sweating and terrified, as if experiencing that agony of fear which the presence of a supernatural being is supposed to impart to the brute creation."

The sacred narrative informs us that the Lord opened the mouth of the ass so that she remonstrated with the prophet for striking her "these three times." It is not stated that Balaam was surprised at this, but there can be no doubt that he was so. Sir Walter employs the incident in illustration of the extreme surprise with which Achilles Tatius, in *Count Robert of Paris*, listens to the accuracy of Hereward's description of the character and personal appearance of Agelastes. "By St. Sophia!" said the officer, "thou astonishest me. The prophet Balaam was not more surprised when his ass turned round her head and spoke to him." And when Lady Binks, in *St. Ronan's Well*, delivered

her opinion of Tyrrel to Lady Penelope, the latter
stared at her ladyship with something like the look of
surprise which "Balaam may have cast upon his ass,
when he discovered the animal's capacity for holding an
argument with him."

One of the best and manliest characters in the whole
gallery of Waverley portraits is Arnold Biederman,
the venerable chief magistrate of one of the Swiss can-
tons. The latter end of this good man, as described
in the novel of *Anne of Geierstein,* was such as Balaam
wished to be his own : for he died "the death of the
righteous," and was universally lamented as a true and
simple-minded chief who wisely ruled the Swiss in times
of peace, and who bravely led and guided them when
war became inevitable.

Though not permitted to set foot in the Land of
Promise, Moses was yet allowed to see it from the top of
Mount Pisgah. In relating the feelings of Darsie Latimer on seeing his native England from the Scottish
shores of the Solway, Sir Walter seems to have had this
incident in his thoughts. "One thing, however, I have
seen," writes Darsie Latimer to his friend Alan Fairford,
in *Redgauntlet,* "and it is with pleasure the more indescrib-
able, that I am debarred from treading the land which
my eyes were permitted to gaze upon like those of the
dying prophet from the top of Pisgah. I have seen, in
a word, the fruitful shores of merry England—merry
England of which I boast myself a native, and on which
I gaze, even while raging floods and unstable quicksands
divide us, with the filial affection of a dutiful son."

And here is another Pisgah view, but upon a very different landscape. The Emperor, in *Count Robert of Paris*, has imprisoned his rival, Ursel, and kept him in a dark dungeon until it was thought his eyesight was destroyed. Instead of cherishing feelings of hatred and anger against the author of all his sufferings, the captive thus speaks of the Emperor to his physician, "It is by his means that the blind and miserable prisoner has been taught to seek a liberty far more unconstrained than this poor earth can afford, and a vision far more clear than any Mount Pisgah on this wretched side of the grave can give us."

TEXTS FROM THE MOSAIC LAW.

In the light of the present day it is deplorable to read in the Waverley Novels, in the pages of Hallam, Lecky, and other historians, of the inhuman cruelties practised upon poor women who, on account of some personal peculiarity, were looked upon as agents of the Evil One, and employed by him to work iniquity and mischief. Such persons were called Witches, and the crimes and mischiefs imputed to them went by the general term of witchcraft. The punishment of witchcraft was considered to be in accordance with the well-known text in the Mosaic Law, "Thou shalt not suffer a witch to live."

This is not the place to enter upon any exposition of the text just quoted.[1] It may suffice to say that in the days of Moses there appear to have been certain persons who traded upon the credulity of their fellows, who insulted the majesty of Jehovah by setting aside His revealed law, and inquiring at some pretended deity or evil spirit concerning future events. Against such

[1] The reader who is interested in this subject will find it discussed at length in Sir Walter Scott's *Letters on Demonology and Witchcraft.*

persons the punishment indicated in the text was directed.

The witch of mediæval and comparatively modern history may be traced to the doctrine of the evil principle as elaborated and credited in the Middle Ages. The Arch-fiend, and his legions of demons, were held to exercise a sway not only over the elements of nature, but also over the bodies and souls of all those who had never been admitted into the Church and protected by its faith and rites. And when witchcraft came to be prosecuted as heresy, the part assigned to woman in the Scriptural account of the fall led to her being looked upon as specially suited to be the instrument or tool of the Evil One.

The subject of witchcraft comes frequently before us in the Waverley Novels. Dominie Sampson, in *Guy Mannering*, was born at a time when a doubt in the existence of witches was considered as a justification of the practices attributed to them. The belief in their existence was an article that could not be separated from his religious faith, and it would, perhaps, have been equally difficult to have induced him to doubt the one as to doubt the other.

Bailie Macwheeble, too, in *Waverley*, is alarmed at the thought of seeing a witch in the person of old Janet Gellatley. He quotes his authorities for the existence of witches. " Right sure am I," he observes to Waverley, " that Sir George Mackenzie says that no divine can doubt there are witches, since the Bible says, ' Thou shalt not suffer them to live ;' and that no lawyer can doubt it, since it is punishable with death by our law. So there's baith law and gospel for it; an' his honour (referring to the Baron Bradwardine, who was sceptical on the subject of witches) winna believe the Leviticus, he might aye believe the statute-book."

One of the saddest incidents in *The Heart of Midlothian* is the seizure of poor Madge Wildfire by the mob at Carlisle, who, thinking they were doing God service in carrying out the injunction of the Mosaic Law on witchcraft, dragged her to a muddy pool and there ducked her, according to the favourite mode of punishment. At the earnest request of Jeanie Deans the poor maniac was rescued by a magistrate, but in a state of insensibility owing to the cruel treatment she had received.

The three old hags in *The Bride of Lammermoor*, who remind us of Shakespeare's three weird sisters in *Macbeth*, though cunning and malevolent creatures, have yet humanity enough in them to claim our sympathy as we hear their names associated with stakes, and chains, and tar-barrels. It is a relief to turn away from such associations to another witch story which has some elements of the ludicrous in it. The story refers to old Janet Gellatley mentioned on the preceding page, and it is related by Rose Bradwardine in *Waverley*.

" Once upon a time there lived an old woman called Janet Gellatley, who was suspected to be a witch, on the infallible grounds that she was very old, very ugly, very poor, and had two sons, one of whom was a poet, and the other a fool, which visitation, all the neighbourhood agreed, had come upon her for the sin of witchcraft. And she was imprisoned for a week in the steeple of the parish church, and sparingly supplied with food, and not permitted to sleep until she herself became as much persuaded of her being a witch as her accusers; and in this lucid and happy state of mind was brought forth to make a clean breast, that is, to make open confession of her sorceries, before all the Whig gentry and ministers in the vicinity, who were no conjurors themselves. My father went to see fair play between the witch and the clergy; for the witch had been born on his estate. And while the witch was confessing that the Enemy appeared and made his addresses to her as a handsome black man —which, if you could have seen poor old blear-eyed Janet, reflected little honour on Apollyon's taste—and while the auditors listened with astonished ears, and the clerk recorded with a trembling hand, she all of a sudden changed the low mumbling tone with which she spoke into a shrill yell, and exclaimed, 'Look to yourselves! look to yourselves! I see the Evil One sitting in the midst of ye!' The surprise was general, and terror and flight its immediate consequences. Happy were those who were next the door; and many were the disasters that befell hats, bands, cuffs, and wigs, before they could get out of the church, where they left the obstinate prelatist (the Baron Bradwardine) to settle matters with the witch and her admirer, at his own peril or pleasure."

From motives of prudence and necessity, allowable under the special circumstances of the case, as narrated in *The Heart of Midlothian*, Jeanie Deans thought it advisable not to acquaint her father with her intention of proceeding to London for the purpose of pleading with the Queen in person for the life of her sister. On her way southward Jeanie rested at York, from which city she wrote to her father, "I make my present pilgrimage more heavy and burdensome," she writes, "through the sad occasion to reflect that it is without your knowledge, which, God knows, was far contrary to my heart; for Scripture says that the vow of the daughter should not be binding without the consent of the father, wherein it may be I have been guilty to take the wearie journey without your consent."

The vow here alluded to is that recorded in the thirtieth chapter of Numbers, and has reference to that part of the Mosaic or Levitical law which declares that a woman shall be free of a vow, from the direct consequences of which her father or parents may dissent.

This vow is quoted at length, in *The Bride of Lammermoor*, in the strikingly dramatic scene where Ravenswood suddenly returns to the castle and demands from Lucy Ashton's own lips her renunciation of the engagement between her and himself. Lucy's bloodless lips could only falter out the words, "It was my mother."

"She speaks truly," said Lady Ashton, "it *was* I who, authorised alike by the laws of God and man, advised her and concurred with her to set aside an unhappy and precipitate engagement, and to annul it by the authority of Scripture itself."

"Scripture!" said Ravenswood, scornfully.

"Let him hear the text," said Lady Ashton, appealing

to the divine (Rev. Mr. Bide-the-Bent), "on which you yourself, with cautious reluctance, declared the nullity of the pretended engagement insisted upon by this violent man."

The clergyman took his clasped Bible from his pocket, and read the following words :—"*If a woman vow a vow unto the Lord, and bind herself by a bond, being in her father's house in her youth ; and her father hear her vow, and her bond wherewith she hath bound her soul, and her father shall hold his peace at her : then all her vows shall stand, and every vow wherewith she hath bound her soul shall stand.*"

"And was it not even so with us ?" interrupted Ravenswood.

"Control thy impatience, young man," answered the divine, "and hear what follows in the sacred text :—*But if her father disallow her in the day that he heareth; not any of her vows, or of her bonds wherewith she hath bound her soul, shall stand ; and the Lord shall forgive her, because her father disallowed her.*"

"And was not," said Lady Ashton, fiercely and triumphantly breaking in, "was not ours the case stated in the holy writ ?   Will this person deny, that the instant her parents heard of the vow, or bond, by which our daughter had bound her soul, we disallowed the same in the most express terms, and informed him by writing of our determination ? "

"And is this all ? " said Ravenswood, looking at Lucy, "are you willing to barter sworn faith, the exercise of free will, and the feelings of mutual affection, to this wretched hypocritical sophistry ? "

"Hear him !" said Lady Ashton, looking to the clergyman, "hear the blasphemer !"

"May God forgive him," said Bide-the-Bent, "and enlighten his ignorance."

As David Deans, in *The Heart of Midlothian*, recovers from the shock occasioned by the arrest of his daughter Effie for the alleged crime of child-murder, his neighbours crowd around him with their appropriate sources of consolation and sympathy—the Laird of Dumbiedykes with his purse, Jeanie with burnt feathers, and the women with their exhortations. "O neighbour—O Mr. Deans, it's a sair trial, doubtless—but think of the Rock of Ages, neighbour—think of the promise !"

"And I do think of it, neighbours—and I bless God that I can think of it, even in the wrack and ruin of a' that's nearest and dearest to me.—But to be the father of a castaway—a profligate—a bloody Zipporah—a mere murderess !—O how will the wicked exult in the high places of their wickedness."

Dumbiedykes again offers his purse. "Davie—winna siller do't ?" But Deans sternly rejects any such offer in tones which ring with the stern old law of retaliation. "I tell ye . . . if a dollar, or a plack, or the nineteenth part of a boddle, wad save her open guilt and open shame frae open punishment, that purchase wad David Deans never make ! Na, na; *an eye for an eye, a tooth for a tooth*, life for life, blood for blood—it's the law of man, and it's the law of God.—Leave me, sirs—leave me—I maun warstle wi' this trial in privacy and on my knees."

The wily Gilbert Glossin, in *Guy Mannering*, who had

wormed himself into possession of the Ellangowan estate, expresses his feigned surprise to Dominie Sampson that the latter had never come down to see the old place.

"You never come down to see your old acquaintance on the Ellangowan property, Mr. Sampson, you would find most of the old stagers still stationary there. I have too much respect for the late family to disturb old residenters, even under pretence of improvement. Besides, it's not my way. I don't like it. I believe, Mr. Sampson, Scripture particularly condemns those who oppress the poor, *and remove landmarks.*"

"Or who devour the substance of orphans," subjoined the Dominie. "Anathema! Maranatha!"

Hobbie Elliot, in *The Black Dwarf,* asks Earnscliff's opinion upon the subject of marriage with a cousin. "I heard the priest of St. John's," continues Hobbie, "and our minister bargaining about it at the winter fair, and troth they baith spak' very weel. Now the priest says it is unlawful to marry ane's cousin; but I cannot say I thought he brought out the Gospel authorities half sae weel as our minister—our minister is thought the best divine and the best preacher atween this and Edinburgh. Dinna ye think he was likely to be right?"

"Certainly," replies Earnscliff, "marriage by all Protestant Christians is held to be as free as God made it by the Levitical law; so, Hobbie, there can be no bar, legal or religious, betwixt you and Miss Armstrong."

In *Kenilworth* there is allusion made to an injunction which is mentioned at least three times in the Pentateuch —"Thou shalt not seethe a kid in its mother's milk."

And the meaning of it comes out in the following tragic incident. The villain Varney imitates the peculiar whistle of his master, the Earl of Leicester, and entices the unsuspecting Countess Amy out of her own apartment at Cumnor Place on to a trap, down which she falls, and is instantaneously killed. "I dreamed not I could have mimicked the Earl's call so well," says Varney to Anthony Foster, who replies :

"Oh, if there be judgment in Heaven, thou hast deserved it, and wilt meet it. Thou hast destroyed her by means of her best affections. *It is a seething of the kid in the mother's milk.*"

THE BOOK OF JUDGES.

IF we except a few references of a passing nature to the taking of Jericho, the sin of Achan, the cities of refuge, the avenger of blood, and the fraud of the Gibeonites which led to their being made "hewers of wood and drawers of water," we shall find, in connection with our present study, that there is nothing more to detain us in the Book of Joshua. But it is otherwise when we come to the Book of Judges, with its simple but graphic details of military operations, its stirring trumpet-calls and battle-cries, and its interesting narratives of the achievements of the men, and the women also, who were specially selected by God to deliver their country from invasion and oppression. Details and narratives such as these, whether in the Bible history or elsewhere, always seemed to affect Sir Walter Scott very deeply; and, accordingly, we meet with much in the Book of Judges which arrested his attention and, probably also, suggested some of the incidents which we are about to place before our readers.

The novel of *Old Mortality*, in particular, contains many of these apparently suggested incidents. After the battle of Drumclog Lord Evandale was made prisoner by the Covenanters, but, at the intercession of Henry Morton, he was allowed to escape. Riding away for dear life, he sought refuge in the cottage of Bessie Maclure, a poor blind widow. Long after the incident took place Henry Morton called at the cottage, and to him she told the story in the following words :—

"Ae nicht, sax weeks or thereby afore Bothwell Brigg, a young gentleman stopped at this puir cottage, stiff and bleeding with wounds, pale and dune oot wi' riding, and his horse sae weary he couldna drag ae foot after the other, and his foes were close ahint him, and he was ane o' our enemies. What could I do, sir?—You that's a sodger will think me but a silly auld wife; but I fed him, and relieved him, and keepit him hidden till the pursuit was over."

"And who," said Morton, " dare disapprove of your having done so?"

"I kenna," answered the blind woman. "I gat ill-will about it among some o' our ain folk. They said I should hae been to him what Jael was to Sisera. But well I wot, I had nae divine command to shed blood, and to save it was baith like a woman and a Christian." What is this but the story of Jael and Sisera told and acted in the light, and under the beneficent influence, of the teaching of the New Testament?

Of a very different spirit from the blind widow is Mause, the mother of our old friend Cuddie Headrigg. Animated by the fire and zeal of the extreme Cameronian, she has no hesitation in seeking to act the part of

Deborah, the prophetess, who celebrated the victory over Jabin's host and the death of Sisera in the sublime and magnificent ode associated with her name. As Mause witnesses the victory at Drumclog, and the flight of Claverhouse and his dragoons, she exclaims in ecstasy—

"They flee! they flee! . . . See how the clouds roll and the fire flashes ahint them, and goes before the chosen of the Covenant, e'en like the pillar o' cloud and the pillar o' flame that led the people of Israel out of the land of Egypt. This is indeed a day of deliverance to the righteous, a day of pouring out of wrath to the persecutors and the ungodly."

Here Mause was interrupted by her son, who dutifully advised her to sit down under the shelter of a cairn or heap of stones, so as to be out of the range of the bullets which were still flying about. But she replies—

"Fear naething for me! . . . I will stand like Deborah on the tap o' the cairn, and tak' up my sang o' reproach against these men of Harosheth of the Gentiles, whose horse-hoofs are broken by their prancing."

The enthusiastic old woman would have accomplished her purpose of mounting the cairn had not Cuddie, with more filial tenderness than respect, detained her with as much force as his shackled arms permitted him to exert.

When Gideon was called to rise and deliver his country from the invading Midianites, he was assured of his success by the sign of a fleece being wet when all around was dry, and again dry when all around was wet. Sir Walter employs this incident in illustration of

at least one of the points in the character of Donald
M'Leish, Mrs. Baliol's guide during her tour in the Highlands. He was unable to resist the showers of hospitality
which descended rather too copiously on him in the shape
of "mountain dew." Poor Donald! "He was on such
occasions," writes Mrs. Baliol in the memorandum which
contains the tale of *The Highland Widow,* "like Gideon's
fleece, moist with the noble element which, of course,
fell not on us."

As the novelist brings us amid scenes of conflict and
assault, we can hear, in imagination, the memorable
battle-cry of "The sword of the Lord and of Gideon."
We hear it as Balfour and Bothwell approach each other
in mortal struggle at Drumclog; and we hear it again as
Gilfillan, the Cameronian officer, on his way to Stirling,
is suddenly attacked by a party of Highlanders, who rush
out of ambush, and rescue the wounded and helpless
Waverley.

The many varied associations which cluster round the
name of Samson come frequently before us in the pages
of the Waverley Novels. There is his strength to begin
with. When Dwining, the crafty apothecary, in *The
Fair Maid of Perth,* advises Sir John Ramorny to keep
clear of Henry Smith, on account of the latter being regarded as the strongest, the boldest, and the best swords-
man in Perth, Sir John replies, "Fear nothing; he shall
be met with, had he the strength of Samson."

Then there is Samson's riddle. Henry Morton, in
Old Mortality, is bold enough to visit Balfour in his secret
place of retreat for the purpose of inducing him to use

his influence in restoring the possessions unlawfully held
by Basil Olifant.

"For whom," Balfour asks, "hast thou ventured to
do this great thing, to seek to rend the prey from the
valiant, to bring forth food from the den of the lion, and
to extract sweetness from the maw of the devourer?
For whose sake hast thou undertaken to read this riddle,
more hard than Samson's?"

"For Lord Evandale's, and that of his bride," Henry
generously and unselfishly replies.

In our introductory chapter we had occasion to refer
to the green *withs* which Samson said would bind his
strength, and make him as another man. The withs
were tried and new ropes as well, but both were snapped
asunder like a thread. As we read the account of Arthur
Philipson, in *Anne of Geierstein*, being immured in the
dungeon of La Ferette we cannot help wishing that,
like Samson, he could as easily have snapped the bonds
which rendered him utterly helpless against the knife
of the hired assassin who might, at any moment, come
upon him. His own sufferings, and the thought that his
father might also be sharing the same fate, wrought the
young man up to the verge of madness. "He started
up, and struggled so hard to free himself from his bonds
that it seemed they should have fallen from him as from
the arms of the mighty Nazarene. But the cords were
of too firm a texture, and after a violent and unavailing
struggle, in which the ligatures seemed to enter his flesh,
the prisoner lost his balance, and fell to the ground with
great force."

There is another reference to the binding of Samson, this time in *The Monastery*, where the White Lady of Avenel tells Halbert Glendinning to

> " Look on my girdle—on this thread of gold—
> 'Tis fine as web of lightest gossamer,
> And, but there is a spell on't, would not bind,
> Light as they are, the folds of my thin robe.
> But when 'twas donn'd, it was a massive chain,
> Such as might bind the champion of the Jews,
> Even when his locks were longest."

In allusion to Delilah inducing Samson to "sleep upon her knees," and while in this position getting some one to cut his locks of hair, the Duke of Burgundy, in *Anne of Geierstein*, says to Philipson, "Edward (IV. of England) is indeed my brother-in-law, but I am a man little·inclined to put my head under my wife's girdle." And in describing the appearance of Thomas De Vaux, in *The Talisman*, the faithful attendant upon King Richard, Sir Walter says of his hair that "in thickness it might have resembled that of Samson, though only after the Israelitish champion's locks had passed under the shears of the Philistines, for those of De Vaux were cut short, that they might be enclosed under his helmet."

The phrase, "in the hands of the Philistines," descriptive of Samson's captivity, is one which very frequently occurs in the Waverley Novels. As it crops up, however, in the conversation of every-day life, and is now of such general application, there is no need or occasion here to produce any instances of the way in which Sir Walter employs the expression.

In the preliminary chapter of *The Bride of Lammermoor* the author refers to the fate of Samson when he says of himself that he is not to be tempted out of his seclusion or lionised in any way. "Like the imprisoned Samson, I would rather remain, if such must be the alternative, all my life in the mill-house grinding for my bread, than be brought forth to make sport for the Philistine lords and ladies." A passage in *Woodstock* brings us up to the culminating point in the history of Samson when, placed between the pillars, he for the last time exerted his heaven-given strength and brought down the building, entombing himself and his tormentors in the general ruin. There is a great noise heard at the palace of Woodstock, as of an explosion of gunpowder, followed by the fall of a turret with which it had been connected by a mine. Thinking that his son must have perished, Sir Henry Lee exclaims, "Ah! my brave boy, perhaps thou art thyself sacrificed like a youthful Samson among the rebellious Philistines."

Toward the end of the Book of Judges, the sacred historian describes, in minute detail, the circumstances which led to the first civil or tribal war in Israel. He narrates how, on one particular occasion, the men of Jabesh-Gilead were all destroyed in order that the unmarried females of the place might be obtained as wives for the surviving men of the nearly-exterminated tribe of Benjamin. As Jabesh-Gilead did not furnish a sufficient number, the unprovided Benjamites were directed to lie in wait, and carry off the maidens of Shiloh as they came out of the city to dance at one of the great annual festivals. It is to this latter incident that the following extract from *Ivanhoe* refers :—

The Norman Knight, De Bracy, dresses or disguises himself as an English yeoman. Fitzurse impatiently asks—

"What on earth dost thou purpose by this absurd disguise at a moment so urgent?"

"To get me a wife," answered De Bracy, coolly, "after the manner of the tribe of Benjamin."

"The tribe of Benjamin?" said Fitzurse, "I comprehend thee not."

"Wert thou not in presence yester-even," said De Bracy, "where we heard the Prior Aymer tell us a tale in reply to the romance which was sung by the minstrel? He told how, long since in Palestine, a deadly feud arose between the tribe of Benjamin and the rest of the Israelitish nation; and how they cut to pieces well-nigh all the chivalry of that tribe; and how they swore by our blessed Lady that they would not permit those who remained to marry in their lineage; and how they became grieved for their vow, and sent to consult his Holiness the Pope how they might be absolved from it; and how by the advice of the Holy Father, the youth of the tribe of Benjamin carried off from a superb tournament all the ladies who were there present, and thus won them wives without the consent either of their brides or their brides' families."

"I have heard the story," said Fitzurse, "though either the Prior or thou hast made some singular alterations in date and circumstances."

"I tell thee," said De Bracy, "that I mean to purvey me a wife after the tribe of Benjamin; which is as much as to say that in this same equipment I will fall upon that herd of Saxon bullocks, who have this night left the castle, and carry off from them the lovely Rowena."

The sacred historian closes the Book of Judges with the reflection, induced not only by this story of the tribe of Benjamin, but also by the prevalence of disorder throughout the land, and the low state into which the national religion had fallen, "In those days there was no king in Israel: every man did that which was right in his own eyes." Sir Walter uses the historian's saddening reflection in describing the state of Scotland when, by the departure of James VI. to assume the richer and more powerful crown of England, it, too, had no king. The country was distracted by contending parties among the aristocracy; the administration of justice was made the subject of the grossest partiality; and even judges lent their sacred authority either to support a friend or crush an enemy. Such was the state of Scotland as described in the opening chapter of the tragic story of *The Bride of Lammermoor.*

THE BOOK OF RUTH.

As the story of Ruth forms a supplement to the Book of Judges, we may here give an extract from the former, in connection with an interesting incident in the novel of *Guy Mannering*. After the death of the Laird of Ellangowan, and the breaking-up of the household there, Colonel Mannering generously offered a home to Lucy Bertram. As she gratefully accepted the offer, her old friend and tutor, Dominic Sampson, began to realise for the first time that he was to be parted from her. Such an idea had never occurred to the simplicity of his understanding. In an impassioned appeal, the longest speech he had ever been known to make, he thus addressed his old pupil :—

"No, Miss Lucy Bertram, while I live I will not separate from you. I'll be no burden—I have thought how to prevent that. But, as Ruth said unto Naomi, 'Entreat me not to leave thee, nor to depart from thee : for whither thou goest, I will go ; and where thou dwellest, I will dwell ; thy people shall be my people, and thy God shall be my God. Where thou diest, will I die, and there will I be buried. The Lord do so to me, and more also, if aught but death do part thee and me.'"

And, while we write of the affections, we are reminded of a Scriptural expression which occurs not only in the narrative of Ruth and Naomi, but also in several other places of the Old Testament. In the scene where Jeanie Deans goes to visit Effie in prison, in *The Heart of Midlothian*, the sisters walked together to the side of the pallet-bed, and sat down side by side, taking hold of each other's hands, looking in each other's face, but without speaking a word. In this position they remained for a minute, while the gleam of joy gradually faded from their features, and gave way to the most intense expression, first of melancholy, and then of agony, till, throwing themselves again into each other's arms, they, to use the language of Scripture, "lifted up their voices and wept bitterly."

LEAVING the Book of Judges and the story of Ruth, we come now to the Books of Samuel, with all their interesting narratives of Samuel himself, of Saul, and of David. Among our Waverley references we do not find many that relate to the prophet-judge personally, but a great number to the outstanding incidents recorded in the two Books which bear his name. There is an affecting scene in *Ivanhoe* which reminds us of the dying mother's request to call her newly-born child Ichabod, as she hears of the defeat of her countrymen and the ark of God having fallen into the hands of the Philistines. Isaac of York learns that his daughter Rebecca has been carried off by the fierce and dissolute Templar. One of the outlaws, who has conveyed this information to the distracted father, adds that he had drawn his bow to send an arrow after the Templar, but, fearing lest he should harm the lady instead, he had not shot.

"Oh," answered the Jew, "I would to God thou hadst shot, though the arrow had pierced her bosom. Better the tomb of her fathers than the dishonourable couch of the licentious and savage Templar. Ichabod! Ichabod! the glory hath departed from my house!"

We hear this agonising cry of grief and sorrow from the sorely-afflicted David Deans during the trial of his daughter at Edinburgh, as related in *The Heart of Midlothian.* And when the father of Nanty Ewart, in *Redgauntlet,* heard of the misconduct of his son while a student at the University of the same city, "he did nothing for six days but cry out, Ichabod! Ichabod! the glory is departed from my house!"

When Saul joined the company of prophets and prophesied among them, the people of Israel wonderingly asked of each other, "Is Saul among the prophets?" This proverb, ever since used to express surprise at seeing some one in a place or company where he was least expected to appear, is so employed by Sir Walter in *Peveril of the Peak.* A side door in Bridgenorth's house in London, where a conventicle is being held, suddenly opens, and Christian enters the apartment. He starts and colours as he sees Julian Peveril; then, turning to Bridgenorth with an assumed air of indifference, he asks, "Is Saul also among the prophets? Is a Peveril among the saints?"

The proverb is also employed to express surprise on learning that some one is possessed of gifts or qualifications which he did not before get the credit of possessing. It is used in this sense by Brown in writing to a friend when he states that, in addition to other accomplishments, Colonel Mannering had also those of drawing and poetry; for, to a set of sketches by the Colonel, there was added a short poetical description by the same hand. Well might Brown write—"Is Saul, you will say, among the prophets? Colonel Mannering write poetry!"

In *The Heart of Midlothian* there is a graphic description of one of the well-known traditions of Edinburgh—the Porteous mob. Captain John Porteous, of the Town Guard, had given orders to the troops to fire on the crowd, and for this excess of his commission he was afterwards tried, found guilty, and sentenced to be hanged. He was reprieved, however, and the general belief was that he would finally be pardoned. Exasperated at the escape of the object of their fury, the mob forced open the prison door and set fire to the building. Unconscious of what was going on, Porteous felt relieved from anxiety by his reprieve, thinking in the emphatic words of Scripture, on an occasion in somewhat similar circumstances, that surely the bitterness of death was past.

Sir Walter here alludes to the incident of Samuel desiring Saul to bring before him Agag, the captive king of Amalek. The captive approached with every mark of deference and respect, feeling that the bitterness of death was surely past; but neither in the Scriptural case nor in that of the Edinburgh tragedy was the dreaded bitterness over, for death was inflicted in both instances.

There are, at least, two other scenes in the Waverley Novels where this "bitterness of death" was not past, but fully expected by two unhappy persons in very trying circumstances. In *Quentin Durward*, the Duke of Burgundy receives an unexpected visit from his Lord Paramount, Louis XI. of France. Hearing of the murder of the Bishop of Liege, and believing it to have been done at the instigation of the King, the Duke orders His Majesty to be arrested and lodged in the Castle of Peronne. The scene at the meeting of the two potentates is a striking one. Well might the King get a foretaste of the bitterness of death as he stood in the presence of "the most passionate prince who ever lived," while "under the dominion of one of his most violent paroxysms of fury." In *The Fortunes of Nigel*, Lord Dalgarno seizes hold of the dark-haired scrivener and shakes him so violently that the trembling caitiff "felt at that moment all the bitterness of the mortal agony." But king and caitiff both escaped.

Oppressed and saddened by the fate foretold by Samuel, and troubled by an evil spirit, the mind of Saul gave way, and he sank into a deep and dangerous melancholy. The youthful David's music was the only charm which could bring the King to himself again. Under its sweet and soothing influence he "was refreshed, and was well, and the evil spirit departed from him." We have, throughout the Waverley Novels, numerous instances of kings, princes, generals, and persons in almost every rank of life, under such fits of melancholy as those which troubled Saul. The old soldier in *Woodstock* asks Captain Pearson if he intends to carry out, to the letter, the commands of General Cromwell with reference to the execution of the prisoners. With an air of doubt the Captain replies that he fears there is no other course open to him.

"Be assured," said the old man, "that if thou dost

this folly, thou wilt cause Israel to sin, and that the
General will not be pleased with your service. Thou
knowest, and none better than thou, that Oliver, though
he be like unto David the son of Jesse in faith, and
wisdom, and courage, yet there are times when the evil
spirit cometh upon him as it did upon Saul, and he
uttereth commands which he will not thank any one for
executing."

The poor simpleton, David Gellatley, in *Waverley*, was
extremely fond of music, deeply affected by that which was
melancholy, but transported into extravagant gaiety by
light and lively airs. Louis XI., King Rene, the Duke of
Rothesay, and Mordaunt, had all their dark and troubled
hours. But in *The Legend of Montrose* we are specially
reminded of the melancholy moods of Saul, and the
influence of music in dispelling them. Allan MacAulay,
brother of the chief, was subject both to fits of despond-
ency and, occasionally, to mental aberration. It was
observed that the beauty of Annot Lyle and her skill
in music, "produced upon the disturbed spirits of
Allan, in his gloomiest moods, beneficial effects similar
to those experienced by the Jewish monarch of
old."

Here is Sir Walter's graphic description of Allan
recovering from one of these moods under the soothing
influence of Annot's harp.

"As the strain proceeded, Allan MacAulay gradually
gave signs of recovering his presence of mind, and attention to the objects around him. The deep-knit furrows
of his brow relaxed and smoothed themselves; and the

rest of his features, which had seemed contorted with internal agony, relapsed into a more natural state. When he raised his head and sat upright, his countenance, though still deeply melancholy, was divested of its wildness and ferocity ; and in its composed state, although by no means handsome, the expression of his features was striking, manly, and even noble. His thick brown eyebrows, which had hitherto been drawn close together, were now slightly separated, as in the natural state ; and his gray eyes, which had rolled and flashed from under them with an unnatural and portentous gleam, now recovered a steady and determined expression."

"Thank God," he said, after sitting silent for about a minute, until the last sounds of the harp had ceased to vibrate, "my soul is no longer darkened—the mist hath passed from my spirit."

The story of David and Goliath is one of those incidents in the sacred narrative to which we may expect frequent and varied reference in the pages of the Waverley Novels. It is to Sir Walter what some favourite doctrinal text is to the theologian, for it furnishes him, as a novelist, with abundance of material for illustration both in its details and as a whole. As the name of Samson suggests strength, so that of Goliath suggests size. The mirror in which Mr. Holdenough, in *Woodstock*, imagined he saw the reflection of his friend Joseph Albany, was so large in size that it "might have served Goliath of Gath to have admired himself in, when clothed from head to foot in his brazen armour."

The mention of the Philistine's armour reminds us of

a remark which Isaac the Jew made to his daughter about the lance of Ivanhoe. "It was," he said, "like that of Goliath, and might vie with a weaver's beam."

In response to the giant's demand that the Israelites should send him a

"Foeman worthy of his steel,"

David comes upon the scene. Saul reminds him of his youth and inexperience, and suggests that if he will fight the Philistine he should put on a suit of armour and take a sword in his hand. David tried the armour and the sword, but immediately put off the one and laid down the other, feeling that they were only

"Encumb'ring and not arming him."

In the *Legend of Montrose*, Sir Walter describes the warlike habits of the Highlanders and their peculiar mode of warfare as compared with that practised by the Lowlanders. Anything that the former "had been taught of discipline was like Saul's armour upon David, a hindrance rather than a help, because they had not proved it."

When, in *Anne of Geierstein*, Arthur Philipson and Rudolph Donnerhugel, the gigantic Swiss, met to fight the pre-arranged duel, the latter offered Arthur a huge two-handed sword, which the Englishman looked at with some surprise, as he had never been accustomed to the use of such a weapon.

"He who fights on a Swiss mountain, fights with a Swiss brand," said Rudolph. "Think you, our hands are made to handle pen-knives?"

"Nor are ours made to wield scythes," said Arthur;

and as the Swiss still continued to offer the sword, he refused it on the same ground as David did the armour of Saul—it was only an encumbrance.

Rudolph then asks if Arthur repents having accepted the challenge. "If so, cry craven, and return in safety."

"No, proud man," replied the Englishman, "I ask thee no forbearance. I thought but of a combat between a shepherd and a giant, in which God gave the victory to him who had worse weapons of odds than falls to my lot to-day. I will fight as I stand; my own good sword shall serve my need now as it has done before."

The fight, accordingly, began; but it was interrupted by the appearance of Arnold Biederman, who, in stern tones which rose above the clash of swords, commanded them at once to forbear. Towards the end of the novel this gigantic Swiss again challenges the Englishman. This time they met each other on horseback, and in the encounter the Swiss met the fate of Goliath. The Duke of Burgundy was greatly delighted to hear the news. Taking a ponderous chain of gold from off his own neck, he hung it round Arthur's, saying as he did so, "Why, thou forstallest all our honours, young man—this was the biggest bear of them all. . . . I think I have found a youthful David to match their huge thick-headed Goliath."

When Henry Smith, in *The Fair Maid of Perth*, resolved upon taking the place of the missing man in the approaching battle between the two clans at Perth, he presented himself within the lists, and announced that he was ready to fight on the part of the clan Chattan. Like Saul, the Provost advised Henry to put on armour,

offering him at the same time his own Milan hauberk and
Spanish sword. But Smith replied:

"I thank your noble Earlship. . . . I am little used to
sword or harness that I have not wrought myself, because
I do not know what blows the one will bear without
being cracked, or the other lay on without snapping."

Sir Geoffrey Hudson, the Dwarf in *Peveril of the Peak*,
in his own amusing way, states to Julian Peveril that he
admires and respects him now that he has "killed one
of those gigantic fellows who go about swaggering as if
their souls were taller than ours, because their noses are
nearer to the clouds by a cubit or two." He recommends
Julian, however, not to plume himself too much on having
accomplished such a feat, or to consider it as anything
unusual, for, he says, "I would have you know it hath
been always thus; and that in the history of all ages,
the clean, tight, dapper little fellow hath proved an over-
match for his bulky antagonist. I need only instance
out of Holy Writ the celebrated downfall of Goliath,
and of another lubbard who had more fingers to his
hand, and more inches to his stature, than ought to
belong to an honest man, and who was slain by a nephew
of good King David." The dwarf hero refers to the
historical incident mentioned in the twentieth chapter
of First Chronicles, "And yet again there was war at
Gath, where a man of great stature, whose fingers and
toes were four and twenty, six on each hand and six on
each foot, and he also was the son of the giant. But
when he defied Israel, Jonathan, the son of Shimea,
David's brother, slew him."

The love and esteem which Saul seems to have felt, at one time at least, for David gradually gave way to hatred and jealousy. After the defeat and death of Goliath, the fits of jealousy increased in number and intensity, until at length David had to leave the Court and flee for his life to the country, whither he was followed and hunted "like a partridge on the mountains."

The Baron Bradwardine remarked to Waverley, when the latter came to visit him at his place of concealment, that the Government "have sent soldiers to abide on the estate and hunt me like a partridge on the mountains, as Scripture says of good King David." In *Woodstock*, Everard asks Wildrake if he has heard any news of "the young man, King of Scotland as they call him."

"Nothing," was the reply, "but that he is hunted like a partridge on the mountains."

In the course of David's wanderings in his endeavour to keep out of the reach of Saul, he found refuge in one of the caves among the limestone rocks near Adullam. When Henry Morton, in *Old Mortality*, visited Burley in his hiding-place, the latter remarked, "I like my place of refuge—my cave of Adullam, and would not change its rude ribs of limestone rocks for the fair chambers of the castle of the Earls of Loudon with their broad bounds and barony."

In this cave of Adullam, David established himself as an independent chief, and was soon joined by a number of followers, drawn chiefly from those classes who are ever ready for revolt from the restraints of civilised society. In *The Fortunes of Nigel* there is a description given of the state of Whitefriars, adjacent to the Temple. In the time of James I., and for nearly a century afterwards, this particular district of London, known by the cant name of Alsatia, had the privilege of sanctuary, unless against the writ of the Lord Chief Justice, or of the Lords of the Privy Council. One may easily imagine the class of persons likely to be found in this modern cave of Adullam. "The place abounded," says Sir Walter in the novel just named, "with desperadoes of every description—bankrupt citizens, ruined gamesters, irreclaimable prodigals, desperate duellists, bravoes, homicides, and debauched profligates of every description, all leagued together to maintain the immunities of their asylum." During the march of the Highland army into England, as narrated in *Waverley*, Prince Charles Edward was joined by a number of very sorry-looking recruits. On being asked his opinion of them, the Baron Bradwardine replied, "that he could not but have an excellent opinion of them, since they resembled precisely the followers who attached themselves to the good King David at the cave of Adullam ; *videlicet*, every one that was in distress, and every one that was in debt, and every one that was discontented, which the Vulgate renders bitter of soul; and doubtless" he said, "they will prove mighty men of their hands, and there is much need that they should, for I have seen many a sour look cast upon us."

In the course of Alan Fairford's wanderings in search of his friend Darsie Latimer, as told in *Redgauntlet*, the former is taken on board the Jumping Jenny. The skipper, Nanty Ewart, tries to draw out of his passenger some information as to where he is going, and what is the object of his travels. Thinking that he is one of the adherents of Charles Stewart, and that he is on his way to join the desperate cause, Nanty repeats the verse just quoted by the Baron Bradwardine, and then asks "Have I touched you now, sir?"

But Alan, in search only of his friend, and having nothing whatever to do with the distressed and discontented who were joining the cause of the Pretender, could reply, with a clear conscience, "You are as far off as ever."

One evening in the twilight, alone and hungry from having tasted no food all day, Dominie Sampson, in *Guy Mannering*, was suddenly confronted by the gipsy, Meg Merrilies, in the deserted hamlet of Derncleugh.

"I kenn'd ye wad be here," she said in a harsh and hollow voice, "I ken wha ye seek, but ye maun do my bidding."

Resisting all attempts at silencing her, Meg forced the unwilling Dominie into a vault, pushed him into a broken chair, and, like the Witch of Endor persuading the forlorn and broken-hearted King of Israel to take food, she placed before him a dish of goodly stew, and sternly commanded him at once to eat.

Afraid of the mixture, the poor man had determined not to taste it, hungry though he was; but the savoury smell soon began to tell upon his obstinacy. He thought, too, of what Saul had done in the cave, and so he not only ate the stew, but drank the modern witch's health in a cupful of brandy, after which he felt "mightily elevated, and afraid of no evil which could befall unto him."

Keeping in mind the particular direction of our present study of the Waverley Novels, we may note here that *Redgauntlet* always reminds us of the friendship which bound David and Jonathan so closely together. The correspondence contained in the letters which pass between the two friends, Alan Fairford and Darsie Latimer, is the chief charm of this novel; and when the letter-writing stops and the narrative begins, we feel how intense is the affection which unites the two young men. What a striking instance of devotion to his friend does Alan present when, during the great trial of *Peebles against Plainstanes*, the young advocate throws aside everything when he incidentally learns that Darsie is in imminent personal danger, forgets fame and fortune, hazards even the serious displeasure of his father, and sets out in search of his beloved companion.

In language uttered under the influence of great emotion, the Rev. Mr. Holdenough, in *Woodstock*, thus apostrophises the memory of the friend of his youth— "Oh, Albany, my brother, my brother, I have lamented for thee even as David for Jonathan."

In *The Fair Maid of Perth*, we have a wonderfully touching description of the love which "passes the love of women." Conachar enters the lists with sore misgivings as to his fate, but is encouraged by his foster-father and eight foster-brothers, who do their utmost to protect him until they themselves are, one after another, struck down. As the last falls, Conachar loses heart altogether, madly takes refuge in flight, and plunges into the Tay. He afterwards presents himself before Catherine Glover at the waterfall, and in utter despair he exclaims—"I have lost honour, fame, and friends; and such friends! . . . Oh! their love surpasses the love of women! . . . The faithful nine are still pursuing me; they cry with feeble voice, 'Strike but one blow in our revenge, we all died for you.'"

After the great wrong done by David "in the matter of Uriah," the prophet Nathan was sent to the king to reprove him. This he did by means of the parable of the rich man who spared his own flocks, but seized the one ewe-lamb of his poor neighbour. Simon Glover refers to this, when speaking to Henry Smith of Catherine's notion of entering the Convent. "I love and honour the Church," said the Glover, crossing himself, "I pay her rights duly and cheerfully . . . but I cannot afford the Church my only and single ewe-lamb, that I have in the world."

The Duke of Rothesay and Sir John Ramorny are discussing a project they have in hand to carry off this same only daughter of the Glover. The Duke states his scruples in the matter, and then asks Ramorny—"Dost thou remember when we went to hear Father Clement preach, or rather to see this fair heretic, that he spoke as touchingly as a minstrel about the rich man taking away the poor man's only ewe-lamb?"

This parable was also, we think, in Sir Walter's mind when he makes Foster say to Varney, in *Kenilworth*, that he will be no party to having his child's soul placed in peril either for Varney or Varney's master. "I may," he continued, "walk among snares and pitfalls myself, because I have discretion, but I will not trust the poor lamb among them."

The application of the parable is employed in *The Abbot*, where Roland Græme is joined one morning on the battlements of Loch Leven Castle by the chaplain, Elias Henderson. Looking across the country, with its villages and hamlets enjoying the blessings of peace and security, the chaplain asks the page what that man would deserve who should bring fire, civil war, and slaughter over those peaceful scenes.

Roland replies that he does not know to what the chaplain refers, nor can he form any idea who the person can be, that could ever dream of bringing such calamities upon the land.

"God forbid!" replied the preacher, "that I should say to thee, 'Thou art the man.'" He then proceeded to warn the page that in serving Queen Mary, and in seeking to get her once more seated on the throne of Scotland, he might be the person on whose head would fall the due curse and punishment in having been the means of bringing about such a change for the worse.

During the sickness of his child, David prayed and fasted, refusing all consolation from his attendants ; but, to their great surprise, when he was told that the child was dead, he rose up, washed himself, put off all signs of mourning, and then sat down to eat. In *Peveril of the Peak*, Bridgenorth expresses his gratitude to Lady Peveril for her attention and kindness to his child, and adds,

"David, the man after God's own heart, did wash and eat bread when his beloved child was removed. Mine is restored to me, and shall I not show gratitude under a blessing, when he showed resignation under an affliction?"

As David Deans and Jeanie, in *The Heart of Midlothian*, sit down to their homely meal, during the time they are under a great cloud of sorrow, he exhorts his daughter to eat and be comforted. "The man after God's own heart," he said, "washed and anointed himself, and did eat bread, in order to express his submission under a dispensation of suffering, and it did not become a Christian man or woman so to cling to creature comforts of wife or bairns . . . as to forget the first duty — submission to the Divine will."

In describing the taking of Rabbah, one of the Ammonite cities, the sacred historian records the terrible punishment inflicted by David upon the unfortunate prisoners of war. To this punishment the poor Jew, in *Ivanhoe*, alludes when the Palmer wakes him from his sleep and warns him of his danger. When Isaac learns that the Templar has ordered his Mussulman slaves to seize him and carry him off, either to the castle of Malvoisin or that of Front-de-Bœuf, he exclaims in the extremity of consternation, "Holy God of Abraham . . . the dream is not dreamed for nought, and the vision cometh not in vain. I feel the rack pass over my body like the saws, and harrows, and axes of iron over the men of Rabbah, and of the cities of the children of Ammon."

In the stratagem employed by Joab to get Absalom's banishment recalled, he sent to Tekoah and instructed a wise woman of that place what to say when she stood before the king. He "put the words in her mouth." There is a reference to this incident in *Kenilworth*, where the Countess secretly leaves Cumnor Hall for Kenilworth Castle under the protection of Wayland Smith. Janet Foster, who remains behind, is instructed what to say in the event of her mistress being missed next morning. Before setting out, Smith reminds the maid that if she remembers her lesson, there will be no pursuit in search of the Countess. To this reminder, Janet replies that she will no more forget her instructions "than the wise widow of Tekoah forgot the words which Joab put into her mouth."

During the trial of Effie Deans, in *The Heart of Mid-lothian*, her sister Jeanie is under examination, and as counsel interrogates her, the proceedings are suddenly interrupted by her father, who exclaims, "Na, na, my bairn is no like the widow of Tekoah—nae man has putten words into her mouth."

The affecting cry of David when he received the news of Absalom's death, is an incident which Sir Walter could scarcely fail to quote. When Robert of Scotland, in *The Fair Maid of Perth*, hears that the Duke of Rothesay has been found dead in his apartment—"from sudden illness, as I have heard"—the unhappy and broken-hearted king gave expression to his grief and sense of bereavement almost in the words of the King of Israel—in somewhat similar circumstances—"O Rothesay! O my beloved

David! Would to God I had died for thee, my son—my son!"

When the son of Sir Henry Lee devotes his life to the cause of King Charles, and seeks, at great personal risk, to effect his Majesty's escape from Woodstock, we feel that much as the old knight is concerned for the safety of his sovereign, his anxiety for that of his son is still more so. While Sir Henry consents to the risk being undertaken, we hear him thus communing with himself, "But at what a cost do I this? Oh, Absalom, Absalom, my son, my son!"

Among the last recorded acts of David was the charge to Solomon with reference to Shimei who, on one occasion, had deeply injured and publicly insulted the king. Though the offender had been forgiven, and though allowed to stay in Jerusalem, he was yet warned that the brook Kedron was the boundary of his liberty, and that if he ventured across it he would incur the penalty of death. In narrating the experience of Chrystal Croftangry, in *Chronicles of the Canongate*, Sir Walter refers to this incident. After a course of dissipation, Chrystal was obliged to take refuge in the sanctuary at Holyrood. Day by day he had to keep within the boundary line, or kennel, which divides the sanctuary from the unprivileged part of the Canongate. "To a stranger, or an indifferent person, either side of the line would have seemed much the same; but to Croftangry, the gutter or kennel was what the brook Kedron was to Shimei — death was denounced against him who should cross it."

SOLOMON AND THE KINGS OF JUDAH
AND ISRAEL.

THERE is, perhaps, no Bible name which occurs more
frequently in the Waverley Novels than that of Solomon.
Again and again we meet it in connection with his
wealth and magnificence; with his wisdom, which has
become proverbial; with his sagacious judgment; with
the gold which he brought from Ophir; and with the
famous visit of the Queen of Sheba. But the references
are generally of such a passing nature, that they appear
to little advantage when lifted out of their context and
laid before the reader as extracts. We have marked a
few for quotation, however; and the first we see is from
The Fortunes of Nigel, where George Heriot places before
King James the massive silver plate which has for its
engraved ornamentation the subject of the Judgment
of Solomon. The King thus criticises the artist's
work :—

"It is a curious and vera artificial sculpture, but yet,
methinks, the carnifex or executioner there is brandishing
his gully ower near the King's face, seeing he is within
reach of his weapon. I think less wisdom than Solomon's wad have taught him that there was danger in

edge-tools, and that he would have bidden the smaik either sheath his shabble, or stand further back."

In Donnerhugel's narrative, as related in the novel of *Anne of Geierstein*, there is mention made of a Persian girl named Hermione, who came to reside at the Castle of Arnheim. There were wonderful reports of her great wisdom and learning, so much so that the Bishop of Bamberg resolved, like the Queen of Sheba, to visit Hermione and prove her with hard questions. "He conversed with her, and found her deeply impressed with the truths of religion, and so perfectly acquainted with its doctrines, that he compared her to a doctor of theology in the dress of an Eastern dancing-girl. When asked regarding her knowledge of languages and science, he answered that he had been attracted to Arnheim by the most extravagant reports on these points, but that he must return, confessing 'the half thereof had not been told unto him.'"

But as in the Bible, so also in Waverley, we meet with much that reminds us of the faults and failings of the later years of Solomon's life. "The beauty of a fair woman caused Solomon Ben David to stumble in his path," says the Nawaub in the story of *The Surgeon's Daughter;* and in many other novels of the series we find similar allusions. Thus, in *Kenilworth,* Varney asks his master, the Earl of Leicester, if he will allow himself to be driven frantic about Amy Robsart, because, said he, "you have not been wiser than the wisest man whom the world has ever seen." And Sir Patrick Charteris observes to Henry Smith, in *The*

Fair Maid of Perth, when he brings the latter disappointing news of Catherine Glover, that women are but weather-cocks, "as Solomon and others have proved before you."

Leaving Solomon, we come to his son, Rehoboam, who began his reign under circumstances which associate his name with setting aside old and experienced counsellors and seeking advice, instead, from the younger men who had grown up with him at the court of his father. Frank Osbaldistone, in *Rob Roy*, is warmly commended for not taking such a course, when he goes to Bailie Nicol Jarvie to ask his advice as to the best way of furthering the interest of Mr. Osbaldistone senior. "Ye're right, young man, ye're right," said the worthy magistrate. "Aye take the counsel of those who are wiser and aulder than yourself, and binna like the godless Rehoboam who took the advice o' a wheen beardless callants, neglecting the auld counsellors who had sate at the feet of his father Solomon, and, as it was weel put by Mr. Meiklejohn in his lecture on the chapter, were doubtless partakers of his sapience."

Here is another instance in which an aged counsellor's advice is proposed to be taken. It occurs in *Woodstock*, where King Charles says that "in Scotland, the Presbyterian ministers when thundering in their pulpits on my own sins, and those of my house, took the freedom to call me to my face Jeroboam, or Rehoboam, or some such name, for following the advice of young counsellors." Then referring to his old friend, Sir Henry Lee, the king proceeds, "I will take that of the gray beard for once, for never saw I more sharpness and decision than in the countenance of that noble old man."

"Like the unwise son of the wisest of men," Richard Middlemass, in *The Surgeon's Daughter*, valued the advice of his young friend, Tom Hillary, more than that of his elder friends and counsellors.

We come now to Elijah, "the blessed Elias," as the monk in *The Talisman* says, "even him who was translated without suffering the ordinary pangs of mortality." Our first mention of him, in connection with our present study, is in *Peveril of the Peak*, and the reference is to his being fed by ravens. One morning Major Bridgenorth was reposing in his easy chair, thinking of former times, and recalling the feelings with which he was wont to expect the recurring visits of Sir Geoffrey Peveril, who brought him news of the welfare of his child. "Surely," Bridgenorth said, thinking as it were aloud, "there was no sin in the kindness with which I then regarded that man."

Solsgrace, who was in the apartment, and guessed what was passing through his friend's mind, replied, "When God caused Elijah to be fed by ravens, while hiding by the brook Cherith, we hear not of his fondling the unclean birds, whom, contrary to their ravening nature, a miracle compelled to minister unto him."

"It may be so," answered Bridgenorth, "yet the flap of their wings must have been gracious in the ear of the famished prophet, like the tread of Peveril's horse in mine. The ravens, doubtless, resumed their nature when the season was passed, and even so it has fared with him."

After leaving his place of concealment by the brook Cherith, the prophet was directed to go to Zarephath, where he was to lodge and be sustained by a poor widow. Henry Morton, in *Old Mortality*, knocks at the door of Bessie Maclure's cottage and inquires if she can give him accommodation for the night.

"I can, sir, if you will be pleased with the widow's cake and the widow's cruize."

Morton gratefully accepts the poor widow's hospitality, with the remark that, having been a soldier, nothing can come amiss to him in the way of entertainment.

Widow Maclure was blind in addition to being poor. Struck by her loneliness, Morton asks if she has no one beside her except the little girl whom he observed in the cottage.

"None, sir," said his old hostess; "I dwell alone, like the widow of Zarephath."

Elijah's restoring to life the widow's son, forms the subject of an argument on the intercession of saints between Father Eustace and Henry Warden, in *The Monastery*. The supposed death of Halbert Glendinning has naturally thrown his mother's household into grief and mourning; but when he was afterwards discovered to be alive and well, Father Eustace says to Edward Glendinning, "Let thy sorrowing mother know that her son is restored to her from the grave, like the child of the widow of Zarephath, at the intercession," he added, looking at Henry Warden, "of the blessed saint whom I invoked in his behalf." "Deceived thyself," said Warden instantly, "thou art a deceiver of others. It was no dead man, no creature of clay, whom the blessed Tishbite invoked when, stung by the reproach of the Shunammite mother, he prayed that her son's soul might come unto him again."

There is a reference in Warden's reply to another of the miracles wrought by Elijah; for that of raising the widow's son at Zarephath is a distinct and separate act from the restoring to life the child of the Shunammite mother.

In *The Fortunes of Nigel*, we have the adventures of a young Scottish nobleman who went to London in the hope of obtaining, from King James, a sum of money which His Majesty, when James VI. of Scotland, had borrowed from Nigel's father. The payment of this money was necessary to prevent the sale of the castle and estate of Glenvarloch. Nigel finds a friend at Court in the person of Lord Huntinglen, who, from the fact of his having saved James from threatened assassination, was privileged to ask an annual boon of the king. His lordship lays the petition of Nigel before James, who thinks there need be no difficulty about the money, but as regards the estate he had a strong wish to retain it, seeing that "it contained the best hunting-ground in Scotland." Lord Huntinglen listened with great composure, and answered: "An' it please your Majesty, there was an answer yielded by Naboth when Ahab coveted his vineyard: 'The Lord forbid that I should give the inheritance of my fathers unto thee.'"

This application of the Scripture narrative had the desired effect upon the king, for he hastily wrote an order on the Scottish exchequer for the amount of the loan, saying, as he did so, "Ye see, my Lord of Huntin-glen, that I am neither an untrue man to deny you the boon whilk I became bound for, nor an Ahab to covet Naboth's vineyard."

In *Woodstock*, Albert Lee is brought before Cromwell, and, after a brief interview, is ordered to be tried before a court-martial. "One word," said young Lee as he was led from the room.

"Stop, stop," said Cromwell; "let him be heard."

"You love texts of Scripture," said Lee. "Let this be the subject of your next homily—'Had Zimri peace who slew his master?'" This bold allusion to Cromwell's share in the execution of Charles I. is quoted from the question asked by Jezebel of Jehu, when the latter arrived at Jezreel after slaying Joram, the King of Israel.

In those volumes of the Waverley Novels which are mainly devoted to describing times of great religious excitement either in England or Scotland, there is a wonderful profusion and wealth of Scripture language and reference. Such volumes specially indicate how accurately and how intimately Sir Walter knew the Sacred History. No one who did not know the Bible thoroughly, could have written such books as *Old Mortality* and *Woodstock.* Those two novels contain numerous and powerfully-drawn portraits of clergymen, preachers, re-ligious enthusiasts, and men of moderate views in religion. Some of these people preach sermons, others make long prayers, and almost all of them speak in language savour-ing strongly of that of Scripture; and the particular portion of Scripture which they seem most frequently to employ is that of the time of the Kings of Judah and Israel. Kettledrummle, in his sermon to the Cameronians after the battle of Drumclog, enlarges on the doctrine of armed resistance to Charles II., and as he warms up to his subject, he confers on the king such names as "Jeroboam, Omri, Ahab, Shallum, Pekah, and every other evil monarch recorded in the Chronicles." Balfour calls Bothwell a "railing Rabshakeh;" the poor blind widow Maclure speaks of the dragoons billeted in her cottage as "men of Belial;" and such expressions as "the priests of Baal," "flattering Ziphites," "the sons of Zeruiah," and many more like these are of frequent occurrence in *Old Mortality.* Expressions of this kind are used by the extreme section of the Cameronians, who, according to Sir Walter, have no hesitation whatever in detaching from their context many of the commands given to the Jews, and use such commands against all whom they consider the oppressors of Scotland. For example, the more moderate among the clergymen propose that, previous to making an attack on Tillietudlem, the ladies should be summoned to surrender, on the strength of an offer to send them under a safe escort in peace and quietness as far as Edinburgh. Mucklewrath, however, on hearing such a proposal cries out, "Who talks of safe conduct and of peace? . . . I say, take the . . . daughters and the mothers of the house, and hurl them from the battlements of their trust, that the dogs may fatten on their blood, as they did on that of Jezebel, the spouse of Ahab."

In the same novel there is another scene in which

Mucklewrath again appears. The scene we refer to is, to our thinking, at once the most dramatic and the most exciting in all the Waverley Novels; and it comes into its place here, in its historical order, as having reference to King Hezekiah. Henry Morton escapes from Both-well Bridge after an unsuccessful attempt to rally the forces under his command. Seeking refuge in a farm-house, he finds it filled with fugitives like himself, but of the extreme section of the Cameronians. They regard the entrance of Morton with anything but favour, and so far forget themselves, in their zeal for the Covenant, as to seize hold of him and sentence him to be slain when the hand on the clock-face announces that the Sabbath is past. Fearing that the enemy may come up before the hour, the "maniac preacher" starts to his feet ex-claiming, "I take up my song against him. As the sun went back on the dial ten degrees for intimating the recovery of holy Hezekiah, so shall it now go forward, that the wicked may be taken away from among the people, and the Covenant established in its purity."

The preacher then sprang to a chair with the attitude of frenzy, in order to anticipate the fatal moment by putting the index of the clock forward : while several of the party began to make ready for the immediate execu-tion of their victim. The trampling of horses, however, was heard, and the timely arrival of Claverhouse with a party of dragoons prevented the slaughter of Henry Morton.

There is another reference to Hezekiah where Hugo de Lacy, in *The Betrothed*, stands before the Prelate,

overwhelmed in doubt lest his preference of the con-
tinuance of his own house to the rescue of the Holy
Sepulchre should be punished by the disease which
threatens his nephew's life. "Come," said the Prelate,
"noble De Lacy, the judgment provoked by a moment's
presumption may be even yet averted by prayer and
penitence. The dial went back at the prayer of the good
King Hezekiah—down, down upon thy knees, and doubt
not that, with confession, and penance, and absolution,
thou mayest atone for thy falling away from the cause
of Heaven."

We have in the Waverley Novels several interesting
references to Naaman the Syrian. On her journey to
London, as described in *The Heart of Midlothian*, Jeanie
Deans hears and sees for the first time the Episcopalian
service in church. Unlike all that she has been accustomed
to observe in the act of public worship, she felt confused
by the change of position adopted in different parts of the
ritual. She prudently resolved, however, to imitate as
nearly as she could the postures and observances of her
fellow-worshippers. "The prophet," she thought, "permitted Naaman the Syrian to bow even in the house of
Rimmon. Surely if I, in this streight, worship the God
of my fathers in mine own language, although the manner
thereof be strange to me, the Lord will pardon me in this
thing."

While soldiering on the Continent, our old friend
Captain Dalgetty, in *A Legend of Montrose*, was "pricked
in conscience" as to going to church and hearing mass.
Asking advice from the reformed Dutch pastor on the

matter, the clergyman replied " that he considered there would be no harm done in Dalgetty's going to mass, seeing that the prophet permitted Naaman, a mighty man of valour, and an honourable cavalier of Syria, to follow his master into the house of Rimmon, a false god or idol to whom he had vowed service, and to bow down when the king was leaning upon his hand."

Observing that Jeanie Deans was a seriously-disposed young woman, the Rector, the Rev. Mr. Staunton, invited her to attend family worship in the hall. Her Presbyterian scruples, however, made her hesitate before accepting the invitation, which induced the Rector to remark that he had no wish to force anything on her conscience, but to remind her that Divine grace does not confine its streams only to Presbyterian countries like Scotland, but that it extends its springs, various in character, yet alike efficacious in virtue, throughout the Christian world.

"Ah, but," said Jeanie, "though the water may be alike, yet, with your worship's leave, the blessing upon them may not be equal. It would have been in vain for Naaman the Syrian leper to have bathed in Pharpar and Abana, rivers of Damascus, when it was only the waters of Jordan that were sanctified for the cure."

In the story of *The Surgeon's Daughter*, the Fakir expresses himself greatly astonished at Hartley's refusal to accept of a present. "A Feringi can then refuse gold! I thought they took it from every hand, whether pure as that of an Houri, or leprous like Gehazi's."

SHORT as the Book of Esther is, we have several allusions in the Waverley Novels to the outstanding incidents of its interesting narrative. There is the beauty of Esther, the divorce of Vashti, the gallows for Haman, the unchanging laws of the Medes and Persians, and the Oriental magnificence of Ahasuerus.

Gwenwyn, the fierce and warlike Welsh chief in *The Betrothed*, while visiting the Garde Doloureuse, sees for the first time Eveline, the only daughter of Sir Raymond Berenger. Greatly struck by her beauty, he resolves upon asking her hand in marriage, after divorcing his childless wife Brengwain. Taking his chaplain into confidence, the chief instructs him how to proceed in the matter; and in the letter which the former wrote to Sir Raymond, there was a moral application in which were many allusions to Vashti, Esther, and Ahasuerus.

"Hang as high as Haman" is an expression which Sir Walter frequently uses. Cromwell tells Wildrake, in *Woodstock*, that if he betrays counsel he shall "hang as high as Haman;" and when in the Tolbooth of Glasgow, and temporarily a prisoner by the flight of Dougal,

Bailie Nicol Jarvie, in *Rob Roy*, calls out for hammers, and threatens when again at liberty that he "will hang the Highland blackguard as high as Haman."

In *The Heart of Midlothian*, Reuben Butler does all he can to dissuade Jeanie Deans from going to London alone to plead her sister's cause before the king and queen in person. He points out the difficulties which she will have to encounter, pictures the grandeur and magnificence surrounding the throne, and expresses his fears that she will find it next to impossible even to see their Majesties. But Jeanie replies, "I have thought of a' that, Reuben, and it shall not break my spirit. Nae doubt their claiths will be very grand, wi' their crowns on their heads, and their sceptres in their hands, like the great King Ahasuerus when he sat upon his royal throne fornent the gate o' his house, as we are told in Scripture. But I have that within me that will keep my heart from failing, and I am amaist sure that I shall be strengthened to speak the errand I came for."

HAVING indicated, in the preceding chapters, how largely and how frequently Sir Walter draws upon the historical portion of the Old Testament for illustration, let us now turn to the poetical and prophetical books to see in what way they are employed in the pages of the Waverley Novels.

Beginning with the Book of Job, we find that the first reference to it is connected with our old acquaintance, David Deans, who once more comes before us with his family trials and sorrows. The reference is to Satan making his appearance among the sons of God, as described in the opening chapter of the sacred poem. When Deans sees the officers of justice arrive at his cottage with a warrant to search for and apprehend his unfortunate daughter, Effie, the old man falls senseless on the floor. As his consciousness returns, he raises himself from the ground and, addressing his other daughter, Jeanie, gives expression to these terrible words, "Where is she that has no place among us, but has come foul with her sins, like the Evil One, among the children of God? Where is she, Jeanie? Bring her before me, that I may kill her with a word and a look."

In *The Monastery*, Father Eustace relates to the Abbot the adventures and mishaps of Philip the Sacristan on his homeward journey from Glendearg. Father Eustace adds that he is inclined to think the Sacristan's brain is affected, seeing he had sung, laughed, and wept in the same breath.

"A wonderful thing it is to us," said the Abbot, "that Satan has been permitted to put forth his hand thus far on one of our sacred brethren."

"True," said Father Eustace, "but for every text there is a paraphrase; and I have my suspicions that if the drenching of Father Philip cometh of the Evil One, yet it may not have been altogether without his own personal fault."

"How!" said the Father Abbot, "I will not believe that thou makest doubt that Satan in former days hath been permitted to afflict saints and holy men, even as he afflicted the pious Job."

In his argument with God, Satan insinuates that Job had come so far out of his trials with honour only because he had not been touched in his own person. "Skin for skin," said the tempter, "all that a man hath will he give for his life." We can never read these words without thinking of a scene in *Rob Roy*, where Morris, the timid revenue officer, begs in the most piteous terms for his life when he falls into the hands of Helen Macgregor. In the dreadful situation of the moment he would indeed have given all that he had for his life. Morris fell prostrate before the female chief with an effort to clasp her knees, from which she drew back, as if his touch had been pollution, so that all he could do in token of the extremity of his humiliation was to kiss the hem of her plaid. "I never heard entreaties for life poured forth with such agony of spirit," says Frank Osbaldistone, who witnessed the scene. "The ecstasy of fear was such that instead of paralysing his tongue, as on ordinary occasions, it even rendered him eloquent; and, with cheeks pale as ashes, hands compressed in agony, eyes that seemed to be taking their last look of all mortal objects, he protested, with the deepest oaths, his total ignorance of any design on the person of Rob Roy, whom, he swore, he loved and honoured as his own soul. . . . He prayed but for life—*for life he would give all he had in the world*—it was but life he asked— life, if it were to be prolonged under tortures and privations, he asked only breath, though it should be drawn in the damps of the lowest caverns of their hills."

The wretched petitioner for the poor boon of simple existence pleaded in vain. Half naked and manacled, he was thrown over a cliff into the lake below, and " the unit of that life, for which he had pleaded so strongly, was for ever withdrawn from the sum of human existence."

Crushed to the dust by the successive calamities which befell Job, he had yet the wisdom to see God's hand in all that had happened. His words of faith and resignation are quoted by Sir Walter in *A Legend of Montrose*, where the clergyman replies to the broken-hearted Lady Campbell of Ardenvohr, when something in her husband's speech to Dugald Dalgetty reminded her of the loss of their children :

"He who gave," said the clergyman, addressing her in a solemn tone, "hath taken away. May you, honourable lady, be long enabled to say, Blessed be His name."

In *The Surgeon's Daughter*, Dr. Hartley is called to the residence of General Witherington to prescribe for his two sick children. When able to announce the welcome news to the General and his wife that the children are likely soon to recover, the lady, in the fulness of her joy, yet trembling with emotion, exclaims "May the God of Israel bless thee, young man ; thou hast wiped the tear from the eye of the despairing mother. And yet—alas ! alas ! still it must flow when I think of my cherub Reuben. Oh, Mr. Hartley ! why did we not know you a week sooner ? my darling had not then died."

"God gives and takes away, my lady," answered Hartley, "and you must remember that two are restored to you out of three."

The poverty of Job is often referred to, or used as an illustration. Thus Baby Yellowley, in *The Pirate*, declares she never knew a witch, such as Norna, who was not "as poor as Job." Alan Fairford, in *Redgauntlet*, describes Peter Peebles to be not only as "poor as Job, but as mad as a March hare," and Dame Ursula says to Margaret Ramsay, with reference to Lord Nigel, that "a Scots nobleman is as proud as Lucifer, and as poor as Job."

Though Job came out of his trials with patience and resignation, his wife lost heart and hope. There is a reference to her in *Woodstock*, where Sir Henry Lee angrily replies to his daughter Alice, who had communicated to him her uncle's advice that it might be well for the old knight to act courteously to the commissioners appointed to sequestrate the parks and property at Woodstock. "By the blessed Rood, thou hast well-nigh led me into the heresy of thinking thee no daughter of mine. Ah! my beloved companion, who art now far from the sorrows and cares of this weary world, couldst thou have thought that the daughter thou didst clasp to thy bosom, would, like the wicked wife of Job, become a temptress to her father in the hour of affliction, and recommend him to make his conscience truckle to his interest, and to beg back at the bloody hands of his master's, and perhaps his son's murderers, a wretched remnant of the royal property he has been robbed of !"

Describing how wretchedly disappointed he was in his friends, Job complains that they had dealt deceitfully with him, and passed away like the summer-dried brook. So David Deans, in *The Heart of Midlothian*, bewails the loss of the loved associations that had clustered round his daughter Effie. Sternly resolved never again to see her, he says to Jeanie, "She was the bairn of prayers, and may not prove an utter castaway. But never, Jeanie, never more let her name be spoken between you and me. She hath passed from us like the brook which vanisheth when the summer waxeth warm; as patient Job saith, let her pass and be forgotten."

Job upbraids his friends for their unkind usage of him. "Miserable comforters are ye all," he says. In *The Fortunes of Nigel* there is a "Job's Comforter" in the case of Sir Mungo Malagrowther, a crabbed old

Scotch courtier, who visits Lord Nigel while confined in the Tower of London, and comforts him, after his fashion, with a minute account of the process of mutilation of the hand—a punishment to which Nigel had rendered himself liable for his offence against Lord Dalgarno. And, in *Quentin Durward*, Louis XI. is arrested by the Duke of Burgundy, on hearing of the murder of the Bishop, and imprisoned in the fortress of Peronne. The old warder or seneschal intimates to the King that the apartment, set apart for his Majesty's use, is one which had never been inhabited by any prisoner since the time of King Charles the Simple.

"King Charles the Simple!" echoed Louis; "I know the history of the tower now—— He was here murdered by his treacherous vassal. . . . *Here*, then, my predecessor was slain!"

"Not here, not exactly here," said the warder, a garrulous old man, "not *here*, but in the side chamber a little onward, which opens from your Majesty's bedchamber."

The seneschal then conducts the King into the small chamber. "If it please your Majesty," he says, "to look upon this little wicket behind the arras, it opens into the little old cabinet in the thickness of the wall where Charles was slain; and there is a secret passage from below which admitted the men who were to deal with him. And your Majesty, whose eyesight is better than mine, may see the blood still on the oak floor, though the thing was done five hundred years ago." A Job's comforter, truly!

Replying to Job, Eliphaz relates in sublime and striking language the manner in which a vision had appeared before him. Many scenes and incidents in the Waverley Novels have apparently been suggested to Sir Walter by this vision of Eliphaz. Thus Master Holdenough tells Colonel Everard how he had seen a vision of an old college companion, while sitting writing in a half-furnished apartment in the Lodge of Woodstock. He had been so employed for about three hours, when " a strange thrilling came over my senses, and the large and old-fashioned apartment seemed to wax larger, more gloomy, and more cavernous, while the air of the night grew more cold and chill. I know not if it was that the fire began to decay, or whether there cometh before such things as were then about to happen, a breath and atmosphere, as it were, of terror, as Job saith in a well-known passage, 'Fear came upon me, and trembling, which make my bones to shake;' and there was a tingling noise in my ears, and a dizziness in my brain, so that I felt like those who call for aid when there is no danger, and was even prompted to flee, when I saw no one to pursue."

Fergus MacIvor relates to Waverley that he had seen the Bodach Glas or Gray Spectre, and that, consequently, he would be either captive or dead before the morning. Downcast and dispirited by the disastrous march of the Highland army into England, Fergus one evening left his quarters, and walked out in hopes that the keen frosty air would brace his nerves and revive his spirits. To his great surprise he saw a tall figure in the moonlight, and keep what pace he would, the figure kept regularly about four yards in advance. The description which Sir Walter gives of the poor chief's terror was evidently suggested by that of the sacred poet in the vision of Eliphaz. "I felt an anxious throbbing at my heart," said MacIvor, . . . "my hair bristled, and my knees shook." The figure spoke and told the chief to "beware of to-morrow." The following evening Fergus was made a prisoner, and he and Waverley never again met each other until the fatal day at Carlisle, a little while before the former was led out to execution.

When Jeanie Deans, in *The Heart of Midlothian,* went to visit her sister in the prison of Edinburgh, "O Effie," she said, "how could you conceal your situation from me ? . . . Had ye spoke but ae word—sorry we might hae been, and shamed we might hae been, but this awfu' dispensation had never come ower us."

"And what gude wad that hae dune ?" answered the prisoner. "Na, na, Jeanie, a' was ower when ance I forgot what I promised when I faulded down the leaf of my Bible. See," she said, producing the sacred volume, "the book opens aye at the place o' itsell. O see, Jeanie, what a fearfu' Scripture."

Jeanie took her sister's Bible, and found that the fatal mark was made at this impressive text in the Book of Job : "He hath stripped me of my glory, and taken the crown from my head. He hath destroyed me on every side, and I am gone ; and mine hope hath he removed like a tree."

"Isna that ower true a doctrine ?" said the prisoner —"isna my crown, my honour, removed ? And what am I but a poor, wasted, wan-thriven tree, dug up by the roots, and flung out to waste in the highway, that man and beast may tread it under foot."

The well-known description of the horse in the Book of Job is frequently used by Sir Walter while relating battle-scenes, or drawing the portrait of some of his military heroes and adventures. In *The Betrothed*, Genvil's love of battle, "like that of the war-horse of Job, kindles at the sight of the spears, and at the sound of the trumpet." Henry Wynd or Smith, in the *Fair Maid of Perth*, says to Simon Glover, "St. John knows I have heard a summons to battle as willingly as war-horse ever heard the trumpet;" and when Claverhouse, in *Old Mortality*, was informed that the Whigs were gathering at Drumclog, one of his officers, Bothwell, welcomed the news, for, "like the war-horse of Scripture, he snuffed the battle afar off."

The sea-monster, too,

"By his titles
Of Leviathan, Behemoth, and so forth,"

is, in these lines, referred to in the motto to the thirtieth chapter of *The Antiquary*. And, in *Quentin Durward*, Louis XI. thus speaks of his approaching interview with the Duke of Burgundy: "I am to face this Leviathan, Charles, who will presently swim hitherward, cleaving the deep before him."

We close these illustrations from the Book of Job by quoting one well-known verse, which is introduced in Henry Morton's reflections, in *Old Mortality*, when he had finished looking at the papers, and reading the verses, which he had found in the secret pocket of Both-

well, who was killed in the skirmish at Drumclog : "Our
resolutions, our passions, are like the waves of the sea,
and, without the aid of Him who formed the human
breast, we cannot say to its tides, 'Thus far shall ye
come, and no farther.'"

THE Book of Psalms contains much that seems to have interested Sir Walter, for we find him frequently referring to or quoting from it. Many of its expressions and illustrations appear to glide into the composition of his novels, and prove by their presence, if any proof were wanted, how thoroughly the Sacred Scriptures, as a whole, were known to the author of Waverley. Thus the Bishop of Lincoln, in *Kenilworth*, speaks of the Queen's countenance being *a lamp to the paths* of her ministers; and the pedlar, in *Waverley*, congratulates Gilfillan on *the lines* of the latter *having fallen in pleasant places* in being the owner of some fertile land in Ayrshire.

In the story of *The Black Dwarf* there is an incident which was no doubt suggested to Sir Walter by the expression, "Thou shalt dash them in pieces like a potter's vessel," occurring in the second Psalm. Declaring what he would do to the person, were any such to be found, who could do him the greatest possible harm either in body or soul, the Dwarf in one of his fierce and misanthropic moods says to Earnscliff, "Were that man's fortunes and life in my power as this frail potsherd"—

he snatched up an earthen cup which stood beside him
—"I would not dash him into atoms thus"—he flung
the vessel with fury against the wall—"No! I would
pamper him with wealth and power," the Dwarf went
on to say, "until his enemy were as friendless and as
miserable as himself."

In *The Fair Maid of Perth,* Catherine Glover administers a rebuke to Father Clement when he persuades
her to receive the addresses of the Duke of Rothesay,
and tempts her with the possibility of her being thereby
in a position to help forward the reformation of the
Church. But she repudiates the idea as unprincipled,
and the Father confesses himself corrected by her admonition. "By the mouths of babes and sucklings,"
said he, quoting an expression from the eighth Psalm,
" hath He rebuked those who would seem wise in their
generation. I thank Heaven, that hath taught me better
thoughts than my own vanity suggested, through the
medium of so kind a monitress."

In *The Abbot,* Queen Mary, while a prisoner in Loch
Leven Castle, turns to one of her ladies-in-waiting, and
says with reference to the youthful Roland Græme and
Catherine Seyton, "Are they not a lovely couple, my
Fleming? and is it not heartrending to think that I
must be their ruin?"

"Not so," said Roland, "it is we, gracious Sovereign,
who will be your deliverers."

"*Ex oribus parvulorum!*" said the Queen looking upward; "it is by the mouths of these children that
Heaven calls me to resume the stately thoughts which

become my birth and my rights; Thou wilt grant them Thy protection, and to me the power of rewarding their zeal."

From the same Psalm the following quotation is made, and it occurs in *The Pirate*, where Sir Walter, at the close of the novel, describes the last days of the high-minded and imaginative Minna Troil. After all her trials and disappointments she turned her thoughts from the world, and gave her time and her heart to minister to those who needed help and comfort; and when she died, her friends were consoled " by the fond reflection that the humanity which she then laid down, was the only circumstance which had placed her, in the words of Scripture, 'a little lower than the angels.'"

In *The Betrothed*, there is an incident which forms an interesting commentary on the character of the righteous or godly man, as brought out in the fifteenth Psalm in the form of question and answer. Wilkin, the Fleming, goes to Father Aldrovand and asks his advice in the following circumstances. Stating his case, Wilkin says that he had promised to his neighbour, Jan Vanwelt, that he would give him his daughter Rose in marriage. He had also accepted of a sum of money which was to be the earnest of his promise being carried out. The Fleming, however, came to feel that he could not give away his daughter, and he wished to know if he could, in conscience, withdraw from the promise he had made. The Father thought that in the circumstances Wilkin might withdraw, but if he did so, he must at the same time pay back the money he had received from his neighbour. This Wilkin could not see his way to do, as the Welsh had destroyed his substance, and the money was all he had wherewith to begin the world anew.

"Nevertheless, son Wilkin," said Aldrovand, "thou must keep thy word, or pay the forfeit; for what saith the text? *Quis habitabit in tabernaculo, quis requiescet in monte sancto?*—Who shall ascend to the tabernacle, and dwell in the holy mountain? Is it not answered again, *Qui jurat proximo et non decipit?* Go to, my son—break not thy plighted word for a little filthy lucre—better is an empty stomach and a hungry heart, with a clear conscience, than a felled ox with iniquity and word-breaking."

In *Old Mortality*, Bothwell brings his rearguard and prisoners along very rough and uneven ground. Among the prisoners are Kettledrummle the preacher, and old Mause Headrigg, both of whom are sorely distressed at the brutality of the troopers compelling them to leap their horses over drains and gullies. Thinking of the Psalmist's troubles and deliverances, as recorded in the eighteenth Psalm, Mause exclaims, "Through the help of the Lord I have luppen ower a wall," as her horse was, by a rude attendant, brought up to leap the turf enclosure of a deserted field.

The well-known expression in the twenty-third Psalm, "the valley of the shadow of death," affords Sir Walter some interesting illustrations in a variety of ways. An incident in *The Talisman* brings before us the valley in its literal form and aspect. The Crusader

and the Saracen are riding together across "the awful
wilderness of the forty days' fast, and the scene of the
actual personal temptation, wherewith the Evil Principle
was permitted to assail the Son of Man." As they pene-
trate the gloomy recesses of the mountains, the Crusader
remonstrates with his fellow-traveller on the ill-timed
and misplaced frivolity of singing a love song. "I blame
not," he said, "the love of minstrelsy, and of the *gaie
science;* albeit we yield unto it even too much room in
our thoughts when they should be bent on better things.
But prayers and holy psalms are better fitting than lays
of love, or of wine-cups, when men walk in this Valley
of the Shadow of Death, full of fiends and demons, whom
the prayers of holy men have driven forth from the
haunts of humanity to wander amidst scenes as accursed
as themselves."

In the *Legend of Montrose,* the Valley is referred to in
illustration of the force of fear or unwillingness to face
a particular danger. Thus, among the Highlanders
assembled at the house of Angus MacAulay, ready to
take up arms under Montrose, no one could be found to
undertake the perilous duty of accompanying Sir Duncan
Campbell on an embassy to the Marquis of Argyle.
"One would have thought," observes Sir Walter, "Inveraray had been the Valley of the Shadow of Death,
the inferior chiefs showed such reluctance to approach it."

Before setting out for London, and while Reuben
Butler was searching for the papers for MacCallum More,
Jeanie Deans, in *The Heart of Midlothian,* took up her
lover's Bible; "I have marked a Scripture," she said, as

she again laid it down, "with your kylevine pen, that will be useful to us baith." After she had gone "Butler flew to the Bible, the last book which Jeanie had touched. To his extreme surprise, a paper, containing two or three pieces of gold, dropped from the book. With a black lead pencil she had marked the sixteenth and twenty-fifth verses of the thirty-seventh Psalm—'A little that a righteous man hath, is better than the riches of the wicked.' 'I have been young, and now am old, yet have I not seen the righteous forsaken, nor his seed begging their bread.' Deeply impressed with the affectionate delicacy which shrouded its own generosity under the cover of a providential supply to his wants, he pressed the gold to his lips with more ardour than ever the metal was greeted by a miser." This twenty-fifth verse is again quoted in *The Bride of Lammermoor*, in connection with the scene where Caleb Balderstone made off to Wolf's Crag with the wild-fowl which was roasting on the spit, and intended for the Christmas dinner in the house of Gilbert the cooper. The cooper could have borne the loss more complacently had the savoury roast been given to "some poor body," or, indeed, to any one but Caleb's master, the descendant of that Ravenswood who "rade in the wicked troop o' militia when it was commanded out against the sants at Bothwell Brig." "Aweel, Gilbert," said the minister, "and dinna ye see a high judgment in this ?—The seed of the righteous are not seen begging their bread—think of the son of a powerful oppressor being brought to the pass of supporting his household from your fulness ! "

Following Jeanie Deans on her way to London, we find her falling into the hands of a lot of ruffians, who detained her as their prisoner in an old hovel or barn. Left to her own sad reflections, she sought refuge in religion, and felt much strengthened as she thought of her father's winter evening tales, with their numerous instances of how the martyrs of the suffering Church of Scotland had been preserved from dangers infinitely greater than her own. "I bethought myself," Jeanie thus continues her reflections, "that the same help that was wi' them in their strait, wad be wi' me in mine, an' I can but watch the Lord's time and opportunity for delivering my feet from their snare; and I minded the Scripture of the blessed Psalmist, whilk he insisteth on, as weel in the forty-second as in the forty-third Psalm, 'Why art thou cast down, O my soul, and why art thou disquieted within me? Hope in God, for I shall yet praise Him, who is the health of my countenance, and my God.'"

In her letter to the unfortunate Master of Ravenswood, in *The Bride of Lammermoor*, Lady Ashton desires him to banish from his mind all thoughts of marrying her daughter Lucy. Brighter though his prospects now appear to be, yet she says with reference to this, and to the fact of Ravenswood's ancestors having been on different sides of religion and politics from those of her own family, "It is not a flightering blink of prosperity which can change my constant opinion in this regard, seeing it has been my lot before now, like holy David, to see the wicked great in power, and flourishing like a green bay tree; nevertheless I passed, and they were not, and the place thereof knew them no more."

In the opening chapter of *Woodstock* there is a remarkable scene in the church where the Presbyterian preacher, Mr. Holdenough, is rudely pulled down the pulpit stairs by a soldier, one of Cromwell's "military saints." A violent struggle ensues, and in the end the preacher leaves the church, while the soldier mounts to the pulpit. Taking a Bible from his pocket he selected his text from the forty-fifth Psalm—"Gird thy sword upon thy thigh, O most mighty, with thy glory and thy majesty; and in thy majesty ride prosperously." Upon this theme the novelist tells us that the "military saint" commenced one of those wild declamations common at the period, in which men were accustomed to wrest and pervert the language of Scripture, by adapting it to modern events. In its literal sense, the language of this Psalm applies to King David, and, typically, to the coming of the Messiah; but in the opinion of the military orator it was most properly applicable to Oliver Cromwell, and to him he therefore applied it in the course of a long and rambling sermon.

In the novel of *Kenilworth*, there is an interesting illustration of the meaning of that expression in the seventy-third Psalm which states that the wicked "have no bands in their death"—that is, they appear to feel neither pain nor agony, remain firm to the end, and scarcely feel themselves to be in the last mortal struggle. After a life of villainy, Varney was arrested for his share in the murder of the Countess Amy. He showed no remorse. "I was not born," he said, "to drag on the remainder of life a degraded outcast—nor will I so die, that my fate shall make a holiday to the village herd." He was found dead in his cell from the effects of poison which he had concealed about his person. "Nor did he appear to have suffered much agony, his countenance presenting, even in death, the habitual expression of sneering sarcasm which was predominant while he lived. 'The wicked man,' saith Scripture, 'hath no bonds in his death.'"

In his vivid description of the skirmish at Drumclog, Sir Walter reproduces the historical account of the Cameronians uniting their voices and reciting, in solemn modulation, the two first verses of the seventy-sixth Psalm, according to the metrical version of the Church of Scotland:

> " In Judah's land God is well known,
>   His name's in Israel great ;
> In Salem is his Tabernacle,
>   In Zion is His seat.

> " There arrows of the bow He brake,
>   The shield, the sword, the war ;
> More glorious Thou than hills of prey,
>   More excellent art far."

After a short pause the third and fourth stanzas were recited by the Covenanters, who applied the destruction of the Assyrian host to their own impending conflict :

> " Those that were stout of heart were spoil'd,
>   They slept their sleep outright ;
> And none of those their hands did find,
>   That were the men of might.

" When Thy rebuke, O Jacob's God,
   Had forth against them past,
   Their horses and their chariots both
   Were in a deep sleep cast."

This incident reminds us of another occasion on which one of the Psalms was recited on the eve of battle. This time the incident is narrated in the novel of *Peveril of the Peak*, where the Puritans, before their assault on Martindale Castle, lift up their voices and recite one of those triumphant songs in which the Israelites used to celebrate their victories over the heathen inhabitants of the promised land :

" Let God arise, and then His foes
   Shall turn themselves to flight,
   His enemies for fear shall run,
   And scatter out of sight.

" And as wax melts before the fire,
   And wind blows smoke away,
   So in the presence of the Lord,
   The wicked shall decay.

" God's army twenty thousand is
   Of angels bright and strong,
   The Lord also in Sinai
   Is present them among.

" Thou didst, O Lord, ascend on high,
   And captive led'st them all,
   Who, in times past, Thy chosen fold
   In bondage did enthral."

These stanzas form part of Sternhold's version of the sixty-eighth Psalm, with some slight variations.

In a variety of ways Sir Walter illustrates one of the verses of the hundred and fourth Psalm, "Wine that maketh glad the heart of man." Inviting Jeanie Deans to his mansion in London, the Duke of Argyle presented her to the Duchess and her daughters, by whom she was received with much kindness and attention. Before leaving, the Duke poured out a glass of wine and offered it to his guest. But Jeanie declined it, saying that she never tasted wine in her life.

"How comes that, Jeanie?" said the Duke; "wine maketh glad the heart, you know."

"Ay, sir, but my father is like Jonadab, the son of Rechab, who charged his children that they should drink no wine."

In *The Talisman*, King Richard speaks of wine as "that lightener of the human heart." Wilkin, the Fleming, in *The Betrothed*, feels the want of this reviving property of wine as he asks the butler for a flagon of Rhenish, "for," says he, "my heart is low and poor within me." Watch the delight of the poor lay brother as he takes with a trembling hand a cup of wine which the Abbot, in the novel of the same name, pours out for him. "He drained the cup with protracted delight, as if bidding adieu in future to such a delicious potation." But, perhaps, the finest instance in Sir Walter's writings of the exhilarating power of wine is to be found in *The Lay of the Last Minstrel*. Exhausted by the effort in reciting his Lay, the Duchess tells her page to bring a goblet of wine for the aged minstrel:

> " The precious juice the minstrel quaff'd,
>   And he, embolden'd by the draught,
>   Look'd gaily back to them and laugh'd ;

The cordial nectar of the bowl
Swell'd his old veins and cheer'd his soul."

But with all this mention of the exhilarating property of wine, Sir Walter does not fail to point out that there is enjoyment in its use, only in so far as that use is not abused. "The juice of the grape," says the Crusader, in *The Talisman*, to the Saracen Emir, "is given to him that will use it wisely, as that which cheers the heart of man after toil, refreshes him in sickness, and comforts him in sorrow. He who so enjoyeth it may thank God for his wine-cup as for his daily bread; and he who abuseth the gift of Heaven, is not a greater fool in his intoxication than thou in thine abstinence."

Adam Woodcock, in *The Abbot*, advises Roland Græme to "beware of the pottle-pot—it has drenched the judgment of wiser men than you."

The Baron Bradwardine, in *Waverley*, detested those who swallowed wine for the "mere delectation of the gullet," and approved of it only in so far as it "cheered the heart and gladdened the face." And what a social wreck is poor Nanty Ewart, in *Redgauntlet*, who gave way to the desire for strong drink, and came to realise for himself the melancholy truth that brandy was slowly but surely killing him.

Before leaving the hundred and fourth Psalm, we are reminded, in *Waverley*, of an interesting reference to the conies mentioned in the eighteenth verse. The Baron Bradwardine remarks to Waverley, when the latter came to visit him while still a fugitive after the disasters of 1745, "Now I have gotten a house that is not unlike a *domus ultima,*"—they were standing at the time below the Baron's hiding-place in the face of a rock,—"We poor Jacobites are now like the conies in Holy Scripture (which the great traveller Pococke calleth Jerboa), a feeble people, that make our abode in the rocks."

Having succeeded in her mission to London, and obtained a pardon for her sister, Jeanie Deans is welcomed home by her father in the most touching and affectionate terms. The old man gives expression to his gratitude and joy in language borrowed from, or at least suggested by, that of the hundred and twenty-sixth Psalm. "Jeanie, my ain Jeanie—my best—my maist dutiful bairn—the Lord of Israel be thy father, for I am hardly worthy of thee! *Thou hast redeemed our captivity* —brought back the honours of our house. Bless thee, my bairn, with mercies promised and purchased! But HE *has* blessed thee, in the good of which He has made thee the instrument."

In *Ivanhoe* there is also a reference to this Psalm. At the close of her trial for the imputed crime of sorcery, Rebecca piteously looks round the court of the Grand-Master and asks, in an imploring tone, if there is any one present who, either for the love of a good cause or for ample hire, will do the errand of one in great straits. Higg, the son of Snell, offers his services. "I will do thine errand," he said, addressing Rebecca, "as well as a crippled object can." To which she gratefully replies, "God is the Disposer of all. *He can turn the captivity of Judah,* even by the weakest instrument. To execute His message, the snail is as sure a messenger as the falcon."

The gracious manner in which Lady Peveril received the Puritans at Martindale Castle had a singularly soothing effect upon the sectaries, who had expected a very different reception. Even Solsgrace, the Presbyterian parson, did not escape the sympathetic infection, for he recited aloud the first verse of the hundred and thirty-third Psalm, as best expressive of the feelings of all present on the occasion :—

> "O what a happy thing it is
> And joyful for to see
> Brethren to dwell together in
> Friendship and unity."

There is a text in the hundred and twenty-fourth Psalm which Sir Walter quotes very frequently—"Our soul is escaped as a bird out of the snare of the fowlers." When arrested for alleged complicity in the assault upon Dousterswivel, old Edie Ochiltree, in *The Antiquary*, thanked his friends for their sympathy and offers of assistance. He assured them, at the same time, that he had "gotten out o' mony a snare when I was waur deserving o' deliverance. I shall escape like a bird from the fowler."

Describing the feelings of Isaac the Jew when he was thrown into the dungeon of Torquilstone Castle, Sir Walter explains that the Jews in England at the time of the story, *Ivanhoe*, had, by the very frequency of their fears on all occasions, their minds prepared for every sort of tyranny which could possibly be practised upon them. Nor was this the first time that Isaac had been placed in circumstances so dangerous. "He had therefore experience to guide him, as well as hope, that he might again, as formerly, be delivered as a prey from the fowler."

When Alan Fairford arrives at Mount Sharon, in *Redgauntlet*, he is kindly and hospitably received by Miss Geddes. She informs him that her brother has gone to Cumberland to get the magistrates of that county interested in the case of Darsie Latimer. Beset by many dangers, both by land and sea, the gentle lady yet expresses the hope that her brother will be preserved by "Him who directeth all things, and ruleth over the waves of the sea, who overruleth the devices of the wicked, and who can redeem us even as a bird from the fowler's net."

When Darsie Latimer was made a prisoner by Redgauntlet he was closely confined, and allowed to see no one. But he contrived to open a communication with Wandering Willie, the blind musician, whom he heard playing beneath the window of his apartment. Among musical people there is a sort of freemasonry by means of which they can, by the mere choice of some particular tune or song, express a great deal to the hearers. Darsie commenced the experiment by selecting something more expressive of his captivity than any song which he could recollect. He therefore sang two or three lines of the hundred and thirty-seventh Psalm—

"By Babel's streams we sat and wept"—

the meaning of which was instantly caught up by the musician outside, who replied by playing a tune, the words of which conveyed hope and encouragement to the prisoner.

We close this chapter by pointing out one or two interesting illustrations of the text, "Put not your trust in princes," in the hundred and forty-sixth Psalm. The Earl of Leicester, in *Kenilworth*, in a conversation which he has with Varney, observes—"And so men talk of the Queen's favour toward me?"

"Ay, my good lord," said Varney, "of what can they else, since it is so strongly manifested?"

"She is indeed my good and gracious mistress," said Leicester after a pause, "but it is written, 'Put not thy trust in Princes.'"

In *The Fair Maid of Perth*, Sir John Ramorny twice quotes the text to the Prince of Scotland himself, who would not listen to the ambitious designs which the former ventured to propose, and dared him to renew the theme on peril of his life. To which Sir John replied, "If I have said anything which could so greatly exasperate your Highness, it must have been by excess of zeal mingled with imbecility of understanding. . . . Alas! my only future views must be to exchange lance and saddle for the breviary and the confessional. The convent of Lindores must receive the maimed and impoverished Knight of Ramorny, who will have ample leisure to meditate upon the text, 'Put not thy faith in Princes.'" And further on in the story, Sir John is asked to state where he was, or what he was doing, on the night when Oliver Proudfute was murdered. He replies that he can prove by the evidence of his late royal master that he was in his own lodgings, lying ill at ease, on the night in question. The Prince confirmed this statement, but said, further, that he knew nothing of what Sir John's attendants might be doing, and that it was quite possible some of them may have committed the crime. Angry at the insinuation contained in the latter portion of the Prince's speech, Ramorny replied, "I thank your Highness for your cautious and limited testimony in my behalf. He was wise who wrote, 'Put not your faith in Princes.'"

The proud and ambitious MacIvor, in *Waverley*, states his claims and expectations to Prince Charles Edward, who graciously listens, but desires him, as a personal favour, not to press them at that particular time. This request so offended the chief that, in relating to his friend Waverley an account of the interview, he closes by saying, in bitter irony and disappointment, "*After this, put your trust in Princes.*"

OUR present study has brought us up to those Poetical Books of the Bible which bear the name of Solomon as their author; and the first reference to them in our Waverley notes is to the text, "Wisdom's ways are ways of pleasantness, and all her paths are peace." In our introductory chapter we had occasion specially to refer to Sir Walter's use of this text, so that we do not require to say more about it now, but proceed to the consideration of others requiring our attention.

"In the multitude of counsellors there is safety," says the royal sage. This text is quoted in *Kenilworth* in connection with the incident of Wayland Smith prescribing for the Earl of Sussex, on condition that the patient is not disturbed during the period of lethargy produced by the medicine. When Queen Elizabeth's physician calls at her request to see the Earl, he is, of course, refused admittance. At this the Queen expresses great surprise; but when she learns that the patient has risen from his sleep, greatly strengthened and refreshed, she says to Raleigh, "By my word, I am glad he is better. But thou wert over bold to deny the access of my Doctor Masters. Know'st thou not that Holy

Writ saith, 'In the multitude of counsel there is safety'?"

"Ay, madam," said Walter, "but I have heard learned men say that the safety spoken of is for the physicians, not for the patient."

"By my faith, child, thou hast pushed me home," said the Queen, laughing, "for my Hebrew learning does not come quite at a call." Here her Majesty asked the Bishop of Lincoln if Raleigh had rightly interpreted the text; but the Bishop replied in such a rambling sort of way as to show that he, too, was not sure of his Hebrew, and so the Queen graciously interrupted him, and passed on to another subject.

When Tyrrel arrives at St. Ronan's he observes to our old friend, Mrs. Dods, the landlady of the inn, that while she is arranging about the rooms he is to occupy, he will go to the stable and see after his horse.

"The merciful man," said Mrs. Dods, when her guest had left the kitchen, "is merciful to his beast." In this way Sir Walter invariably paraphrases the text, "The righteous man regardeth the life of his beast."

Fond of animals as the author of *Waverley* always was, this verse seems to have been a great favourite with him, for it is quoted, or illustrated in some way or other, in almost every novel he wrote. We have just seen how he makes Meg Dods quote it; and when he tells us, in another part of the story of *St. Ronan's*, that Meg sternly refused to connive at the postilions exchanging, for porter and whisky, the corn which should feed their horses, we have the meaning of the text brought out in the landlady's consideration for the animals, and her regard for their health and strength in the work they had to do.

It is delightful to meet so many varied illustrations of this text cropping up, every now and again, in every novel of the Waverley series. In her flight from Loch Leven, in *The Abbot*, Queen Mary tells Roland, her page, to see to the comfort of Rosabelle, her pony. Christie of the Clinthill, in *The Monastery*, chafes impatiently at Sir Piercie Shafton keeping the horses standing so long in the cold after the hard riding they have had. When the Master of Ravenswood and Bucklaw arrive at Wolf's Crag, in *The Bride of Lammermoor*, it is their horses that they request old Caleb to look after first, before attending to themselves or to anything else. The Baron Bradwardine, in *Waverley*, fondly strokes his reeking horse after the victory and pursuit at Preston, and as he dismounts and gives him in charge to the groom, he warns the man to mind the charger and not to leave him to look for plunder on the field. While Dandie Dinmont, in *Guy Mannering*, is enjoying his own dinner at the little roadside inn, he casts an eye from time to time to see how his horse, Dumple, is getting on. Before Hayraddin the Bohemian is led off to execution, he has a request to make of Quentin Durward. "Tell me thy request," says Quentin, "I will grant it if it be in my power."

"Nay, it is no mighty demand—it is only in behalf of poor Klepper, my palfrey, the only living thing that may miss me. . . . Take him and make much of him. . . . He will never fail you at need—night and day, rough and smooth, fair and foul, warm stables and the winter sky, are the same to Klepper. . . . Will you be kind to Klepper?"

"I swear to you that I will," answered Quentin, affected by what seemed a trait of tenderness in a character so hardened.

It is not, however, until we take up the *Legend of Montrose* that we find the fullest development of the meaning of the text in Dugald Dalgetty's extraordinary attachment to his horse. He calls him his companion, and refuses to let any of M'Aulay's grooms rub him down or attend him in any way; he does everything himself. This companionship between man and horse continues all through the story: to such a degree, indeed, that there is an impression left on the mind of the reader that this particular novel of the Waverley series is specially illustrative of Sir Walter's paraphrase, "The merciful man is merciful to his beast."

But Sir Walter does not confine the text to horses. Mary Avenel, in *The Monastery*, nurses her pigeons "with the tenderness of a mother." The Black Dwarf is greatly affected as he sees his favourite goat throttled by Hobbie Elliot's deer-hound. While dining at the country inn, the Cat and Fiddle, a mastiff came and sat down before Julian Peveril, licking his chops, and following with his eye every morsel which the traveller raised to his mouth.

"Here, my poor fellow," said Peveril, "thou hast had no fish, and needest this supernumerary trencher-load more than I do. I cannot withstand thy mute supplication any longer." When Jeanie Deans returns from

London, and is being conducted over the new farm-yard by old May Hettly, the cows acknowledge the presence of their mistress by lowing, turning round their heads, and exhibiting visible signs of pleasure as she approaches to caress each in their turn.

"The very brute beasts are glad to see ye again," said May, "but nae wonder, Jeanie, for ye were aye kind to beast and body."

We have several very interesting illustrations of the truth contained in the text, "Hope deferred maketh the heart sick." The gentle and amiable girl, Jenny Caxon, in *The Antiquary*, is every day expecting a letter from her lover, Lieutenant Taffril, who is absent on duty. She summons courage to go to the Post Office to make inquiry, but is told by the gossiping and heartless postmistress to come back next morning at ten. The poor girl "could only draw her cloak about her to hide the sigh of disappointment, and return meekly home to endure, for another night, the sickness of the heart occasioned by hope delayed."

Sir Halbert Glendinning, in *The Abbot*, has been several weeks absent from Avenel Castle, and now he is daily expected home. But day after day passes, and still he does not come. The date which his affectionate wife had fondly calculated in her own mind for meeting her husband has long since passed, and so hope delayed began to make the heart grow sick. Alan Fairford is wearying to have his friend Darsie Latimer back to Edinburgh once more. "I am sick at heart," he writes, "and cannot keep the ball up." And further on, in the same book, *Redgauntlet*, Alan, in pleading the cause of poor Peter Peebles, describes his client as "a victim to protracted justice, and to that hope delayed which sickens the heart."

The Highland widow experiences this sickness of heart as she anxiously waits and longs for the return of her beloved son. And, in *Anne of Geierstein*, Queen Margaret's head gets giddy and her heart sick, as she wearily waits for the restoration of the line of Lancaster.

At the interview between the Duke of Argyle and Jeanie Deans, in *The Heart of Midlothian*, his Grace tells Jeanie to hold herself in readiness to attend him in the course of next day, or the day after, for the purpose of accompanying him to the Queen's presence, there to plead for a pardon to Effie Deans. The day after the interview was spent in that "hope delayed which maketh the heart sick." As "minutes glided after minutes—hours fled after hours—it became too late to have any reasonable expectation of hearing from the Duke that day; yet the hope which she disowned she could not altogether relinquish, and her heart throbbed, and her ears tingled with the casual sound in the shop below. It was in vain. The day wore away in the anxiety of protracted and fruitless expectation." But this heart-sickness fled when next day brought the welcome summons for Jeanie to attend upon the Duke; and so suddenly did the messenger come, that there was no time allowed even for a change of dress.

As poor Madge Wildfire lay on her death-bed, in the same novel, she found relief in singing some of her old snatches of song and obsolete airs. But as her end approached, reason seemed to dawn; and as if feeling weary and wanting to be at rest, she gave expression to her sickness of heart by singing, in soft and affecting tones, two stanzas of a hymn :—

> " When the fight of Grace is fought,
> When the marriage vest is wrought,
> When Faith hath chased cold doubt away,
> *And hope but sickens at delay,*
>
> " When Charity, imprisoned here,
> Longs for a more expanded sphere,
> Doff thy robes of sin and clay ;
> Christian, rise, and come away."

Sir Arthur Wardour, addressing an old domestic with reference to an incident which had happened some time previously, says, "Robert, I was angry and you were wrong : go about your work, and never answer a master that speaks to you in a passion."

"Nor any one else," said the Antiquary, "for a soft answer turneth away wrath."

When the Duke of Argyle was expected at Roseneath, in *The Heart of Midlothian*, his fussy and self-important agent, Captain Knockdunder, advised Jeanie Deans to tell her father to put his Cameronian nonsense out of his head for a few days, and get his beasts all in order. But to this imprudent advice Jeanie turned away the wrath that might have been stirred by an angry reply, for she only smiled, and expressed the hope that his Grace would find everything to his entire satisfaction.

In a lonely part of the King's Park at Edinburgh, Reuben Butler sees the figure of a man approaching, and thinking it probable that the person had come there to settle some affair of honour, he resolves to speak—a resolution formed, no doubt, as he recollects the text, "A word spoken in due season how good is it." "There are times," thought Butler to himself, "when the slightest interference may avert a great calamity—when a word spoken in season may do more for prevention than the eloquence of Tully could do for remedying evil." Butler, accordingly, spoke and relieved his mind by giving the stranger the advice which we have already had occasion to quote, while writing on the subject of Cain killing his brother Abel.

In *Woodstock*, there is a discussion between Cromwell and Mr. Holdenough, the Presbyterian divine, regarding the merits of lay and ordained preaching. Holdenough naturally exalts the latter, while Cromwell prefers the former, and in doing so says : "You may talk of your regular Gospel-meals, but a word spoken in season by one whose heart is with your heart just, perhaps, when you are riding on to encounter an enemy, or about to jump a breach, is to the poor spirit like a rasher on the coals, which the hungry shall feel preferable to a great banquet, at such times when the full soul loatheth the honey-comb."

Old Edie Ochiltree, in *The Antiquary*, quotes a well-known text as he muses over what particular place he will select for his lodging that night. He had been at Glenallan House, and as he returns, he soliloquises in the following strain :—"I dinna ken how it is, but I am nicer about my quarters this night than ever I mind having been in my life. I think, having seen a' the braws yonder, and finding out ane may be happier without them, has made me proud o' my ain lot. But I wuss it bode me

gude, for *pride goeth before destruction.* . . . Sae I'll e'en
settle at ance, and put in for Ailie Sim's."

In *The Fortunes of Nigel* there is an affecting scene,
where old John Christie goes in search of his wife, who
had eloped with Lord Dalgarno. He at length finds her
beside the lifeless body of her seducer. She sinks down
at her husband's feet as he thus addresses her, "Kneel
not to me, woman, but kneel to the God thou hast
offended, more than thou could'st offend such another
worm as thyself. How often have I told thee when thou
wert at the gayest and the lightest, that 'pride goeth
before destruction, and a haughty spirit before a fall.'"
It accords not with our present purpose to quote the passage in full, but we commend it to the readers of *Nigel*
for the touching pathos in which the injured and broken-
hearted husband closes his appeal, and expresses his intention not to let her, who had been his first and only love,
be an utter castaway if it lies with him to prevent it.

Among the numerous instances of good advice and
wise counsel given by Solomon in the Proverbs, there is
one which receives several interesting illustrations in the
Waverley Novels. We refer to the text, "Cease, my
son, to hear the instruction that causeth to err from the
words of knowledge." At the ceremony of betrothal
between Lucy Ashton and Bucklaw, in *The Bride of Lammermoor*, the clergyman invites the company to join him
in a short extempore prayer. With the simplicity of
the times, and the privilege of his profession, which
permitted him to make strong personal allusion, Mr.
Bide-the-bent, in the course of his supplication, prayed

"that the bridegroom might be weaned from those follies which seduce youth from the path of knowledge . . . and cease from the society that causeth to err."

Jeanie Deans listens to the story that George Staunton has to tell her about Effie, and when he asks her to be guided by his advice and direction while in London, she replies, "I will do what is fitting for a sister, and a daughter, and a Christian woman to do, but do not tell me any of your secrets. It is not good that I should come into your counsel, or listen to the doctrine which causeth to err."

Solomon compares the laughter of the fool to the crackling of thorns under a pot. This is a favourite simile with Sir Walter. Effie Deans, in speaking to her sister, says, "I can laugh yet sometimes—but God protect you from such mirth. My father—I mean your father—would say it was like the idle crackling of thorns; but the thorns keep their poignancy, they remain unconsumed." The Dwarf, in *Peveril of the Peak*, likens youth with its fashions, follies, and frolics, to the "crackling of thorns under a pot;" and the preacher in *The Abbot* says of life that "it was not lent us to be expended in that idle mirth which resembles the crackling of thorns under the pot." Alan Fairford, in *Redgauntlet*, had too heavy a heart to enjoy the jests and laughter at Provost Crosbie's dinner-party. All the fun was to him "like the idle crackling of thorns under the pot," "with this difference," adds Sir Walter, "that it did not accompany or second any such useful operation as the boiling thereof."

The text which Thackeray loved so much to quote,

and the meaning of which he has illustrated so well, is very seldom used by Sir Walter. We refer to "Vanity of vanities, all is vanity." On the front of the conservatory at Mount Sharon, the house of Joshua Geddes and his sister Rachel, also in *Redgauntlet*, there was carved the armorial scutcheon of the family, with the pious motto, *Trust in God*, and the date 1537. Quaker though Joshua was, he seemed not a little proud of this ancient date, although he declaimed to his guest, Darsie Latimer, upon the vanity usually begotten on the subject of ancient ancestry. "Vanity of vanities," saith the preacher, Joshua began moralising, "if we ourselves are nothing in the sight of Heaven, how much less than nothing must be our derivation from rotten bones and mouldering dust, whose immortal spirits have long since gone to their private account!"

The only other reference to this text which we have met, in the course of our present study, is in *Woodstock*, where Holdenough and Dr. Rochecliffe recognise each other after a long separation. Talking over old memories and their associations, the former asks his friend if he remembers Caius College?

"Remember Caius College!" said Rochecliffe, "Ay, and the good old ale we drank, and our parties to Mother Huffcap's."

"Vanity of vanities," said Holdenough, smiling kindly at the same time, and still holding his recovered friend's arm enclosed and hand-locked in his.

But though we have the text quoted in its literal form in only a few instances we have, throughout the Waverley Novels, numerous instances of its spirit and meaning. In

Guy Mannering, Godfrey Bertram allows himself to be worried out of all serenity by the thought, which vexes and annoys him, that he has not been made a justice of the peace. Glossin gets what he had long set his heart upon—possession of the Ellangowan estate; but when he does enter upon possession, he finds nothing in it but vexation of spirit. The Earl of Leicester, in *Kenilworth*, moves heaven and earth to gain the favour of Queen Elizabeth, and when he has succeeded beyond his utmost expectation, it is only to experience the bitterness and the wrath of the Queen, as she hears of his secret marriage and his duplicity towards herself. And though Effie Deans, in *The Heart of Midlothian*, rises to be Lady Staunton—"the ruling belle, the blazing star, the universal toast of the winter, . . . and really the most beautiful creature that was seen at Court upon the birthday," she yet experiences, to the full, the truth of the sacred text, "Vanity of vanities; all is vanity."

We have some interesting illustrations of the text, "Curse not the king, no not in thy thoughts : and curse not the rich in thy bed-chamber; for a bird of the air shall carry the voice, and that which hath wings shall tell the matter." Two of these illustrations are to be found in *Rob Roy*. The first is where Die Vernon quietly advises Frank Osbaldistone to take her advice, when he has anything to say about Rashleigh, and "go up to the top of Otterscope Hill, where—when you can see for twenty miles around you in every direction—stand on the very peak and speak in whispers ; and, after all, don't be too sure that the bird of the air will not carry the matter."

Bailie Nicol Jarvie thus paraphrases the text, when he says to Frank that he has no wish to "speak ony ill of this MacCallum More :—'Curse not the rich in your bed-chamber,' saith the son of Sirach, 'for a bird of the air shall carry the clatter, and pint-stoups hae lang lugs.'" Here is another paraphrase of the text—this time by Louis XI., who advises Quentin Durward to mind what he is saying while in the neighbourhood of the Castle of Plessis-les-Tours : "One great danger of these precincts is, that the very leaves of the trees are like so many ears which carry all which is spoken to the King's own cabinet." In *Peveril of the Peak,* Alice Bridgenorth advises Julian Peveril to leave the Isle of Man, to be on his guard, to distrust everything, and trust not even "the very stones of the most secret apartment in Holm Peel, for that which hath wings shall carry the matter." In the same novel we have an instance of Solomon's warning being transgressed. Mrs. Chiffinch determines, contrary to her husband's caution, to attend King Charles on his excursion down the Thames. To her great chagrin, however, she was ordered to fall out of the royal pro-cession, which so vexed and mortified her that she cried for very spite, and cursed the king most heartily.

According to Solomon, the slothful man excuses him-self from the performance of duty by the presence of imaginary difficulty or danger in the way—"There is a lion in the path." The Regent Murray, in *The Abbot,* is the "lion in the path" which bars the road against Queen Mary's army attempting to reach Dumbarton. The widow Maclure, in *Old Mortality,* advises Burley not to go the

L

way he had indicated to Morton. "If you be of our ain folk," she says, "gangna up the pass the night for your lives. There is a lion in the path that is there. The curate of Brotherstone and the soldiers have beset the path to hae the lives of any of our puir wanderers that venture that gate." Allan M'Aulay, in the *Legend of Montrose*, is about to pass his broadsword through the prostrate body of Ranald MacEagh, when the point of his weapon is suddenly struck upward by Dalgetty, who suddenly interposes.

"Fool," said Allan, "stand aside, and dare not come between the tiger and his prey."

But Dalgetty stepped across the body of MacEagh, and gave Allan to understand that if he called himself a tiger, he was likely to find a lion in his path.

The insatiable appetite of the leech is referred to in *Peveril of the Peak*, where Sir Walter describes the needy adventurers who were to be found haunting the ante-chambers of the Duke of Buckingham, as "genuine descendants of the horse-leech, whose cry is Give, give!"

In a note added to his last edition of the Waverley Novels, Sir Walter tells his readers that these tales will, in all probability, be the last which it will be his lot to submit to the public. On the eve of going abroad for the sake of rest and change, he feels that had he continued to prosecute his literary labours, it seems probable that at his advancing years "the bowl, to use the pathetic language of Scripture, would have been broken at the fountain."[1]

[1] Eccles. xii. 6.

THE PROPHETICAL BOOKS.

AN incident in *The Heart of Midlothian* introduces us to the Book of the Prophet Isaiah. On her journey to London, Jeanie Deans experiences much kindness from the Rev. Mr. Staunton, who recommends her to the care of his housekeeper, Mrs. Dalton. This good and kind-hearted woman was so much pleased with Jeanie, and with her staid and quiet demeanour, that one day after dinner she took up a Bible and asked, at the same time, if she could read this Book?

"I hope sae, madam," replied Jeanie; "my father wad hae wanted mony a thing ere I had wanted *that* schuling."

"The better sign of him, young woman. . . . Take thou the Book then, for my eyes are something dazed, and read where thou listest—it's the only book thou canst not happen wrong in."

Jeanie was at first tempted to turn up the parable of the Good Samaritan, but her conscience checked her, as if it were a use of Scripture, not for her own edification, but to work upon the mind of others for the relief of her worldly afflictions. Under this scrupulous sense of duty she selected, in preference, *a chapter of the prophet Isaiah,* and read it, notwithstanding her northern accent and tone, with a devout propriety which greatly edified Mrs. Dalton.

Scattered throughout the Novels, we find a great many of the well-known texts from Isaiah woven into Sir Walter's sentences. In *The Abbot,* for example, the old gardener advises Roland Græme to leave the public service, *beat his sword into a pruning-hook,* and make a dibble of his dagger. That dissolute and swaggering cavalier, Wildrake, in *Woodstock,* was the first to announce to Charles II. the news of the Restoration, and as he did so, he borrowed an expression from a well-known text in Isaiah, "I bring good news," he said, "glorious news—the King shall enjoy his own again. My *feet are beautiful on the mountains,*" adding, as an explanation of his unwonted use of Scripture figures, that he had lived with Presbyterians so long that he had caught their language.

Towards the close of *The Pirate,* Sir Walter describes the great change which passed over Norna, who now lived a very different life, abandoned all her former pretensions, and gave herself up to the study of the Bible. To the poor ignorant people who came, as formerly, to invoke her power over the elements, the only reply she would give them was, in the sublime words of the prophet, " *The winds are in the hollow of His hand.*"

Through the prophet Isaiah, God gives expression to His utter detestation of the mere ritual or outward observance of public worship. " Bring no more vain oblations; incense is an abomination to me; the new moons and Sabbaths, the calling of assemblies, I cannot away with; it is iniquity, even the solemn meeting." These words seem to be in the thoughts of old Edie Ochiltree, in *The Antiquary*, as Lovel and he are among the ruins of St. Ruth one moonlight night. "I wad like a wise man to tell me," Edie says, "whether Heaven is most pleased wi' the sight we are looking upon—thae pleasant and quiet lang streaks o' moonlight that are lying sae still on the floor o' this auld kirk, and glancing through the great pillars and stauchions o' the carved windows, and just dancing like on the leaves o' the dark ivy as the breath o' wind shakes it—I wonder whether this is mair pleasing to Heaven than when it was lighted up wi' lamps, and candles, nae doubt, and roughies (links or torches), and wi' the mirth and the frankincent that they speak of in the Holy Scripture, and wi' organs assuredly, and men and women singers, and sackbuts, and dulcimers, and a' instruments of music—I wonder if that was acceptable, or whether it is of these grand parafle o' ceremonies that holy writ says, 'It is an abomination to me.'"

As the Countess Amy, in *Kenilworth*, opens a small parcel from her husband, and displays to view a set of rare and costly jewels, the lady's maid gazes with admiration on the articles. "Surely," said Janet, looking at the string of pearls, "surely, the daughters of Tyre wore no fairer neck-jewels than those." And, afterwards, as the Earl of Leicester himself offers a ring to Janet, with the request that she will wear it for the sake of her mistress, and for his own as well, the Puritanic maid refuses the offered gift. "We of the precious Master Holdforth's congregation," she says, "seek not, like the gay daughters of this world, to twine gold around our fingers, or wear stones upon our necks, like the vain women of Tyre and Sidon."

The military preacher, in the opening chapter of *Woodstock*, drags into his discourse an extraordinary number of Scripture references and incidents, and he finishes up by an illustration of the meaning of Mahershalalhashbaz—the name by which the prophet Isaiah was directed to call his son. "Ye shall have no comfort or support," says the preacher to the congregation, "neither from the sequestrated traitor Henry Lee, who called himself Ranger of Woodstock, nor from any on his behalf; for they are coming hither who shall be called Mahershalalhashbaz, because he maketh haste to the spoil." The preacher here refers to Cromwell and the Parliamentary Commissioners appointed for the sequestration of Woodstock.

Old David Deans laments to Reuben Butler the sad "defections of the times," and enumerates, one by one, the shortcomings of the National Church. Unwilling to interrupt him, Reuben listens patiently, but takes the first opportunity of slipping in a word of encouragement. "You have been," says Reuben, "one of those to whom the tender and fearful souls cry during the midnight solitude, '*Watchman, what of the night? Watchman, what of the night?*' And, assuredly, this heavy dispensation as it comes not without divine permission, so it comes not without its special commission and use."

In predicting the final overthrow of Tyre, the prophet Isaiah speaks of that ancient place as " the crowning city, whose merchants are princes, whose traffickers are the honourable of the earth." This description comes to be naturally applicable to the famous countries, cities, and merchants of modern history. Thus, in *Anne of Geierstein*, the Duke of Burgundy refers to England as he thus addresses the Earl of Oxford, who was travelling in the disguise of an English merchant—" Welcome, you of a nation whose traders are princes, and their merchants the mighty ones of the earth." And in *The Fortunes of Nigel* the Lady Hermione, while relating her personal history to Margaret Ramsay, says of her father that he was a merchant, " but of a city whose merchants are princes—Genoa."

We have already referred to Kettledrummle's sermon to the Covenanters after the battle of Drumclog. On that occasion, the preacher chose for his text the last two verses of the forty-ninth chapter of Isaiah—" Even the captives of the mighty shall be taken away, and the prey of the terrible shall be delivered : for I will contend with him that contendeth with thee, and I will save thy children. And I will feed them that oppress thee with their own flesh, and they shall be drunken with their own blood, as with sweet wine ; and all flesh shall know that I the Lord am thy Saviour and thy Redeemer, the Mighty One of Jacob." The first part of this text was applied by Kettledrummle to the incident of his own deliverance and to that of his companions ; while the second was employed to describe the punishment which, according

to the preacher, was soon to be meted out to the per-
secuting government.

When Kettledrummle finished his discourse, his place
was occupied by another preacher, but one of a very
different stamp.   He was a young man, hardly twenty
years of age.   But young as he was, he had been twice
imprisoned for several months, and suffered many seve-
rities, which gave him great influence over those of his
own sect.   His audience listened to an impassioned
address with an eagerness like that of "the famished
Israelites collecting the heavenly manna."   He painted
the desolation of the Church, during her time of persecution, in the most affecting colours.   He described her
like Hagar watching the waning life of her infant in the
fountainless desert; like Judah under the palm-tree
mourning for the devastation of the temple; like Rachel
weeping for her children and refusing to be comforted.
But the youthful preacher rose to sublimity when describing the men yet reeking from the battle.   Calling on
them to remember what great things God had done for
them, and to persevere in the career which their victory
had opened, he proceeds, in language suggested by the
opening verses of the sixty-third chapter of Isaiah, " Your
garments are dyed—but not with the juice of the
wine-press; your swords are filled with blood, but not
with the blood of goats or lambs; the dust of the desert
on which ye stand is made fat with gore—but not with
the blood of bullocks, for the Lord hath a sacrifice in
Bozrah, and a great slaughter in the land of Idumea."

In the conversation between Burley and Henry Morton, as narrated in the opening chapters of *Old Mortality,* there are many Scriptural illustrations employed. Here are two from the prophecies of Jeremiah. Since Morton cannot see things in the light that Balfour sees them, the latter tells him that he is "yet in the dungeon-house of the law, a pit darker than that into which Jeremiah was plunged, even the dungeon of Malchiah, the son of Hammelech, where there was no water but mire." And speaking of the restoration of King Charles, Balfour declares emphatically that it was accomplished, not by Montrose and his Highland caterans, but by the Covenanters, "the workers of the glorious word—the reformers of the beauty of the tabernacle." Then Balfour asks what has been their reward? "In the words of the prophet," he continues; "We looked for peace, but no good came, and for a time of health, and behold, trouble. The snorting of his horses was heard from Dan, the whole land trembled at the sound of the neighing of his strong ones; for they are come, and have devoured the land, and all that is in it."

The prophet Jeremiah abandons himself to sorrow as he thinks on the condition of his country. "Oh that my head were waters, and mine eyes a fountain of tears." This plaintive wail is re-echoed by David Deans, in *The Heart of Midlothian,* who exclaims—"Woe to me were I to shed a tear for the wife of my bosom, when I might weep rivers of waters for this afflicted church, cursed as it is with carnal seekers and with the dead of heart." And when Isaac the Jew, in *Ivanhoe,* in the extremity of his distress for Rebecca, is asked to read the scroll brought by grateful Higg, the son of Snell, he says to Ben Samuel, "Do thou read, brother, for mine eyes are as a fountain of water."

In the eighteenth chapter of Jeremiah, the prophet, under the type of breaking a potter's vessel, presages the desolation of the Jews. It was this chapter which Major Bridgenorth, in *Peveril of the Peak*, selected as the subject of his lecture at Moultrassie Hall. Though not naturally eloquent, the Major seemed so convinced of the truth of what he was stating, that the chapter "supplied him with language of energy and fire, as he drew a parallel between the abominations of the worship of Baal, and the corruptions of the Church of Rome —so favourite a topic with the Puritans of that period; and denounced against the Catholics, and those who favoured them, that hissing and desolation which the prophet directed against the city of Jerusalem."

Addressing Pashur, who had put Jeremiah into the stocks, the prophet says, "The Lord hath not called thy name Pashur, but Magor-missabib. For thus saith the Lord, Behold, I will make thee a terror to thyself, and to all thy friends." The insane preacher in *Old Mortality* applies this latter name to himself. "Am I not Habakkuk Mucklewrath, whose name is changed to Magor-missabib, because I am made a terror unto myself, and unto all that are around me? I heard it—when did I hear it? Was it not in the tower of the Bass that over-hangeth the wide, wild sea? And it howled in the winds, and it roared in the billows, and it screamed, and it whistled, and it clanged with the screams, and the clang, and the whistle of the sea-birds as they floated and flew, and dropped and dived, on the bosom of the waters."

When Ezekiel received the divine command to reprove the people of Israel for their rebellious conduct toward God, there appeared to the prophet, in vision, a hand holding a roll, on both sides of which were written "lamentation, and mourning, and woe." Sir Walter frequently refers to this roll of the prophet. As Lord Nigel finds himself a prisoner in the Tower of London, he sets himself the melancholy task of deciphering the names, mottoes, verses, and hieroglyphics with which his predecessors in captivity had covered the walls of their prison. He saw the names of many a forgotten sufferer, mingled with others which will never be forgotten so long as English history is read. This record of signatures and inscriptions, Sir Walter says, "was like the roll of the prophet, a record of lamentation and mourning, and yet not unmixed with brief interjections of resignation and sentences expressive of the firmest resolution." Describing the tomb-paved churchyard surrounding the Cathedral of Glasgow, Frank Osbaldistone, in *Rob Roy*, says of the inscriptions on the stones, with their sad records of mortality, that they reminded him of the roll of the prophet, on which was written "lamentation, and mourning, and woe."

The Lady Hermione, in *The Fortunes of Nigel*, relates her personal history to Margaret Ramsay; and in the course of doing so, she employs an illustration borrowed from a passage in Ezekiel. Speaking of the state of Scotland, the Lady proceeds—"You have heard of the bitterness of the ancient Scottish feuds, of which it may be said, in the language of the Scripture, 'The fathers eat sour grapes, and the teeth of the children are set on edge.' Some such bitterness had divided the lady's house from that of her lover's, and, accordingly, when he came to ask Hermione's hand in marriage, her mother raked up the memory of every injury which the rival families had inflicted on each other, and rejected his proposal of alliance as if it had come from the basest of mankind."

The Book of Daniel, with its striking historical records, is frequently referred to by Sir Walter.

While the knight and the hermit, in *Ivanhoe*, are enjoying their repast in the cell, the former compliments the latter on his looking so well on his diet of "parched pease and cold water."

"Sir Knight," answered the hermit, "your thoughts, like those of the ignorant laity, are according to the flesh. It has pleased our Lady and my patron saint to bless the pittance to which I restrain myself, even as the pulse and water were blessed to the children Shadrach, Meshach, and Abednego, who drank the same, rather than defile themselves with the wine and meats which were appointed them by the King of the Saracens."

With the greatest possible indignation, the Lady Margaret Bellenden listens to the following exposition of Scripture by Mause Headrigg, who had resolutely refused to allow her son to attend the Wappenschaw, or military gathering, as described in the opening chapter of *Old Mortality*. "There was ance a king in Scripture,"

Mause proceeds to say, "they ca'd Nebuchadnezzar, and he set up a golden image in the plain of Dura, as it might be in the haugh yonder by the waterside, where the array were warned to meet yesterday; and the princes, and the governors, and the captains, and the judges themsells, forby the treasurers, the counsellors, and the sheriffs, were warned to the dedication thereof, and commanded to fall down and worship at the sound of the cornet, flute, harp, sackbut, psaltery, and all kinds of music."

"And what o' a' this, ye fule wife? Or what had Nebuchadnezzar to do with the Wappenschaw of the Upper Ward of Clydesdale?"

"Only just thus far, my leddy," continued Mause, firmly, "that prelacy is like the great golden image in the plain of Dura; and that as Shadrach, Meshach, and Abednego were borne out in refusing to bow down and worship, so neither shall Cuddie Headrigg, your leddy-ship's puir pleughman, at least wi' his auld mither's consent, make murgeons or jennyflections, as they ca' them, in the house of the prelates and curates, nor gird him wi' armour to fight in their cause, either at the sound of kettle-drums, organs, bagpipes, or ony other kind of music whatever."

In *The Abbot*, Father Ambrose is informed from an anonymous letter, placed in his hand by a pilgrim, that a child educated in the Catholic faith is in the Castle of Avenel, whose owner has embraced the cause of the Reformation. The letter expresses the utmost concern for the spiritual safety of the child, whose situation the writer conceived to be as critical and dangerous as that of "the three children who were cast into the fiery furnace of persecution."

Among the spectators at the coronation of George III. were Lilias and her uncle Redgauntlet. The latter becomes greatly excited, not on account of the splendour of the scene, but because, being a Jacobite, he looked upon the vast assembly as only slaves and sycophants bending before the throne of a new usurper. "See," he said to his terrified niece, who entreated him to remember where they were, "yonder bows Norfolk, renegade to the Catholic faith; there stoops the Bishop of ——, traitor to the Church of England. . . . But a sign shall be seen this night amongst them—*Mene, Mene, Tekel, Upharsin,* shall be read on these walls, as distinctly as the spectral handwriting made them visible on those of Belshazzar."

At the feast given by the usurping Prince John, in *Ivanhoe,* the Saxon Cedric produces something like consternation in the assembly as he quaffs his goblet to the health of the absent King of England—Richard the Lion-hearted. After the guests disperse, Prince John is greatly affected. In reply to his counsellor, who tries to encourage him, the Prince says, "In vain—they (the Norman nobles) have seen *the handwriting on the wall*— they have marked the path of the lion in the sand—they have heard his approaching roar shake the wood—nothing will reanimate their courage."

Intent on the safety and welfare of his daughter, Isaac the Jew, in *Ivanhoe,* proposes to go to the Preceptory of Templestowe, in the hope that the Grand

Master may be able to turn aside Bois Guilbert from his evil designs upon Rebecca.

"Go," said his friend, Nathan Ben Israel, "and be wise, for wisdom availed Daniel in the den of lions into which he was cast; and may it go well with thee, even as thine heart wisheth."

In the coronach sung over Duncan's "lowly bier," in *The Lady of the Lake*, Sir Walter employs some illustrations which seem to have been suggested to him by the prophet Hosea. "As for Samaria, her king is cut off as the foam upon the water," and "they shall be as the morning cloud, and as the early dew that passeth away." How delicately and how effectively is this imagery of the prophet reproduced in the following lines of the coronach referred to :—

> " Like the *dew on the mountain*,
>   Like the *foam on the river*,
>   Like the bubble on the fountain,
>   *Thou art gone, and for ever !* "

In *The Heart of Midlothian*, David Deans employs the figure or imagery of "foam upon the water," and quotes, at the same time, another passage from Hosea. In a long letter to Jeanie, during her stay in London, Deans charges his daughter to withdraw her eyes from the vanities of the great city, and not to worship in any of the churches where the Episcopal form of service is used. This service the stern old Cameronian writes of as "an ill-mumbled mass, as it was weel termed by James the Sext, though he afterwards, with his unhappy son, strove to bring it ower back and belly into his native kingdom,

wherethrough their race have been cut off *as foam upon
the water*, and shall be as wanderers among the nations—
see the prophecies of Hosea, ninth and seventeenth, and
the same, tenth and seventh.   But us and our house, let
us say with the same prophet, 'Let us return to the
Lord, for He hath torn, and He will heal us—He hath
smitten, and He will bind us up.'"

In *The Monastery*, there is a text quoted from the
prophet Joel.   Julian Avenel takes his place at the
supper-table, and points to a seat, between himself and
Catherine Græme, for the preacher, Henry Warden, to
occupy.   But notwithstanding the influence of both
hunger and fatigue, the preacher retained his standing
posture, not being satisfied with the relationship in which
his host and Catherine lived together.

"Beshrew me," said Julian, "these new-fashioned
religioners have fast days, I warrant me—the old ones
used to confer that blessing chiefly on the laity."

"We acknowledge no such rule," said the preacher.
"We hold that our faith consists not in using or abstain-
ing from any special meals on special days; and in fasting, *we rend our hearts and not our garments.*"

The Book of Jonah furnishes the author of *Waverley*
with a number of illustrations.   Referring to the flight
of Dousterswivel, the Antiquary says to Sir Arthur Wardour that the scoundrel never reached Edinburgh, for
the coach in which he travelled was upset.   "How could
it go safe with such a Jonah?"

In the motto to chapter seventeen of *The Bride of
Lammermoor*, the father referred to is Sir William Ashton,

through whose head are coursing thoughts and speculations on the probability of his daughter being married to the Master of Ravenswood, and thereby healing the feuds between the two families.

> "Here is a father now,
> Will truck his daughter for a foreign venture,
> Make her the stop-gap to some canker'd feud,
> *Or fling her o'er, like Jonah to the fishes,*
> *To appease the sea at highest."*

In the same novel Lady Ashton, like many other mothers of hot and impatient character, was mistaken in estimating the feelings of her daughter Lucy, "who, under a semblance of extreme indifference, nourished the germ of those passions which sometimes spring up in one night, *like the gourd of the prophet,* and astonish the observer by their unexpected ardour and intensity."

In *Kenilworth,* Varney reminds his master, the Earl of Leicester, that though the latter is strong and powerful, yet he is only so by the reflected light of the Queen's favour. "But let her call back the honour she has bestowed, and *the prophet's gourd did not wither more suddenly."*

There is a fine passage in *Ivanhoe,* where Rebecca, addressing the Templar, says, "Know, proud Knight, we number names amongst us to which your boasted northern nobility is as the *gourd compared with the cedar*—names that ascend far back to those high times when the Divine Presence shook the mercy seat between the Cherubim, and which derive their splendour from no earthly prince, but from the awful voice, which bade their fathers be nearest of the Congregation to the vision."

WHEN Sir Walter has occasion to introduce the name of our Lord in the course of his tales and romances, he always does so by using some such reverent term or title as "the Founder of the Christian religion," "the Author of our holy religion," "the Great Physician," or simply as "the Master." The birth of Christ is described as "the great event which brought peace on earth and good-will to the children of men." The work which He came to do, and which He finished on the Cross, is spoken of as "the redemption of man from his fallen state." The White Lady of Avenel is made to say that this redemption extends to the human family alone:

> "For the children of clay was salvation brought,
> But not for the forms of sea or air."

There is no mistake as to what the gospel is, when it is mentioned in the Waverley Novels, nor is there any doubt as to the freeness and fulness of its offer to every one. "For the sake of Heaven, that hears and sees us," said Jeanie Deans to George Staunton, who was speaking in the despairing tones of one predestined to evil both here and hereafter, "dinna speak in this desperate fashion. The gospel is sent to the chief of sinners—to the most miserable among the miserable."

Using Sir Walter's own words in a passage from *Count Robert of Paris*, we can trace, in the Waverley pages, some reference or allusion to almost all "the great events detailed in the blessed gospel." The birth at Bethlehem, the visit of the Magi, the star in the East, and the blessings which our Lord brought with Him at His birth, are all mentioned, more or less frequently. As Colonel Ashton and Bucklaw, in *The Bride of Lammermoor*, draw their swords and prepare to rush on Ravenswood, the clergyman interrupts them, saying, "In the name of Him who brought peace on earth, and goodwill to mankind, I implore—I beseech—I command you to forbear violence toward each other. God hateth the bloodthirsty man—he who striketh with the sword shall perish with the sword."

At the near approach of Christmas-time, as related in *Anne of Geierstein*, the Duke of Burgundy, addressing Lord Oxford, says, "This is a period of the year when good men forgive their enemies. I know not why—my mind was little apt to be charged with such matters—but I feel an unconquerable desire to stop the approaching combat between you and Campo Basso."

"My Lord," said Oxford, "it is a small thing you ask of me, since your request only enforces a Christian duty."

The Song of Simeon—the *Nunc Dimittis* of the Christian Church—uttered in a transport of joy on seeing the infant Saviour brought into the temple, suggests to Sir

Walter an incident in *Woodstock*. The aged knight, Sir Henry Lee, welcomes King Charles in his royal progress across Blackheath to London. Overjoyed at seeing the king once more, and in safety, the faithful old royalist leans back on his seat and mutters the *Nunc Dimittis.*

As we have now reached that point in the Gospel history where our Lord begins His public ministry, we shall proceed to point out to our readers in what way Sir Walter makes use of some of the outstanding injunctions and illustrations embodied in the Divine teaching, as recorded in the gospels of the four Evangelists.

In the Sermon on the Mount, our Lord says of His true followers that they are "the salt of the earth," and that their influence will be felt only so long as the salt retains its savour and its strength. These preserving properties gone, the salt is useless, and life loses all worth living for. Sir Walter employs this illustration, in *The Bride of Lammermoor*, while describing the effect which the death of the Master of Ravenswood had upon his old servant, Caleb Balderstone. Caleb finds the only vestige that revealed the fate of his master, who perished in the quicksands of the Kelpie's Flow. A large sable feather got detached from Ravenswood's hat, and the rippling waves of the rising tide wafted it to Caleb's feet. The old man took it up, dried it, and placed it in his bosom. Thenceforward the spring of the faithful servant's existence was broken. *"Life to him had lost its savour.* He ate without refreshment, slumbered without repose, and . . . died within a year after the catastrophe."

In His exposition of the Third Commandment under the Christian law, our Lord unfolds its meaning, and teaches that it not only forbids false swearing, but all unnecessary expletives or oaths to which, as mere forms of speech, no one pays any attention, or attaches any value. "Swear not at all," He says conclusively. In *Redgauntlet*, when Joshua Geddes asks Davies, at the fishing-station on the Solway, to call the men together to receive their instructions, the reply is that the men had all gone off, except, said Davies, "little Phil and myself. They have, by —— !"

"'Swear not at all,' John Davies—thou art an honest man ; and I believe, without an oath, that thy comrades love their own bones better than my goods and chattels."

In the same novel, Alan Fairford arrives at Mount Sharon to make inquiry about his friend Darsie Latimer. Rachel Geddes describes how much her brother had interested himself in Darsie's case. "He had gone," she said, "before the Head Judge, whom men call the Sheriff, and would have told him of the youth's peril ; but he would in no way hearken to him unless he would swear unto the truth of his words, which thing he might not do without sin, seeing it is written, 'Swear not at all' —also that our conversation shall be yea or nay."

When Halbert Glendinning fears that he has fatally wounded Sir Piercie Shafton, he is overwhelmed with remorse and grief. He implores the aid of an old man whom he sees coming up the glen, and on returning with him to the place where the duel had been fought, he is surprised to find that the body of Sir Piercie is nowhere to be seen.   Thinking that he has been imposed upon, the old man reproves the youth for having stated what was apparently not true.   But Halbert persists in asserting the truth of what he had said, and was proceding to "swear by the Blessed Heaven——"

"'Swear not at all,'" said the stranger, interrupting him, "neither by heaven, for it is God's throne; nor by earth, for it is His footstool—nor by the creatures whom He hath made, for they are but earth and clay as we are. Let thy yea be yea, and thy nay, nay."

And further on, in the same novel, *The Monastery*, Halbert and this same old man, who turns out to be Henry Warden, the reformed preacher, come before us once more in connection with this same text.   Locked up in different apartments in the Castle of Avenel, they yet find it possible to communicate with each other by means of speech.   The preacher advises his companion to make an attempt at escape ; and as the latter does so, he puts his hand on an iron stanchion of the window more in despair than hope.   To his great surprise, however, the bar parted asunder and came away in his hands.   He immediately whispered, "By Heaven, the bar has given way in my hand ! "

"Thank Heaven, my son, instead of swearing by it," answered Warden from his dungeon.

In *Count Robert of Paris*, the Emperor is asked whether it is still his intention to carry out the sentence of death on his unfortunate and misguided son-in-law.   Replying in the affirmative, he states, in addition, that all the arrangements have been made, "by which I swear——"

"'Swear not at all,'" said the Patriarch. "I forbid thee, in the name of that Heaven whose voice, though unworthy, speaks in my person, to quench the smoking flax, or destroy the slight hope which there may remain."

Cromwell, in *Woodstock*, asks from Wildrake a description of Woodstock House, and hazards the remark that no doubt it has plenty of corners for concealing priests about the premises.

"Your Honour's Excellency," said Wildrake, "may swear to that."

"I swear not at all," replied the General drily.

We get an interesting illustration, in *Old Mortality*, of at least a portion of the meaning which our Lord gives while expounding the second table of the law. Balfour states to Morton and Poundtext, the clergyman, that it has been decided to put their prisoner, Lord Evandale, to death unless Tillietudlem be surrendered by daybreak. Morton asks what law would justify the commission of such an atrocity?

"If thou art ignorant of it," replied Burley, "thy companion is well aware of the law which gave the men of Jericho to the sword of Joshua, the son of Nun."

"But we," answered the divine, "live under a better dispensation, which instructeth us to pray for those who despitefully use us and persecute us."

Both in the Lord's Prayer and in the awful agony in the Garden of Gethsemane, submission to the Divine will is taught in these sublime and tender words, "Thy will bo done." Perhaps there is no New Testament lesson which receives more interesting illustration in the pages of the Waverley Novels than this prayer for submission and resignation. When the two Philipsons lose their way during the snowstorm on the Alps, the elder gives his consent to allow the younger, his son, to go on in advance for the purpose of procuring assistance at the Castle of Geierstein. Terrified by the thundering crash of a falling rock, Philipson dreads that his son is lost. The grief of the father is affecting to the last degree. "Holding up his hands, and lifting his eyes towards heaven, (he) said in accents of the deepest agony, mingled with devout resignation, *Fiat voluntas tua !* (Thy will be done !) He was my last, and loveliest, and best beloved, and most worthy of my love."

In *The Black Dwarf*, Hobbie Elliot reaches home to find that a great calamity has happened in his absence—his house burned down, and Grace Armstrong carried off by a band of armed and masked moss-troopers. Overwhelmed with grief, Hobbie allows himself to be led to a seat by his grandmother, who, with the affecting serenity which sincere piety can throw over the most acute feelings, tried to soothe him under his great trial.

"My bairn," she said, "when thy grandfather was killed in the wars, and left me with six orphans around me, with scarce bread to eat, or a roof to cover us, I had strength—not of mine own—but I had strength given me to say, The Lord's will be done ! . . . My son, . . . pray for strength to say, HIS will be done !"

"Mother ! mother ! urge me not—I cannot—not now

—I am a sinful man, and of a hardened race. Masked —armed—Grace carried off! Give me my sword, and my father's knapsack—I will have vengeance if I should go to the pit of darkness to seek it."

"O my bairn, my bairn! be patient under the rod. Who knows when He may lift His hand off from us?" The aged grandmother then explains that Earnscliff and other friends are away in pursuit of the troopers; but as Hobbie still persists in his intention to follow the robbers, she continues to urge upon him patience and resignation.

"Urge me not, mother—not now." He was rushing out, when looking back he observed his grandmother make a mute attitude of affliction. He returned hastily, threw himself into her arms, and said, "Yes, mother, I *can* say HIS will be done, since it will comfort you."

"May He go forth—may He go forth with you, my dear bairn; and, oh, may He give you cause to say on your return, HIS name be praised!"

Poor Saunders Mucklebackit and his wife, in *The Antiquary*, find it no less hard, than Hobbie Elliot does, to submit with resignation when the hour of trial comes. They have lost their son Steenie, and the grief of the parents is well-nigh uncontrollable. "He has sailed the coble wi' me since he was ten years auld, and there wasna the like o' him drew a net betwixt this and Buchan-ness. *They say folks maun submit—I will try.*" The mother of the drowned fisher-lad tries to listen to the clergyman's attempts at consolation; but from her half-stifled sobs in reply, we feel that she, too, finds it hard to learn the lesson, "Thy will be done." "Yes, sir, yes," she says, as the clergyman pauses. "*It's our duty to submit.* But, oh dear! my poor Steenie, . . . what for is thou lying there! and, oh! what for am I left to greet for ye?"

David Deans, of stronger and sterner feelings than either the Border farmer or the fisherman and his wife, says in reply to a neighbour who inquires what he proposes to do now, when a great family trial has overtaken him—"Nothing," answered Deans firmly, "but to abide the dispensation that the Lord sees meet to send us. O if it had been His will to take the gray head to rest before this awful visitation on my house and name! *But His will be done. I can say that yet, though I can say little mair.*"

An incident in *The Monastery* illustrates the truth expressed by our Lord that "where your treasure is, there will your heart be also." Sir Piercie Shafton, the gay and handsome English Knight, with an especial passion for fine clothing, seeks refuge in Scotland, and while there, receives a letter intimating that there had been forwarded to him two mails filled with wearing apparel, "rich crimson silk doublets slashed out, and lined with cloth of gold," along with numerous other fineries. The Abbot and the Sub-Prior bring these in their train while on a visit to the tower of Glendearg, and when Sir Piercie hears of his clothes, he says to the churchmen, "I pray you, pardon me—I must needs see how matters stand with (the clothes) without further dallying." So saying he left the room. The Sub-Prior, looking after him significantly added, "Where the treasure is, there will the heart be also."

The impossibility of serving two masters is illustrated in various ways by Sir Walter. Elias Henderson, the chaplain in *The Abbot*, seeks to induce Roland Græme to transfer his services from Queen Mary to Lady Lochleven, the latter of whom was ready, even that day, to employ the page in certain important missions on the mainland. But Roland felt that any increase of confidence on the part of Lady Lochleven and her family would only render his situation, in a moral point of view, doubly embarrassing. "One cannot serve two masters," he reasoned, "and I much fear that my mistress will not hold me excused for taking employment under another."

A less conscientious servant than Roland Græme, Michael Lambourne, says that he will at least try the experiment of serving two masters. Prefixed to the fourth chapter of *Kenilworth* are the following lines, which refer to an arrangement by which Lambourne is to enter the service of the Earl of Leicester and Richard Varney:

"'Not serve two masters! Here's a youth will try it—
Would fain serve God, yet give the devil his due:
Says grace before he doth a deed of villainy,
And returns his thanks devoutly, when 'tis acted."

In describing Hereward's ramble through the streets of Constantinople and the terraces along the margin of the Bosphorus, Sir Walter pictures out how the inhabitants of the city were, in various ways, enjoying their ease and whiling away their leisure on the public promenade. Unconsciously, in perhaps the lowest possible sense, they were acting on our Lord's injunction of taking no thought for the morrow; for, adds Sir Walter, the people spent "their time as if their sole object was to make as much of the day as it passed, and let the cares of to-morrow answer for themselves."

Coupled with this injunction is the assurance that "sufficient unto the day is the evil thereof"—a text which Sir Walter often quotes. While Quentin Durward was on guard in the hall, he was strictly enjoined by the king to keep off all intruders, and to remember his secret orders. Perplexing and difficult as these secret orders were to keep in mind, the youthful Scot derived much consolation from the thought that it was time enough to think what was to be done when the emergency actually arrived, and that, in any case, "sufficient for the day is the evil thereof."

Darsie Latimer, in *Redgauntlet*, records in his journal that rarely, in the course of his own experience, has he known what it was to sustain a moment's real sorrow. "What I have called such," he says, "was, I am now well convinced, only the weariness of mind which, having nothing actually present to complain of, turns upon itself and becomes anxious about the past and the future: those periods with which human life has so little connection that Scripture itself has said, 'Sufficient for the day is the evil thereof.'"

Clara Mowbray begs of her brother John not to annoy and worry her with details of the coming private theatricals at St. Ronan's. She will attend and do the part assigned to her, but to think of it beforehand makes both her head and heart ache. She comforts herself, however, with the sacred assurance that "Sufficient for the day is the evil thereof."

Sir Walter had no doubt this text in mind when, in *Rob Roy*, he gives it as his conviction "that of all the propensities which teach mankind to torment themselves, that of causeless fear is the most irritating, busy, painful, and pitiable." And we can trace it in *Woodstock* also, where the good-natured Joliffe tells Phœbe to put her scanty store of wine into a flask and take it to Sir Henry Lee. "The knight," he says, "must not lack his evening draught. . . . There is enough for supper, and *to-morrow is a new day*."

The injunction in the passage "Give not that which is holy to the dogs, neither cast ye your pearls before swine, lest they trample them under their feet, and turn again and rend you," involves the idea of moral fitness and adaptation on the part of the person conveying certain specific information or instruction, and the person or persons to whom such information is to be imparted, or not imparted, as the case may be. Sir Walter illustrates the meaning of the passage in several very interesting examples. In *The Antiquary*, the Earl of Glenallan had a confidential and secret interview with old Edie Ochiltree; and when it was over, his Lordship gave instructions to Francie Macraw, that the mendicant should be seen fairly out of the house and off the grounds, without conversation or intercourse with any of the domestics. Considering, however, that the restriction did not extend to himself, who was the person entrusted with the convoy, Francie used every measure in his power to extort from Edie what had passed at the interview. But Edie had been, in his time, accustomed to cross-examination, and easily evaded that of his quondam comrade. "The secrets of grit folk," said Ochiltree within himself, "are just like the wild beasts that are shut up in cages; keep them hard and fast snecked up, and it's a' very weel or better, but ance let them out, they will turn and rend you."

Conversing with the Marquis of Montrose, Captain Dalgetty thinks that any effort made to instruct the Highlanders in military movements and discipline would only be so much good time thrown away. He grants them to be brave and active, but even supposing he were to try and discipline such a "breechless mob," where, Dalgetty asks, were the chances that he would be understood in the first place, and obeyed in the second? And then he closes his argument by remarking, "Truly, well saith Holy Writ, 'If ye cast your pearls before swine they will turn again and rend ye.'"

In *Ivanhoe*, Prince John haughtily observes that using courtesy to the Lady Rowena and her party of Saxon attendants is only "casting pearls before swine." And the officer in *Count Robert of Paris* says to Hereward, with reference to Eastern affairs, that to show the "fine meshes of Grecian policy to the coarse eye of an unpractised barbarian like thee, is much like casting pearls before swine—a thing forbidden in the blessed Gospel." Sir Philip de Comines intimates to Louis XI., in *Quentin Durward*, that there is a report of the approach of an envoy from La Marck. "This," he said, "is like to drive the Duke (of Burgundy) frantic with rage. I trust he has no letters, or the like, to show on your Majesty's part?"

"Letters to a Wild Boar!" answered the King; "no, no, Sir Philip, I was no such fool as to cast pearls before swine. What little intercourse I had with the brute animal was by message, in which I always employed such low-bred slaves and vagabonds, that their evidence would not be received on a trial for robbing a hen-roost."

Varney and Antony Foster, in *Kenilworth*, meet at dinner, both dressed so much more smartly than usual that the former sarcastically observes: "Thou art gay as a goldfinch, Antony. . . . Methinks thou wilt whistle a jig anon—but I crave your pardon—that would secure your ejection from the zealous butchers, the pure-hearted weavers, and the sanctified bakers of Abingdon, who let their ovens cool while their brains get heated."

"To answer you in the spirit, Master Varney," said Foster, "were—excuse the parable—to fling sacred and precious things before swine. So I will speak to thee in the language of the world which he, who is king of the world, hath taught thee to understand and to profit by no common measure."

The golden rule of equity, as taught by our Lord, is to do to others as we would they should do to us. In *Rob Roy*, Mr. Osbaldistone's managing clerk, Owen, puts the golden rule into the following quaint and curious arithmetical form. Addressing the head of the firm with reference to the case of Frank, Owen says: "Mr.

Francis seems to understand the fundamental principle of all moral accounting, the great ethic rule of three : let A do to B as he would have B do to him ; the product will give the rule of conduct required." And in the same novel, Bailie Nicol Jarvie warmly congratulates old Mr. Osbaldistone and Owen on the return of prosperity, without at the same time affecting to disclaim that he had done his best to serve them when matters looked otherwise. "He had," the worthy magistrate observes, "only just acted as he would be done by."

Simon of Hackburn, in *The Black Dwarf,* looks at the golden rule in a different light from the Bailie. While Hobbie Elliot's friends and neighbours are assembling to form a party to go in pursuit of the moss-trooper who had burned his house and carried off Grace Armstrong, "Ay, ay," exclaimed Simon, "that's the gate to take it, Hobbie ; let women sit and greet at hame, *men must do as they have been done by ;* it's the Scripture says 't."

"Haud your tongue, sir," said one of the seniors, sternly ; "dinna abuse the Word in that gate ; ye dinna ken what ye speak about."

In *Quentin Durward,* Sir Walter draws the picture of a selfish man in the person of Ludovic Lesly, an archer of the Scottish guard. In fact, so utterly selfish was he, that he was seldom able "to proceed far in any subject without considering how it applied to himself, or, as it was called, making the case his own, *though not upon feelings connected with the golden rule, but such as was very different.*" In the same novel, however, there is another character occupying a much more lowly position than the Scottish archer, but of a very different disposition. This is the Flemish guide in attendance upon Quentin Durward and the Lady Isabelle. During their journey towards Brabant the good-natured guide, minding the golden rule, and doing as he desired to be done by, removed from them the restraint of a third party, and left Quentin and the Lady free to continue their conversation. There is, in *Anne of Geierstein*, another character whose name we always associate with the golden rule. Of Annette, the waiting-maid, Sir Walter himself says that she wished "always to do as she would wish to be done by." On one occasion she was delighted with the thought that, by her observance of the golden rule, she had been the means of bringing the two lovers, Arthur Philipson and Anne of Geierstein, together, and that on the eve of what seemed to be their inevitable separation for ever.

In *The Heart of Midlothian*, we are reminded of "the strait gate and the narrow way," through and along which the Divine Teacher urges us all to pass. Addressing Jeanie Deans, Madge Wildfire says, "Ye are a decent man's daughter . . . and may be ye'll can teach me to find out *the narrow way and the strait path*, for I have been burning bricks in Egypt, and walking through the weary wilderness of Sinai for lang and mony a day."

The illustration of the house built on the sand, with which our Lord concludes His Sermon on the Mount, is very frequently employed by Sir Walter. At the close of *The Pirate*, in the parting words on the character of

N

Minna Troil, he tells us that though she had been gifted with much depth of feeling and enthusiasm, yet she had seen both blighted even in early youth, because, with the inexperience of a disposition equally romantic and ignorant, she had built the fabric of her happiness *on a quicksand instead of a rock.*

Varney and Foster are discussing their prospects of advancement in the service of the Earl of Leicester and the Countess Amy. "We must found our future fortunes on her good liking," remarks Varney.

"*We build on sand, then,*" said Foster, "for, supposing that she sails away to court in all her lord's dignity and authority, how is she to look back upon me who am her jailor, as it were, to detain her here against her will, keeping her a caterpillar on an old wall, when she would fain be a painted butterfly in a court garden?"

In *Count Robert of Paris,* Hereward tells us of an old countryman of his who, when too old for the active life of a soldier, passed his time in attending the lectures of the philosophers. "But I have understood from him," Hereward adds, "that the masters of this idle science make it their business to substitute, in their argumentations, mere words instead of ideas. . . . Their theories, as they call them, *are built on the sand, and the wind and tide shall prevail against them.*"

In *Woodstock,* Harrison tries to induce Everard to join him in seeking to "repair the breaches in Zion." He feels certain that they two would be chosen pillars and buttresses, under Cromwell, for supporting and sus-

taining the Church; and were they able to endow her
with proper revenues and incomes, both spiritual and
temporal, there might be hopes of her remaining established and firm; otherwise, it is Harrison's opinion,
"*our foundation will be on the loose sand.*" The grandmother of Roland Græme puts the security of the
Church into the keeping of God alone. Endowed with
strong faith, she says, "God will defend His own,
though it be forsaken and despised of men. *Better to
dwell on the sand under His law, than fly to the rock of human
trust.*"

In sending out the twelve apostles to proclaim that
the kingdom of heaven was near at hand, our Lord
intimates to them that they would have many difficulties
to encounter, trials to face, and unsympathetic audiences
to address. "I send you forth," He says, "as sheep in
the midst of wolves, be ye therefore wise as serpents
and harmless as doves." This text is frequently quoted
by Sir Walter, but not always in the sense in which it
is used in Scripture. Wayland Smith, in *Kenilworth*,
privately warns Janet Foster that an old man is on his
way to Cumnor Place with designs against her mistress.
Describing his appearance, and his manner, Wayland
proceeds to say, "*He brings the venom of the aspic under
the assumed innocence of the dove.* What precise mischief
he meditates towards you I cannot guess, but death and
disease have ever dogged his footsteps."

In *Peveril of the Peak*, the Countess of Derby sends
Julian on a secret mission to London. He expresses
his doubts and fears as to the policy of mixing himself

up with the Catholics of the Metropolis.   In the course
of soothing these fears, and seeking to dispel these
doubts, the Countess observes, "Though you Protestants
deny our priesthood *the harmlessness of the dove*, you are
ready enough to allow us a full share of *the wisdom of the
serpent.*"

Describing to Roland Græme the state of the Catholics
in Scotland at the time of the Reformation, and the
hopelessness of their ever again being able to recover
the supremacy they had lost, the Abbot, in the novel of
that name, despondingly remarks, "As well might the
hound say to the hare, use not these wily turns to
escape me, but contend with me in pitched battle, as
the armed and powerful heretic demand of the down-
trodden and oppressed Catholic to lay aside the *wisdom
of the serpent*, by which alone they may hope to raise up
the Jerusalem over which they weep, and which it is
their duty to rebuild."

Our Lord compares those who had listened unmoved
to the ministry of John the Baptist, to children sitting
in the market-place playing at rejoicing and lamenting.
There was no impression made.   In *Count Robert of Paris*,
the Princess Anna Comnena is attracted by the Count,
and shows him great attention.   He sits, however, in
a fit of apparent abstraction or preoccupation, and has
nothing to say in reply to all that was being done to
interest him.   Unable to endure such conduct any
longer, the Princess says, " *We have piped to you and you
have not danced.*   We have sung to you the jovial chorus
of *Evoe, evoe*, and you will neither worship Comus nor

Bacchus." The Count curtly replies that he is a Christian man, and bids "defiance to Apollo, Bacchus, Comus, and all other heathen deities whatsoever."

In the twenty-third chapter of St. Matthew, our Lord denounces, in scathing and withering terms, the hypocrisy of the Scribes and Pharisees. From this chapter we have numerous quotations scattered throughout the Waverley Novels, and plenty of references to the greetings in the market-place, the long prayers, the tithing of mint and anise and cummin to the omission of much weightier matters of the law, the cleansing of cups and platters, the whited sepulchres, and the generation of vipers.

In the novel of *Redgauntlet*, Sir Walter draws the full-length portrait of a hypocrite in the person of Thomas Trumbull, the sanctimonious smuggler. Alan Fairford, still in search of his friend Darsie Latimer, arrives at the town of Annan, and, with the assistance of a young lad, seeks out the house of Trumbull. Listening at the door they hear, within, the uplifting of a Psalm. "They are at exercise, sir," said the lad, motioning at the same time that it would not be proper to enter until prayers were over.

Alan, however, could not wait, and as he knocked at the door with the end of his riding-whip the singing ceased, and Trumbull himself appeared with his Psalm-book in his hand, demanding to know the meaning of this unseasonable interruption. "Do you want me, sir?" he said to Fairford. "We were engaged, and it is the Saturday night."

Alan's preconceptions as to the man's appearance and manner were so completely dispelled by the reality, that he stood for a moment bewildered, and would as soon have thought of giving a cant pass-word to a clergyman descending from the pulpit, as to the apparently respectable father of a family just interrupted in his prayers. Hastily concluding that some idle jest had been passed upon him, or rather that he had mistaken the person to whom he was directed, he asked if he spoke to Mr. Trumbull.

"To Thomas Trumbull," answered the old man. "What may be your business, sir?" and he glanced his eye to the book he held in his hand with a sigh like that of a saint desirous of dissolution.

Explaining that he had been directed thither by Mr. Maxwell of Summertrees, Alan inquired, "Is there another of your name in this town of Annan?"

"None," replied Trumbull, "since my worthy father was removed; he was indeed a shining light—I wish you good even, sir."

"Stay one single instant," said Fairford, "this is a matter of life and death."

"Not more than the casting the burden of our sins where they should be laid," said Thomas Trumbull, about to shut the door in the inquirer's face.

"Do you know," said Alan Fairford, "the Laird of Redgauntlet?"

"Now Heaven defend me from treason and rebellion!" exclaimed Trumbull: "young gentleman, you are importunate. I live here among my own people, and do not consort with Jacobites and mass-mongers."

Here Alan produced the password with which he had previously been provided. In a low tone of voice he said, "At least you can tell me what age the moon is?"

The pass had the desired effect, and Alan was at once invited to enter the house. Putting his head into an apartment, which the murmurs within announced to be filled with the members of his family, Trumbull said aloud, "A work of necessity and mercy! Malachi, take the book—you will sing six double verses of the hundred and nineteen—and you may lecture out of the Lamentations. And Malachi"—this he said in an undertone—"see you give them a screed of doctrine that will last them till I come back."

Directing Alan to follow him, Trumbull led the way out of the house, through a garden, and eventually into a subterranean vault. Here a conversation took place between Trumbull and another person, to whom he introduced Alan as being bound for Cumberland on pressing business, and desirous of speech with Redgauntlet. We need not follow the details of the narrative, but pass on until Trumbull and Alan arrive, after a perilous progress along the roofs of two or three houses, at an inn, which they enter by an attic room. Here they met Nanty Ewart, to whom Trumbull observed, "It is not my custom, Mr. Ewart, as you well know, to become a chamberer or carouser thus late on Saturday at e'en, but I wanted to recommend to your attention a young friend of ours." Alan was then introduced to Ewart, the captain of a smuggling craft. Sitting down to the bowl of punch, Nanty seized the ladle and proceeded to fill the glasses. Trumbull, however, arrested the smuggler's hand until he had, as the hypocrite expressed himself, *sanctified the liquor by a long grace.* Thoroughly disgusted with such conduct, Alan rose from the table, craved and obtained leave to stretch himself on a couch, and tried to procure some rest before the ship should sail with the morning tide.

After a short and troubled sleep, Alan was requested to leave the house with the two boon companions. As they walked to where the ship was lying, Trumbull reminded Alan that the next day was the honourable Sabbath, and became extremely discursive in an attempt to exhort him to keep it holy according to the commandment. Sensible, perhaps, that from the effects of the liquor he was fast becoming unintelligible, he thrust a volume into Fairford's hand, hiccuping at the same time, "good book, good book—fine hymn-book—fit for the honourable Sabbath, which awaits us to-morrow morning." Here the iron tongue of time tolled five from the townsteeple of Annan, to the further confusion of Mr. Trumbull's already disordered ideas. "Ay? Is Sunday come and gone already? Heaven be praised! Only it is a marvel the afternoon is so dark for the time of the year—Sabbath has slipped ower quietly, but we have reason to bless oursells it has not been altogether misemployed. I heard little of the preaching—a cauld moralist, I doubt, served that out—but eh! the prayer

—I mind it as if I had said the words mysell." Here he repeated one or two petitions, which were probably a part of his family devotions. "I never remember a Sabbath pass so cannily off in my life." Then he recollected himself a little, and said to Alan, "You may read that book, Mr. Fairford, to-morrow all the same, though it be Monday; for, you see, it was Saturday when we were thegither, and now it's Sunday, and it's dark night— so the Sabbath has slipped clean away through our fingers, like water through a sieve, which abideth not; and we have to begin again to-morrow morning, in the weariful, base, mean, earthly employments, which are unworthy of an immortal spirit, always excepting the way of business."

At length Alan got on board the *Jumping Jenny.* After a short and feverish sleep he rises and has recourse to his pocket for the copy of Sallust which he had brought with him, that the perusal of a classic author might help to pass away a weary hour. Instead of Sallust, however, he pulled from his pocket the supposed hymn-book with which he had been presented a few hours before by Trumbull. But what was Alan's astonishment to read on the title-page the following words, "Merry Thoughts for Merry Men: or, Mother Midnight's Miscellany for Small Hours." Turning over the leaves, he was disgusted with profligate tales and more profligate songs, ornamented with figures corresponding in infamy with the letterpress. "Good God!" thought Alan, "and did this hoary reprobate summon his family together, and with such a disgraceful pledge of infamy in

his bosom venture to approach the throne of his Creator?
It must be so.   The book is bound after the manner of
those dedicated to devotional subjects, and doubtless the
wretch, in his intoxication, confounded the book he carried with him as he did the days of the week."   With
unutterable loathing and disgust Alan flung the volume
from him over the ship's side, as far away into the sea
as possible.

We have other hypocrites in the Waverley Novels,
but none so contemptible, out and out, as this same
sanctimonious smuggler.   "If you want a hypocrite,"
says Lambourne to Varney, in *Kenilworth*, "you may
take Anthony Foster who, from his childhood, had some
sort of phantom haunting him which he called religion,
though it was that sort of godliness which always 'ended
in being great gain.'"

Foster himself seems to confirm the truth of what
Lambourne says of him, for, listen to him as he is thinking aloud about his daughter and about the life he leads
at Cumnor Hall.   "No contagious vapour shall breathe
on Janet—she shall remain as a blessed spirit, were it
but to pray God for her father.   I need her prayers, for
I am at a hard pass.   Strange reports are abroad concerning my way of life.   The congregation look cold on me,
and when Master Holdforth spoke of hypocrites being
like *a whited sepulchre, which within was full of dead men's
bones*, methought he looked full at me. . . . I will read
my Bible ere I again open mine iron chest."

In the novel of *The Monastery* we are told that, gloomy
and depressed, the Sacristan leaves the room where the

dying Lady of Avenel lay. Dame Glendinning, afraid at first to speak, at length hazards the hope that the lady had made an easy shrift, for, having lived five years with her, she could safely say that no woman lived better.

"Woman!" said the Sacristan sternly, "thou speakest thou knowest not what! What avails cleaning *the outside of the platter,* if the inside be foul with heresy?"

The poor dame, taking these latter words in a literal sense, began to wipe the imaginary dust from the plates on the table before her; but the Sacristan assured her that the foulness, of which he spoke, was the heresy which was daily spreading and leavening the whole Church.

Speaking of the education which Roland Græme had received at Avenel Castle, the lad's grandmother, stern and enthusiastic Catholic as she was, nevertheless commended it as an effort to train up the young in "strong morality, and choke every inlet of youthful folly." Her companion, however, could see nothing in the education of a youth brought up in a family who had embraced the reformed faith, but *a cleansing of the outside of the cup,* and *a whitening of the sepulchre.* Much in the same spirit, though in exactly the opposite direction from the Church stand-point of view, does Tomkins, the Presbyterian soldier, in *Woodstock,* regret that Sir Henry Lee should be "such a malignant cavalier, and that he should, *like the rest of that generation of vipers,* have clothed himself with curses as with a garment."

In the form of a proverbial saying, our Lord teaches this important truth, that no one can do anything well unless his undivided attention be given to whatever he has taken in hand to do. "No man," He says, "having put his hand to the plough, and looking back, is fit for the kingdom of God." This is a truth which receives several very interesting illustrations in the Waverley Novels. In *Old Mortality* Burley says to Morton, with reference to his joining the Cameronian cause, "When *I put my hand to the plough*, I entered into a covenant with my worldly affections that I should not look back on the things I left behind me." Further on, in the same novel, Morton also joins the same cause; but seeing and hearing much that pained and vexed him, he resolved to sever his connection and have nothing more to do with the party. Burley asks where he is going.

"Anywhere—I care not whither; but here will I abide no longer."

"Art thou so soon weary, young man?" said Burley. "*Thy hand is but now put to the plough*, and wouldst thou already abandon it? Is this thy adherence to the cause of thy father?" Morton indignantly declares, in self-defence, that no cause can prosper where so much bitter feeling exists, and which is broken up into so many parties distrusting and suspecting each other.

In a high strain of enthusiasm, Magdalen Græme devotes her life to the interests of Queen Mary and the Church. She calls upon saints and angels to witness that no earthly consideration will induce her to withdraw her "*hand from the plough* when it shall pass through the devoted furrow." The Prelate, in *The Betrothed*, receives the High Constable very coldly on learning that he seeks

to evade his vows of going to Palestine to fight for the
cross, and characterises such conduct as "a fickle and
selfish wish to *withdraw his hand from the plough.*" The
Crusaders, in *Count Robert of Paris*, unlike the High
Constable, hold to their solemn vow not to turn their
back upon Palestine "now that they had *set their hands
to the plough.*" Resolute or irresolute, Wildrake is told
by Cromwell, in strong and unmistakable terms, that
"whosoever *putteth his hand to the plough* in the great
actings which are now on foot in these nations had best
be aware that he do not look back;" and then the Protector significantly adds, "Rely upon my simple word
that if you fail me, I will not spare on you one foot's
length of the gallows of Haman." In the course of the
same novel of *Woodstock*, Cromwell again uses the text
in addressing Colonel Everard on the lukewarmness of
many of their supporters. "Because we look back after
we have *put our hand to the plough*, therefore is our force
waxed dim."

In his address to the seventy disciples sent out to
preach "into every city and place whither He Himself
would come," our Lord tells them that they need have
no hesitation in accepting of any kindness or hospitality
offered; for, as an equivalent, they bring the blessings
of peace to every house into which they enter. "The
labourer is worthy of his hire"—an expression which
has now become proverbial. Let us see in what way it
comes before us in the Waverley Novels. When one of
Henry Morton's followers was sent to report the evacu-
ation of Tillietudlem Castle, and its occupation by the

insurgent forces, Burley was rather driven to fury than pleased to learn such good news. "I have watched," he said, "I have fought—I have plotted—I have striven for the reduction of this place, . . . and when the men were about to yield themselves to my hand, . . . cometh this youth (Henry Morton), and takes it on him to thrust his sickle into the harvest, and rends the prey from the spoiler. Surely *the labourer is worthy of his hire*, and the city, with its captives, should be given to him that wins it."

In *The Pirate* Yellowley thinks, when he finds a hornful of old coins below the hearthstone in one of the old rooms at Stourburgh, that he has a right to the best share. "Surely the labourer," he reasons, "as one may call the finder, is worthy of his hire." In *St. Ronan's*, Mowbray goes to his legal adviser to negotiate for the loan of a sum of money. Seeing nothing but ruin in store for his family, the agent concludes his expressions of regret and sympathy by saying, "It brings tears into my auld een."

"Never weep for the matter, Mick," answered Mowbray, "some of the money will stick in your pockets if not in mine. Your service will not be altogether gratuitous, my old friend—*the labourer is worthy of his hire.*"

In *Kenilworth*, Foster grumbles at having to undertake both the trouble and the risk of looking after Tressilian, so as to secure and detain him. He thinks that Varney should also take his share of the danger. "But this comes," he says, "of being leagued with one who knows not even so much of Scripture as that *the labourer is worthy of his hire.*"

In the dread predictions uttered by our Lord in the twenty-fourth chapter of St. Matthew, He says that the desolations of the evil day will come as surely as the birds of prey come to a dead carcase that lies exposed in the open field, or, proverbially put, "Wheresoever the carcase is, there will the eagles be gathered together." As the day of adversity came upon Sir Arthur Wardour, in *The Antiquary,* and the crisis of his affairs approached, his affectionate daughter anxiously inquires if they are not now irretrievably ruined. The Antiquary, to whom the question was put, hopes that all is not lost ; but Sir Arthur himself fears the very worst, for his creditors are crowding in with their claims as they scent the ruin that is approaching. " Where the slaughter is," says the unfortunate gentleman, quoting the text, "the eagles will be gathered together." And he adds this commentary from his own experience, "I am like a sheep which I have seen fall down a precipice, or drop down from sickness—if you had not seen a single raven or hooded crow for a fortnight before, he will not be on the heather ten minutes before half a dozen will be picking out his eyes."

"Corbies dinna gather without they smell carrion," says our old friend Andrew Fairservice, by way of paraphrasing the text. The Highland clans, scenting the carnage afar off, "came like eagles to the slaughter" of the insurgent Cameronians. The hungry group of hangers-on in the ante-chamber of the Duke of Buckingham was like a "gathering of the eagles to the slaughter" —a needy lot of adventurers living upon the wants of

greatness, or stimulating the desires of lavish extrava-
gance.

Incensed at the indignity put upon Christ in the
garden of Gethsemane, one of those who stood by
Him drew a sword and struck a servant of the high
priest. Our Lord desired him to desist, and put the
weapon back again to its place, adding, "For all they
that take the sword shall perish by the sword." This
text forms the subject of Henry Warden's sermon before
the assembled household of Avenel Castle—a sermon
preached for the special benefit of Ronald Græme, in the
hope that it might teach him to restrain his violent
temper, and calm his stormy bursts of passion.

Indulging in vain and unavailing regrets about the
fate of her brother, under sentence of death in Carlisle
Castle, and lamenting the share that she had herself
taken in spurring on his fiery temper to join the rebellion,
Flora MacIvor says to Waverley, "Oh that I could recollect that I had but once said to him, '*He that striketh
with the sword shall die by the sword.*'"

The parabolic teaching of our Lord supplies much
valuable material to Sir Walter. Taking the first of the
parables which comes before us, not in its chronological
or harmonised arrangement, but simply in the place
which it occupies in our note-book, we find that it is that
of the sower going forth to sow. We do not, of course,
expect to find that the novelist will treat the parable as
a whole, or in its complete and finished form, with all
the lessons that can be drawn from it; the lecturer or
the preacher will do that. But we find, in great abund-

ance, illustrations suggested by the *good ground, the stony ground, and the thorns which sprang up and choked* the growing corn. Roland Græme states the reason of his interfering in the street brawl at Edinburgh, and going tő the rescue of Lord Seyton, whose life he thought in danger. No one, he imagines, could have stood by and seen an honourable man borne to the earth by overpowering odds if his single arm could help him. Such, at least, was the lesson he had been taught in chivalry at the castle of Avenel.

"*The good seed hath fallen into good ground,* young man," said Seyton, "but, alas, if thou practise such honourable war in these dishonourable days, where right is everywhere borne down by mastery, thy life, my poor boy, will be but a short one."

In *The Chronicles of the Canongate,* Chrystal Croftangry proposes to write a family history when he can find leisure to bring forward evidence in support of the facts which he requires to state. "Mere words," he says, "when they are unsupported by proofs, are like *seed sown on the naked rock,* or like an house biggit on the flitting and faithless sands."

The good clergyman, in the tragic tale of *The Highland Widow,* embraced every opportunity of teaching and instructing the widow's son, and though the seed had, as yet at least, only fallen "*among the brambles and thorns* of a wild and uncultivated disposition, it had not yet been entirely checked or destroyed."

In the motto prefixed to the sixth chapter of *The Monastery,* Sir Walter pictures out in a few lines the whole spirit and meaning of the parable of the tares among the wheat.

" Now let us sit in conclave. That these weeds
  Be rooted from the vineyard of the church,
  That these foul tares be severed from the wheat,
  We are, I trust, agreed. Yet how to do this,
  Nor hurt the wholesome crop and tender vine-plants,
  Craves good advisement."

In the chapter to which these lines are prefixed, there is a description given of the alarm which was agitating and upheaving the Church on account of the rapid spread of the reformed doctrines. The Abbot, in the novel bearing his name, has received instructions from the Primate to seek out all heretical persons within the bounds of his authority, and have them watched or detained under confinement. The difficulty is not so much to point out who these persons are, as how to get at them, and pull up the tares without endangering the life of the surrounding wheat.

Another difficulty crops up further on in the same novel, when Henry Warden, one of the preachers of the reformed faith, is in the power of the Church. How is he to be silenced? The Sub-Prior has misgivings as to the wisdom of sending the preacher to the Monastery, where he would be summarily dealt with and disposed of ; but in the present state of public feeling, and the daily increasing strength of the heretics, the Sub-Prior felt that to take such a measure might only tend to make matters worse. No. Let the tares grow up with the wheat. The consolation is, that if Warden remains at Glendearg and attempts to sow a fresh crop of tares among the wheat, the ground is far too dry and hard and barren for them to take root.

Elsewhere, in the other novels, Sir Walter has the parable in mind when he compares the seeds of disagreement sown among friends to "the tares sown by the enemy among the wheat." Neville, in *The Talisman*, declares that this same enemy "hath most interest to sow tares among the wheat, and bring dissension into our councils." And in *Rob Roy* Sir Walter defines jealousy as that "sentiment which springs up with love as naturally as the tares with the wheat."

In *The Heart of Midlothian* we find a reference to the parable of the leaven where Jeanie Deans, in reflecting upon the incidents of her sister's misfortunes, says, "But who could have expected such a growth of evil from one grain of human leaven in a disposition so kind and candid and generous?" And in *The Abbot* there is another, where the Lady of Lochleven tells Roland Græme of the revels which were being held at Kinross. These revels she describes as the "continued workings of the ancient leaven of folly which the Romish priests have kneaded into the very souls of the Scottish peasantry."

From the parable of the labourers in the vineyard we derive the expression, the eleventh hour, signifying the length, or it may be the shortness, of time in which some one may have been employed. The time is indeed far spent when but one hour remains out of the twelve. In *Woodstock*, Mr. Holdenough entreats Cromwell for the life of Wildrake; and if he will not grant this request he prefers another. "Let me go to him as a divine, to watch with him, in case he may yet be admitted *into the vineyard at the latest hour*—yet brought into the sheepfold, though he has neglected the call of the pastor till time is well-nigh closed upon him."

Great was the consternation in the convent when news arrived of the lost battle near Kennaquhair, in *The Monastery.* Some of the monks counselled flight, others advised that the church plate should be offered to bribe the English officer, but the Abbot himself was unmoved and undaunted. Addressing his clerical brethren, he implored them to remain at the post of duty, and be prepared, if need be, to die under the ruins of the shrines to the service of which they had all devoted themselves. "Highly honoured are we all in this distinguished summons," the Abbot proceeds to say, "from our dear brother Nicholas, whose gray hairs have been preserved until they should be surrounded by the crown of martyrdom, down to my beloved son Edward, who, *arriving at the vineyard at the latest hour of the day,* is yet permitted to share its toils with those who have laboured from the morning."

In *Count Robert of Paris* the Emperor asks Briennius if he has anything to allege why the doom of death should not be executed. Short as the time is, the Emperor reminds him that "even *at this eleventh hour* thy tongue is unloosed to speak with freedom what may concern thy life."

In the parable of the marriage feast one of the guests

is represented as having appeared without the wedding garment. On this subject Major Bridgenorth delivered a long lecture to his adherents while they were the guests, along with a party of the Cavaliers, of Lady Peveril, at the castle of Martindale. The Presbyterian teacher explained to his hearers "that outward apparel was not alone meant by that scriptural expression, but also a suitable frame of mind for enjoyment of peaceful festivity; and therefore he exhorts the brethren, that whatever might be the errors of the poor blinded malignants (the Cavaliers) with whom they were in some sort to eat and drink upon the morrow, they ought not on this occasion to show any evil will against them, lest they should therein become troublers of the peace of Israel."

One of the excuses given for not accepting an invitation to the "great supper" which a certain man made, in another parable, was that he had married a wife, and therefore could not come. When it was feared, in *Old Mortality*, that Lord Evandale would again join "that dreadful Claverhouse and his army," his lordship's sister says to Miss Bellenden, his betrothed bride, "I believe you are the only one who can keep him at home."

"And how is it in my power?" said Miss Bellenden.

"You can furnish him with the scriptural apology for not going forth with the host—*he has married a wife, and therefore cannot come.*"

There are a few scattered allusions to the parable of the ten virgins, but of such a passing nature that they are of little or no interest apart from their context. Let

us, however, introduce one which we find in *The Pirate.*
Mordaunt's old housekeeper and the yagger, or pedlar,
are chaffering over buying and selling. She greatly
delights him by stating that there will be some napery
needed soon, and as there is no mistress of the house,
and none in it who can spin, the goods will require to be
got from the pedlar.

"That's what I ca' walking by the word," said the
yagger. "*Go unto those that buy and sell;* there's muckle
profit in that text."

The parable of the Good Samaritan, from the very
nature of its narrative, comes in for a fair share of quotation by Sir Walter. When Ratcliffe, the turnkey in the
prison of Edinburgh, learns that Jeanie Deans has resolved to go on foot to London, he expresses the fear
that she may meet with "rough customers on the Borders,
or in the Midlands," ere she reaches her destination.
Anxious to be of service to her, and knowing all the
tramps and suspicious characters on the road, he scrawls
a few lines on a piece of paper, as a pass, and directs her
to produce this paper in the event of her having "ony
fasherie wi' ony o' St. Nicholas's clerks."

"Alas," said Jeanie, "I do not understand what you
mean."

"I mean, *if ye fall among thieves,* my precious—that is
a scripture phrase, if ye will hae ane—the bauldest o'
them will ken a scart o' my guse feather."

Disguised as a monk, Wamba, in *Ivanhoe,* gains admittance into the castle of Front-de-Bœuf, and is asked who
and what he is. He replies that he is a poor servant of

St. Francis, travelling through the forest, where *he fell among thieves*, who sent him to the castle to do his ghostly office on two persons suffering imprisonment.

In the opening chapter of *The Heart of Midlothian*, Sir Walter details the narrative of a daring robbery from the person of the Collector of Customs at Pittenweem, in Fife. Several persons were passing in the street at the time; but thinking that the noise they heard was only a dispute between the Collector and the people of the house, they paid no attention to the circumstance, and "like the Levite in the parable, *they passed on the opposite side of the way.*"

The stranger, in *St. Ronan's Well*, acts the part of the good Samaritan when he pulls Touchwood out of the stream. And when Richie Moniplies, in *The Fortunes of Nigel*, is brought into the shop of David Ramsay, severely bruised in a street riot, George Heriot, who happened to be conversing with Ramsay at the time, says, "Come, off with his cloak, and let us bear him to his couch. I will send for Dr. Irving, the king's chirurgeon, he does not live far off, and that shall be *my share of the good Samaritan's duty.*"

Chrystal Croftangry thus describes his medical adviser—"I had left him a middle-aged man; he was now an elderly one; but still the same benevolent Samaritan, who went about doing good, and thought the blessings of the poor as good a recompense of his professional skill as the gold of the rich."

The mention of Chrystal's name reminds us that it is associated with another of our Lord's parables—that of the prodigal son. Consulting some papers connected with the history of the Croftangry family, Chrystal quotes the following passage from an old compiler who says of voluptuaries and fast-livers that they devour the "patrimony bequeathed to them by their forebears in chambering and wantonness, so that they come, with the prodigal son, *to the husks and the swine-trough.*"

On Jeanie Deans' return from London she goes to examine the cow-house at the new home in company with May Hettly, the faithful old domestic servant. The sight of one of the animals brings back many re-collections of Effie. May, who had been watching her with a sympathising expression, observed in an under-tone, "The gudeman aye sorts that beast himsel', and is kinder to it than any beast in the byre. . . . O, if the puir prodigal wad return, sae blithely as the gude-man wad *kill the fatted calf*"—adding with charming simplicity, "though Brockie's calf will no be fit for kill-ing this three weeks yet."

The unjust steward, in the parable of that name, is summoned by his lord to give an account of his steward-ship—an expression which has now passed into the language of every-day life. It comes frequently under our notice in the Waverley Novels.

In *The Fortunes of Nigel*, Richie Moniplies places at the disposal of King James certain sums of money which are to be held free of all pledge or usury, on condition that his Majesty will interest himself in the case of Lord Glenvarnock, then a prisoner in the Tower. Regarding this as a bribe, the king exclaims, "How, man! . . .

country, actually left a great part of your command at a field-preaching?"

Gilfillan smiled scornfully as he made this indirect answer, "Even thus are the children of this world wiser in their generation than the children of light."

As Henry Morton directs his movements towards Bothwell Bridge during the battle, he is followed by about a hundred of those who are devotedly attached to his command. Burley turns to MacBriar and says, "Providence points us the way through the worldly wisdom of this latitudinarian youth.—He that loves the light let him follow Burley." But the preacher dissuades him from going in the same direction as Morton. "I fear treachery to the host from this Nullafidian Achan."

"Hinder me not," replied Burley; "Morton hath well said that all is lost if the enemy win the bridge, therefore let (hinder) me not. *Shall the children of this generation be called wiser or braver than the children of the sanctuary?*"

Continuing His commentary, our Lord says, "Make to yourselves friends of the mammon of unrighteousness" —that is, do as the steward did with his lord's goods in making himself the friend of his lord's debtors.

Prior Aymer, in *Ivanhoe*, falls into the hands of the outlaws, and is told that he must pay a heavy ransom, or his convent would be likely to be called to a new election, and the place that now knows him would soon know him no more.

"Are ye Christians?" said the Prior, "and hold this language to a Churchman?" To which the chief outlaw replies that they are not only Christians, but that they have a chaplain with them who will expound to him a text which has reference to this matter. Friar Tuck then appears and says to the Prior, "*Make to yourself friends of the mammon of unrighteousness,*" adding, "for no other friend is likely to serve your turn." The Prior is afterwards compelled to pay a ransom fixed by the Jew, who, in his turn, is appraised by the Prior, who fixes his price at a thousand crowns. Further on in the same novel Brother Ben Samuel, the physician, tries to soothe the grief of Isaac, whose daughter, Rebecca, is about to be tried as a sorceress. "Be of good comfort, brother," said the physician, "thou canst deal with the Nazarenes as one *possessing the mammon of unrighteousness,* and canst therefore purchase immunity at their hands—it rules the savage minds of these ungodly men, even as the signet of the mighty Solomon was said to command the evil genii."

Miss Geddes relates to Alan Fairford the steps her brother had taken to get Darsie Latimer set at liberty. "I will take my horse, even Solomon," said Joshua, in the narrative related to his sister, "and ride swiftly into Cumberland, and I will make myself friends *with mammon of unrighteousness* among the magistrates of the Gentiles, and among their mighty men; and it shall come to pass that Darsie Latimer shall be delivered, even if it were at the expense of half my substance."

The parable of the rich man and Lazarus supplies

Sir Walter with numerous illustrations. In addressing Albert Lee, but who was supposed to be the fugitive King Charles, Cromwell says, "Thou art weary, young man, and thy nature requires rest and refection, being doubtless dealt with delicately, as one who had fed on the fat, and drunk of the sweet, and who hath been *clothed in purple and fine linen.*"

The difference in worldly position between the rich man and Lazarus comes out in *Redgauntlet*, where Alan Fairford and his father are speaking of the legal profession. Alan states that he is quite aware there is much hard work in store for him ere he attains to any eminence in it, to which his father replies that in the medical profession the young doctor, who would get to the bedside of palaces, must first "walk the hospitals, and *cure Lazarus of his sores*, before he be admitted to prescribe for Dives, when he has got gout or indigestion." And in the weird story that Wandering Willie tells, in the same novel of *Redgauntlet*, we fancy that Sir Walter, while writing it, was thinking of the rich man's torment when he makes Willie say, "Terribly the Laird roared out for cauld water to his feet, and wine to cool his throat: and Hell, hell, hell, and its flames, was aye the word in his mouth."

The "great gulf" which separated Dives and Lazarus is frequently alluded to. Bidding farewell to Frank, Diana Vernon says, in *Rob Roy*, "Yes, Frank, for ever! There is a *great gulf between us*—a gulf of absolute perdition." In *The Abbot*, Catherine Seyton says to Roland Græme that when she returns home to her father's house,

"There is a *gulf between* us you may not pass but with peril of your life." And in *Ivanhoe*, when Rowena entreats Rebecca to remain in England, where she and her father could have nothing to fear, the latter replies, "Thy speech is fair, and thy purpose fairer; but it may not be—*there is a gulf betwixt us.*"

The parable of the unjust judge who feared not God, neither regarded man, is mainly used by Sir Walter in illustration of the character of desperadoes and lawless men. Thus, in *The Monastery*, the vanguard of the Regent Murray's army was composed of "picked wild desperates, resolute for mischief, such as *neither fear God nor regard their fellow-creatures*, but understand themselves bound to hurry from the road whatever is displeasing to themselves." And in the same novel, Dame Glendinning advises her son to keep clear of men who "have broadsword and lance both—there are enow of rank riders in this land that *neither fear God nor regard man.*"

In the letter of Jeanie Deans to her father, there is a reference to the parable of the pounds which the king entrusted to his servants before setting out for a far country. The Laird of Dumbiedykes had lent Jeanie a purse of money to defray her expenses on the journey to London. Referring to this, Jeanie writes, "Will ye let the laird ken that we have had friends strangely raised up to us, and that the talent whilk he lent me will be thankfully repaid? I hae some of it to the fore, and the rest of it *is not knotted up in ane purse or napkin*, but in a wee bit paper, as is the fashion here."

Enraged at the want of hospitality shown by Yellow-

ley and his sister, in *The Pirate*, Norna affronts them by
paying for what she had eaten and drunk. "Beware,"
said Norna, as she saw the astonished pair looking at the
gold coin she had laid down, "Beware how you use it!
It thrives not with the sordid or the mean-souled—it
was won with honourable danger, and must be expended
with honourable liberality. The treasure which lies
under a cold hearth will one day, *like the hidden talent*,
bear witness against its avaricious possessors."

We have already had occasion to refer to the sermon
preached by Henry Warden before the assembled household of Avenel Castle. In it he exhorts his hearers not
to rely on their own strength in fighting against sin or
in resisting temptation; and then he brings in, for the
sake of illustration, the parable of the Pharisee and the
Publican. "The Pharisee," said the preacher, "perhaps
deemed himself humble while he stooped in the temple,
and thanked God that he was not as other men, or even
as this publican. But while his knees touched the
marble pavement, his head was as high as the topmost
pinnacle of the Temple."

There is little to note on the subject of Sir Walter's
use of the miracles as recorded in the four gospels. The
miracles, of course, do not supply materials for the use
of the novelist in the same way, or at least to the same
extent, as the parables do. Accordingly in the Waverley
Novels we meet with little that bears on this portion of
the gospel narrative. The following references are nearly
all that we have been able to find. Mrs. Dods is angry
at the clergyman who, in his sermon, compares the well

at St. Ronan's to the *Pool of Bethesda.* In *Old Mortality* Burley says to Poundtext, "Thou art one of those who reap where thou hast not sowed, and divide the spoil while others fight the battle: thou art one of those that follow the gospel *for the loaves and for the fishes.*" The subject of demoniacal possession is more frequently referred to than any of the other miracles, but in such general terms that we need not here produce the references.

THE ACTS OF THE APOSTLES.

IN *The Chronicles of the Canongate* wo aro reminded of an incident in tho history of tho early Christian Church —tho possessors of lands and houses selling their property, and placing tho proceeds at the feet of the Apostles for tho common good. In the *Chronicles*, Chrystal Croftangry relates that when his mother's affairs underwent somo temporary inconvenience, Christie Steel "stood in tho gap, and having sold a small inheritance which had descended to her, brought the purchaso-money to her mistress, with a senso of devotion as deep as that which inspired tho Christians of tho first age, when they sold all they had, and followed the Apostles of tho Church."

Liko tho early Christians, Ananias and Sapphira sold their possession, but unlike them, they "kept back part of tho price." This incident is employed by Sir Walter as an illustration in *Peveril of the Peak*, whero Major Bridgenorth, under feelings of shamo and anger, refuses to give a hostile meeting to Sir Geoffrey Peveril. Tho Rev. Mr. Solsgraco approaches his friend, grasps him cordially by tho hand, and offers his warmest sympathy. "Noblo brother," he said, with unwonted kindness of manner, "though a man of peace, I can judge what this

P

sacrifice hath cost to thy manly spirit. But God will not have from us an imperfect obedience. We must not, *like Ananias and Sapphira, reserve behind* some darling lust, some favourite sin, while we pretend to make sacrifice of our worldly affections. What avails it to say that we have but secreted a little matter, if the slightest remnant of the accursed thing remain hidden in our tent?"

Henry Warden, a preacher of the reformed faith, is conveyed a prisoner for conscience' sake to Glendearg, where he is brought before the Sub-Prior, who recognises him as an old friend and college companion. Before leaving the tower to return to the monastery, the Sub-Prior entreats the preacher not to teach any of Dame Glendinning's family, or inculcate any of his new doctrines. Warden replies, "Be assured, my old friend, that no willing act of mine shall be to thy prejudice. But if my Master shall place work before me, *I must obey God rather than man*"—an answer which reminds us of Peter's reply to the high priest who also sought to prevent the apostles from teaching the doctrines of Jesus of Nazareth. In almost the same terms old Mause Headrigg replies to Lady Margaret Bellenden, who threatens to turn her and her son off the estate unless they comply with her commands. "I canna prefer the commands of an earthly mistress to those of a heavenly Master," says Mause, "and sae I am e'en ready to suffer for righteousness' sake."

We have several very interesting references to the martyrdom of St. Stephen. The only picture, the only ornament indeed, which the Earl of Glenallan's apartment contained, was a large painting representing the death by stoning of the first Christian martyr. King James, in *The Fortunes of Nigel*, called his favourite, the Duke of Buckingham, by the name of "Steenie," from a supposed resemblance between his handsome countenance and that with which the Italian artists represented the Martyr Stephen. Nanty Ewart's misconduct was the means of hastening his father's death, and one of his companions told him that if he felt sorry for his errors, and wished to atone for them by undergoing the fate of the first martyr, he had only to return to his "native village, where the very stones of the street would rise up against him as his father's murderer." And when Lambourne visits Foster at Cumnor Hall, he addresses his old comrade by a name which Foster would willingly forget, Tony Fire-the-Fagot.

"Why!" said Michael Lambourne, "you were wont to glory in the share you had in the death of the two old heretical bishops."

"That," said Foster, "was while I was in the gall of bitterness and bond of iniquity, and applies not to my walk or my ways, now that I am called forth into the lists. Mr. Melchisedek Maultext compared my misfortune in that matter to that of the Apostle Paul, who kept the clothes of the witnesses who stoned Saint Stephen. He held forth on the matter three Sabbaths past, and illustrated the same by the conduct of an honourable person present, meaning me."

This expression, "gall of bitterness and bond of

iniquity," quoted by Foster from Peter's stern rebuke administered to Simon Magus, crops up very frequently in the Waverley Novels. As Henry Morton is carried off from his uncle's house, a prisoner in charge of Bothwell and a party of dragoons, the faithful old housekeeper, Mrs. Alison Wilson, breaks forth into a torrent of invectives against Mause Headrigg. "Ill luck be to the graning corse o' thee—the prettiest lad in Clydesdale this day maun be a sufferer, and a' for your daft whiggery."

"Gae wa," replied Mause, "I trow ye are *yet in the bonds of sin, and gall of iniquity*, to grudge your bonniest and best in the cause of Him that gave ye a' ye hae."

In *The Bride of Lammermoor*, Ravenswood suddenly appears at the Castle and sternly demands to hear from Lucy's own lips whether or not she has broken off their mutual engagement of marriage. The clergyman is the first to speak, and in the course of his address he says, "Alas, the workings of the ancient Adam are strong even in the regenerate — surely we should have long suffering with those who, being *yet in the gall of bitterness and bond of iniquity*, are swept forward by the uncontrollable current of worldly passion."

Lady Peveril says to Bridgenorth, "You were wont to be moderate in (your religious) sentiments—comparatively moderate, at least, and to love your own religion without hating that of others."

"What I was while *in the gall of bitterness and in the bond of iniquity* it signifies not to recall," he answered ; "I was then like to Gallio, who cared for none of these things." Further on in the novel of *Peveril of the Peak* Bridgenorth again uses the expression, this time in speaking to Julian Peveril. "Farewell," he says, "do not answer me now; thou art yet *in the gall of bitterness*, and it may be that strife (which I desire not) should fall between us."

The mention of the name of Gallio, the Roman proconsul who refused to be a judge of such matters as the Jews brought against Paul, reminds us that the name occurs now and again in the other novels, and on each occasion it is employed as a synonym for indifference or lukewarmness in religious matters. In *Old Mortality*, Burley thus addresses Henry Morton shortly after the skirmish at Drumclog. "The council of the army of the Covenant, confiding that the son of Silas Morton can never prove a lukewarm Laodicean, *or an indifferent Gallio*, in this great day, have nominated you to be a captain of their host, with the right of a vote in their council, and all authority fitting for an officer who is to command Christian men." Morton's sympathies, however, are not with Burley's section of the Covenanting army; accordingly we are not surprised to find that, elsewhere in the same novel, the son of Silas Morton is unjustly termed *a Gallio* for no other reason than that of his avowed toleration for those who hold religious opinions and observances differing from his own.

In *The Heart of Midlothian*, David Deans advises Widow Butler to train her grandson to the work of the Christian ministry. "Never," he says, "was there mair need o' poorfu' preachers than e'en now *in these cauld*

Gallio days, when men's hearts are hardened like the nether millstone, till they come *to regard none of these things.*" And further on in the same book, Deans considers it beneath his notice to argue the subject of preparation for the pulpit with Captain Knockdunder, since he has only got a Gallio to deal with.

We find an interesting reference to the conversion of the Philippian jailor in the incident which we have already had occasion to quote, namely, Henry Warden being brought as a prisoner to Glendearg, and the Sub-Prior's anxiety that he should not teach the new doctrines to any of Dame Glendinning's family. The alarmed priest even hints at imprisonment being resorted to, in the event of the preacher not complying with his request. But Warden bravely replies, "Thou mayest indeed cast me into a dungeon, but can I foretell that my Master hath not task-work for me to perform even in that dreary mansion? The chains of saints have, ere now, been the means of breaking the bonds of Satan. In a prison, holy Paul found the jailor whom he brought to believe the word of salvation, he and all his house."

"Nay," said the Sub-Prior, in a tone betwixt anger and scorn, "if you match yourself with the blessed Apostle, it were time we had done—prepare to endure what thy folly as well as thy heresy deserves. Bind him, soldier."

In *Ivanhoe*, Cedric the Saxon, disguised as a priest, is asked by Front-de-Bœuf to carry a scroll to the castle of Philip de Malvoisin. Leading the way to a postern door the Norman thrusts into Cedric's reluctant hand a piece of gold, adding these threatening words, "Remember, I will flay off both cowl and skin, if thou failest in thy purpose."

Glad of his freedom, Cedric looked round and, throwing the piece of gold back to the donor, exclaimed, "False Norman, thy money perish with thee !"—words which remind us of Peter's indignant rejection of the money which Simon Magus offered for power to bestow the gift of the Holy Spirit.

The effect of Paul's preaching at Ephesus was shown upon his hearers in different ways. Many who were brought to believe the gospel came, "confessed, and showed their deeds. Many of them also which used curious arts brought their books together, and burned them before all men." In *The Pirate* we are told that when Norna of the Fitful Head died, there was found a clause in her will which specially directed that all the books, implements of her laboratory, and other things used in her former studies, should be destroyed by being committed to the flames, like those of Ephesus.

The incident of Eutychus falling from the gallery during the preaching of Paul is quoted in *Woodstock*. Cromwell and some of his soldiers are eagerly engaged in trying to find out the subterranean passages which are reported to be at the Royal Lodge of Woodstock. The spirits of the men begin to sink, and at last absolute terror seizes them as they recollect that, all the while, they may possibly be near a particular apartment which is said to be balanced on an axis, and which precipitates whoever steps upon it into a black and bottomless abyss below. One of the soldiers hints that he had that morning consulted the Scriptures by way of lot, and his fortune had been to alight on the passage, *Eutychus fell down from the third loft, and was taken up dead*—an ominous warning not to go farther in case of reaching this dreadful room and sharing the fate of Eutychus. A few pages further on in the novel, Corporal Grace-be-here is ordered to mount the platform of a window in the tower. Apparently afraid of the height, the Corporal climbs the window very reluctantly, saying as he does so that the place is as high as the pinnacle of the temple, "and it is written, that *Eutychus fell down from the third loft, and was taken up dead.*"

"Because he slept upon his post," answered Cromwell readily.

Searching for King Charles, Cromwell's party came upon Albert Lee, whom they bring before the Protector. The young Royalist is disguised so as to resemble his master as closely as possible. Thinking he is really addressing Charles, Cromwell asks, in the words of the chief captain who rescued Paul from the violence of the Jews at Jerusalem, "Art not thou that Egyptian which, before these days, madest an uproar and leddest out into the wilderness many thousand men who were murderers?" and then Cromwell exultingly adds, "Ha, youth, I have hunted thee from Stirling to Worcester, from Worcester to Woodstock, and we have met at last!"

Scourged and uncondemned, Paul asks the centurion if it is lawful thus to treat a Roman citizen. The centurion refers him to the chief captain, who boasts that with a great sum he had obtained his freedom, to which his prisoner replied, "But I was free-born." This incident is alluded to in *Old Mortality*, where Henry Morton and his faithful servant Cuddie, are lamenting the loss of their liberty in being forcibly detained by Bothwell and his dragoons. Morton speaks of his chartered rights as a free-born British subject, and expresses his determination to use every possible means to regain his freedom.

"Ye speak o' a charter," said Cuddie. "Now, these are things that only belang to the like o' you that are a gentleman, and it mightna bear me through that am but a husbandman."

"The charter that I speak of," said Morton, "is common to the meanest Scotchman. It is that freedom from stripes and bondage which was claimed, as you may read in Scripture, by the Apostle Paul himself, and which every man who is free-born is called upon to defend, for his own sake and that of his countrymen."

"Hegh, sirs," replied Cuddie, "it wad hae been lang or my Leddy Margaret, or my mither either, wad hae fund out sic a wise-like doctrine in the Bible! The tane was aye graning about giving tribute to Cæsar, and the tither is as daft wi' her whiggery."

In *The Talisman*, Saladin sends his own physician to wait upon King Richard during the sickness of the latter. The Laird of Gilsland, the King's devoted attendant, feels burdened in conscience at the thought of his royal master being nursed and tended by an unbeliever. He consults the Archbishop of Tyre, who greatly relieves him by the advice he gives. The Archbishop thinks that "men may use the assistance of pagans and infidels in their need, and there is reason to think that one cause of their being permitted to remain on earth is, that they might minister to the convenience of true Christians. There is no doubt," the Archbishop proceeds to say, and quoting from an incident in the narrative of the shipwreck of St. Paul, "that the primitive Christians used the services of the unconverted heathen—thus, in the ship of Alexandria, in which the blessed Apostle Paul sailed to Italy, the sailors were doubtless pagans; yet what saith the holy saint when their ministry was needful: *Nisi hi in navi manserint, vos salvi fieri non potestis*—unless these men abide in the ship, ye cannot be saved."

In the course of our present study we meet with references to many more incidents recorded in the Acts of the Apostles: such as Peter in prison, Paul at Athens, the appeal to Cæsar, and the declaration of Agrippa that he felt almost persuaded to become a Christian. These are so slight, however, that a single sentence will hold them all. The turnkeys in *Kenilworth* and *Anne of Geierstein* swear by St. Peter of the Fetters; the scene in the Cathedral of Glasgow reminds the readers of *Rob Roy* of what may have been the expression on the faces of those who listened to St. Paul at Athens; the hearing of Nigel's case is appealed from Charles the prince to James the king; and Roland Græme, in *The Abbot*, is almost persuaded to embrace the -reformed faith under the teaching of the chaplain of Lochleven Castle.

One other incident concludes our Waverley references to the Acts of the Apostles, and it is in *The Heart of Midlothian.* On her way to London, Jeanie Deans rests for a short time at York. In a letter written to her father from that city Jeanie says, "The folk here are civil, and, like the barbarians unto the holy apostle, hae shown me much kindness." The citizens of York may not appreciate the comparison ; but in the simplicity of her heart it was perhaps the best compliment that Jeanie Deans could pay them.

THE EPISTLES.

TURNING to the Epistles, and reverently laying aside a great mass of material in the shape of expressions and sentences which seem to have been suggested to Sir Walter by this portion of the New Testament, we find, nevertheless, that as much remains behind as will furnish us with some interesting illustrations, in every-day life, of several of the familiar and outstanding apostolic arguments and injunctions. In stating the great gospel doctrine of justification by faith, St. Paul, in his Epistle to the Romans, points out that the foundation of all justification is in the death of Jesus Christ. And as he proceeds with his argument he reminds us how rarely, in human history, do we find or hear of any one laying down his life for another. But he hazards the peradventure that for a good man some would even dare to die. Keeping to this illustration in its human aspect only, we find in the Waverley Novels numerous instances of noble self-sacrifice and devotion, even to death if need be. It is not likely, we think, that any reader of *The Abbot* will be found who can lightly pass over the self-consecration of Magdalen Græme to the cause of the unfortunate Queen Mary. Threatened by the Lady of Lochleven with the doom of a dreadful death, the queen intercedes with the lady for the life of her faithful adherent. Magdalen interposes, however, and says, "Plead no more for me, my gracious sovereign, nor abase yourself to ask so much as a gray hair of my head at her hands. I knew the risk at which I served my church and my queen, *and was ever prompt to pay away my poor life as the ransom.*"

But there is a much more affecting illustration of self-sacrifice than this. It occurs in *Waverley*, during the trial of Fergus MacIvor at Carlisle. As Evan Dhu Maccombich hears the sentence of death pronounced on his chief, he requests permission from the presiding judge to address the Court. Commanding silence, the Judge encourages Evan to proceed.

"I was only ganging to say, my lord, that if your excellent honour, and the honourable Court, would let Vich Ian Vohr go free just this once, and let him gae back to France, and no to trouble King George's government again, that *ony six of the very best of his clan will be willing to be justified in his stead;* and if you'll just let me down to Glennaquoich, I'll fetch them up to ye mysell, to head or to hang, *and ye may begin wi' me the very first man.*"

Notwithstanding the solemnity of the occasion, a sort of laugh was heard in the Court at the extraordinary nature of the proposal. The Judge checked this indecency, and Evan, looking sternly around when the murmur abated, "If the Saxon gentlemen are laughing," he said, "because a poor man such as me thinks my life, or the life of six of my degree, is worth that of Vich Ian Vohr, it's like enough they may be very right; but if they laugh because they think I would not keep my word *and come back to redeem him,* I can tell them they ken neither the heart o' a Hielandman nor the honour of a gentleman."

In *Quentin Durward,* the Prior describes William de la Marck, the most notorious robber and murderer on all the frontier, as "*lapis offensionis, et petra scandali—a stumbling-stone and rock of offence* to the countries of Burgundy and Flanders." And in *The Talisman* King Richard, addressing the Council, says, in offering to give up the chief command to any one whom the meeting can name, "Let us rather look forward to our future measures, and believe me, brethren, you shall not find the pride, or the wrath, or the ambition of Richard, *a stumbling-block of offence* in the path to which religion and glory summon you, as with the trumpet of an archangel."

In support of his exhortation, "Avenge not yourselves, but rather give place unto wrath," St. Paul quotes this authority from Deuteronomy thirty-second and thirty-fifth, "Vengeance is mine; I will repay, saith the Lord." In our introductory chapter we referred to the latter text as being specially illustrated in the tragic tale of *The Bride of Lammermoor.* But in almost every tale that the great novelist wrote, we find this text quoted or illustrated in some way or other. In *The Heart of Midlothian* and *The Legend of Montrose* we see the effects of indulging the "monstrous passion" of revenge; but we gladly turn from such lawless scenes as the execution of Porteous by the mob of Edinburgh, and the terrible, tenfold vengeance wreaked upon the Children of the Mist, to those other novels of the series, where the restraining influence of God's grace and His divine government of the world are put forth as a check and restraint against the wrath and the cruelty of man. Old Ballenkeiroch may think, now and again, that the time has at last arrived for taking vengeance on the Baron Bradwardine for having slain his fair-haired son in a Highland foray; Fergus MacIvor may let his fury against Prince Charles subside into feelings of deep and burning vengeance to be gratified at the first and earliest opportunity; and Helen Macgregor may declare that everything can be forgotten but the loss of honour and the desire for revenge. But all these have to learn the lesson that vengeance does not belong to them, but to God alone. "Revenge," says the mother of poor Madge Wildfire, "is the best reward the devil gives us for our hire here and hereafter. I have wrought hard for it; I have suffered for it; I have sinned for it; and I will have it, or there is neither justice in heaven nor in hell." Vain and impotent words for any human being to use! It is to God alone that vengeance belongs, no matter who has wrought hard for it, suffered for it, or sinned for it. As George Staunton relates to Jeanie Deans the story of Wilson's execution, he remarks that after his companion's death there remained only one thing to be accomplished, and that was vengeance!

"Oh, sir," said Jeanie, "did the Scripture never come into your mind?—'Vengeance is mine; and I will repay it.'"

But, minister's son though he was, Staunton had to confess that he had never opened a Bible for the last five years.

In *Old Mortality*, Lady Bellenden beseeches Claverhouse for the life of his prisoner, Henry Morton. Claverhouse replies by expressing the hope that she will spare him the pain of resisting her passionate appeal on behalf of a traitor, when she thinks of the noble blood of her own house that has been shed by such as Morton. But the lady nobly refuses to take vengeance. "Colonel Graham," she says, "I leave vengeance to God, who calls it his own. The shedding of this young man's blood will not call back the lives that were dear to me ; and how can it comfort me to think that there has, maybe, been another widowed mother made childless, like myself, by a deed done at my very door-stane?"

In *Kenilworth*, Tressilian relates to the curate that he had at last discovered the place of Amy Robsart's retreat at Cumnor Hall, in the company, as he supposed, of the villain Varney. "But for a strange mishap," continued Tressilian, "my sword had avenged all our injuries, as well as hers, on his worthless head."

"Thank God that kept thine hand from blood-guiltiness, rash young man," answered the curate; "'Vengeance is mine, saith the Lord ; and I will repay it.'"

Hobbie Elliot is speaking to Earnscliff about the fatal quarrel in which the father of the latter had fallen. Hobbie thinks that, notwithstanding the long time that has elapsed since the affair happened, it is not yet too late to have revenge. But Earnscliff thus rebukes him :

"Oh ! For shame, Hobbie ; you that profess religion to stir your friend up to break the law, and take vengeance at his own hands."

As old John Christie looks upon the lifeless body of Lord Dalgarno, he repeats the solemn words of Scripture, "'Vengeance is mine, saith the Lord ; and I will repay it.'" And he continues—"I, whom thou hast injured, will be the first to render thee the decent offices due to the dead."

At the death-bed of Miss Mowbray, Tyrrel is greatly. affected. "My life," he says, "till I avenge her." He hurries downstairs, is about to leave the inn, when he is stopped by Touchwood, who has just alighted from his carriage. Asking Tyrrel where he is going, the latter replies :

"For revenge, for revenge. Give way, I charge you on your peril."

"Vengeance belongs to God," answered Touchwood, "and His bolt has fallen." He then relates how Mowbray had within the last half-hour met the Earl of Etherington, and killed him on the spot.

In *The Fair Maid of Perth*, Simon Glover implores Henry Smith not to avenge the death of the murdered bonnet-maker, as Heaven will take its own time and way in revenging the foul deed. Queen Mary leaves vengeance to God in the matter of old Dryfesdale's attempts to poison her ; and the monk in *The Monastery* advises Edward Glendinning to put aside his Border creed, and leave vengeance to God for the supposed murder of his brother.

In enjoining obedience to lawfully constituted authority, St. Paul reminds us that "the powers that be are
ordained of God," and that the magistrate bears not the
sword in vain when he acts as a terror to evil-doers, and
is a praise to them who do well.   David Deans remarks
to Bailie Middleburgh that whatever the authorities of
Edinburgh may be at the time of his speaking, he is
aware that there was "ance in a day, a just and God-
fearing magistracy in the city, that did not bear the
sword in vain, but were a terror to evil-doers, and a
praise to such as kept the path."   When Mr. Holdenough
is ousted from his pulpit by the Independent soldier,
he appeals to the Mayor of Woodstock for help.
"Master mayor," he cries, "wilt thou be among those
wicked magistrates who bear the sword in vain?   Citizens, will you not help your pastor?   Worthy aldermen,
will you see me strangled on the pulpit stairs by this
man of buff and Belial?"

Bailie Nicol Jarvie explains to Frank Osbaldistone
the then existing state of the Scottish Highlands.   Con-
trasting them with the rest of Scotland generally, and
with his own city of Glasgow in particular, the worthy
bailie proceeds to say: "They are clean another set frae
the like o' huz—there's nae bailie courts among them—
nae magistrates that dinna bear the sword in vain, like
the worthy deacon that's awa', and, I may say't, like
mysell and other present magistrates in this city."

We are reminded of the apostolic injunction, "Owe
no man anything," in the reply which Nigel gives to
George Heriot, who suggests that the poor young Scottish

noblo should appear at Court, and personally plead his case before King James. "I know not why I should bo ashamed of speaking the truth," said Nigel; "I have no dress suitable for appearing at Court. *I am determined to incur no expense which I cannot discharge.*" And in this connection our old friend, Bailie Nicol Jarvie, again appears before us to vindicate his father's good name and memory. Major Galbraith rather disparagingly remarks that tho bailie's father was a prick-eared cur in having fought against the king at Bothwell Brig. "*He paid what he ought, and what he bought,* Mr. Galbraith," said tho Bailie, "and was an honester man than ever studo in your shanks." And when Ravenswood intimates to Caleb, his faithful domestic, his intention of going abroad, he also expresses his desire to go with tho reputation of an honest man, leaving no debt behind him, at least of his own contracting.

Ere venturing to the monastery, Father Philip salutes Dame Glendinning in the apostolic fashion. "I see Martin hath my mule in readiness," he observes to the widow, "and I will but salute you with tho kiss of sisterhood, which maketh not ashamed."

In tho same book, *The Monastery,* tho Sub-Prior expresses the hope that Henry Warden, his former friend and college companion, now a preacher of tho reformed faith, will yet hear the voice of the Good Shepherd, and return to tho fold of what ho believes to bo tho true Church. But tho preacher holds out no hope of such a return. "The errors which I combat," he replies, "aro like those fiends which aro only cast out by fasting and prayer. Alas! not many wise, not many learned, are chosen. The cottage and the hamlet shall in our day bear witness against the schools and their disciples. The very wisdom which is foolishness hath made thee, as the Greeks of old, hold as foolishness that which is the only true wisdom." In this reply the reader will be reminded of St. Paul's words when he describes, in his First Epistle to the Corinthians, the different effects of his preaching upon different hearers. It was to "the Jews a stumbling-block, and unto the Greeks foolishness. . . . But not many wise men after the flesh, not many mighty, not many noble are called."

When the Sub-Prior proposes to leave Henry Warden as a prisoner on parole at the tower of Glendearg, he tries to get this promise from the preacher, "that while thus left at liberty, thou wilt not preach or teach, directly or indirectly, any of those pestilent heresies by which so many of our souls have been in our day won over from the kingdom of light to the kingdom of darkness."

"There we break off our treaty," said Warden firmly, quoting, at the same time, the words of the Apostle when he, too, felt that necessity was laid upon him to speak out, "*Woe unto me if I preach not the Gospel.*"

As Mr Holdenough prepares to mount the pulpit stair in Woodstock Church, he is interrupted by the soldier, who thus addresses him, "Friend, is it thy purpose to hold forth to these good people?" "Ay, marry, is it," replied the clergyman; "and such is my bounden duty. *Woe to me if I preach not the Gospel.*"

In *The Fair Maid of Perth*, Father Clement, a Carthusian monk in danger of persecution from having embraced what were held as heretical opinions, shrinks not from his convictions, even when, as Simon Glover tells him, they savour of "blazing tar." Recounting the hardships he has to endure for conscience' sake, the brave monk has yet the courage to say to his friend the Glover: "But were all these evils multiplied an hundredfold—the fire within must not be stifled ; the voice which says within me speak—must receive obedience. *Woe unto me if I preach not the Gospel*, even should I at length preach it from amidst the pile of flames."

As a set-off against these instances of determination to preach the Gospel under all circumstances and at any cost, we have, in *The Highland Widow*, the case of the clergyman who greatly regrets his shyness and timidity in having done so little in the matter of conversing on religious subjects with the widow's unfortunate son. And as the latter lies under sentence of death in Dumbarton Castle, the clergyman endeavours to make up for his neglect in the past by affording all the spiritual consolation he can give during the few hours the young soldier has yet to live.

The great Apostle of the Gentiles writes of having "fought with beasts at Ephesus"—an expression which is generally accepted as figurative language to express his contention with men of fierce and violent passions. Andrew Fairservice uses the expression figuratively when he says to Frank, who had asked him how long he had been in the service of the Osbaldistone family, "I have been fighting with wild beasts for the best part of these four-and-twenty years." And when Yellowley, in *The Pirate,* is asked by Cleveland what business has brought him to Orkney, he replies, "I am weary of fighting with wild beasts at Ephesus yonder," pointing to Shetland, "and I just came over to see how my orchard was thriving which I had planted four or five miles from Kirkwall, it may be a year by-gane."

In distinguishing between the letter and the spirit of the New Testament, St. Paul states that the former takes away life, while the latter gives it: "the letter killeth, but the spirit giveth life." The monk, in *The Betrothed,* says to the Fleming, "Knowest thou not that *the letter of the Scripture slayeth,* and that it is *the exposition which maketh to live ?*" And, in *The Monastery,* another Churchman says to Dame Glendinning, who had told him how the gentle Lady of Avenel had spent much of her time in reading the Holy Scriptures, "I tell thee, Elspeth, *the word slayeth*—that is, the text alone, read with unskilled eye and unhallowed lips, is like those strong medicines which sick men take by the advice of the learned. Such patients recover and thrive; while those dealing in them, at their own hand, shall perish by their own deed. . . . Of this, good woman, be assured, *the word, the mere word, slayeth.*"

The Christian paradox which the Apostle uses when he says, "When I am weak, then am I strong," is apparently in the thoughts of poor David Deans during an incident in the trial of his unfortunate daughter. As her sister is produced as a witness, the prisoner exclaims through her tears, "O Jeanie, Jeanie, save me." This proves too much for the old man, their father. He changes his seat, sits down by the side of Dumbiedykes, and says, " Ah, laird, this is warst of a'—if I can but win ower this part—I feel my head unco dizzy : but *my Master is strong in His servant's weakness.*"

In his Epistle to the Ephesians, St. Paul exhorts them to be no longer without any fixed resolution—"tossed to and fro and carried about with every wind of doctrine." This exhortation is very frequently quoted by Sir Walter. Mr. Holdenough imagines that he has still some influence with the mayor, the aldermen, and the better classes of Woodstock, but as for the lower classes of the town he declares that *they are blown about by every wind of doctrine.* Mr. Fairford senior considers Darsie Latimer so unsettled in his opinions concerning kirk and State, that any moment *some sudden wind of doctrine* might produce an entire change. And in the same novel of *Redgauntlet,* Squire Foxley is described as an old magistrate possessed of so little resolution and strength of character that he is *blown about by every wind of doctrine.*

"Be ye angry and sin not," writes the Apostle in his Epistle to the Ephesians. But as one great and common danger in anger is to allow it to sink deeper and deeper into the heart until it settles into a fixed desire for vengeance, St. Paul adds, "Let not the sun go down upon your wrath." George Heriot admits that Nigel has good cause to be angry at Richie Moniplies in having presented his own supplication to King James instead of his master's ; but he advises Nigel to overlook the fault, "and I judge you will have the better service of him another time."

Sir William Ashton and his daughter are forced during a thunderstorm to seek shelter at Wolf's Crag, the impoverished home of Sir William's mortal enemy, the Master of Ravenswood. The Master entertains them to the best of his power; but it is not without considerable apprehension that he dreads there may something happen ere the day closes. Sir William has his apprehensions too, for he thus addresses Ravenswood, with some embarrassment, "I hope you understand the Christian law too well *to suffer the sun to set upon your anger.*" But the Master quietly replied that he had no occasion that evening to exercise the duty enjoined upon him by the Christian faith.

Sir Walter gives us several interesting illustrations of the apostolic injunction to "redeem the time," and make the most of every opportunity to improve it. In *The Antiquary,* Lovel awakes after a troubled night's rest, and hears through the half-open window of his apartment a female voice singing with much taste and simplicity something between a hymn and a song, in words to the following effect :—

> "'Why sitt'st thou by that ruin'd hall,
> Thou aged carle so stern and gray?
> Dost thou its former pride recall,
> Or ponder how it passed away?
>
> "'Know'st thou not me!' the deep voice cried
> 'So long enjoyed, so oft misused—
> Alternate, in thy fickle pride,
> Desired, neglected, and accused?

> "' Before my breath, like blazing flax,
>   Man and his marvels pass away ;
>   And changing empires wane and wax,
>   Are founded, flourish, and decay.
>
> "' *Redeem mine hours*—the space is brief—
>   While in my glass the sand-grains shiver,
>   And measureless thy joy or grief,
>   When TIME and thou shalt part for ever !'"

During divine service in Glasgow Cathedral, Frank Osbaldistone's thoughts, as he tells us in *Rob Roy*, fell a-wandering among other themes and memories than those suggested by the preacher. This mood of inattention recalled the time of his boyhood when, with his father's hand in his, he used to walk to the chapel of Mr. Shower, who often laid upon him the earnest injunction to "redeem the time because the days are evil." And in *The Heart of Midlothian*, Robertson and Wilson, two criminals under sentence of death, are, according to the custom of the time, taken to church to hear and join in public worship on the Sunday before execution. It was supposed that the hearts of these unfortunate persons, however hardened before against feelings of devotion, could not but be accessible to them upon uniting their thoughts and voices, for the last time, along with their fellow-mortals, in addressing their Creator. The clergyman specially directed part of an affecting discourse to the two criminals, and reminded them that the next congregation they must join would be that of the just, or of the unjust; that the psalms they now heard must be exchanged, in the space of two brief days, for eternal hallelujahs or eternal lamentations. "Therefore," urged the good man, his voice trembling with emotion, "*redeem the time* which is yet left : and remember that, with the grace of Him to whom space and time are but as nothing, salvation may yet be assured, even in the pittance of delay which the laws of your country afford you."

In exhorting the Philippians to work out their own salvation, St. Paul adds, "with fear and trembling." This latter clause is used by the chaplain of Lochleven, in *The Abbot*, when he hears Queen Mary tell her page to make the most of his time during a visit to Kinross. "Dance, sing, run, and leap—all may be done merrily on the mainland." "Alas, madam," said the chaplain, "to what is it you exhort the youth, while time presses and eternity summons? Can our salvation be ensured by idle mirth, or our good work wrought out without fear and trembling?"

The Queen replies that she can neither fear nor tremble; but if weeping and sorrow on her part will atone for the page's enjoying an hour of boyish pleasure, she will cheerfully pay the penance. On this the chaplain remarks that our tears and sorrows are all too little for our own faults and follies, and that they cannot be transferred to others to bear for us.

The expression "filthy lucre" occurs three times in the Epistles, and in each case it is used while stating negatively the qualifications of a bishop. One holding such an office, the Apostle says, should not be given to filthy lucre : should be above accepting such an office for the sake of worldly preferment or gathering money. David Deans asks Reuben Butler if he were to receive the offer of a presentation to "a regular kirk under the present establishment," would he be free to accept it? Butler thinks he would be free, provided he proved acceptable and useful to the parish calling him.

"Right, Reuben, very right, lad," answered Deans; "your ain conscience is the first thing to be satisfied— for how sall he teach others that has himsell sae ill learned the Scriptures as to grip for the *lucre of foul earthly preferment*, sic as gear and manse, money and victual, that which is not his in a spiritual sense—or wha makes his kirk a stalking-horse from behind which he may take aim at his stipend?"

When Reuben is at length comfortably settled as the parish minister of Knocktarlitie, another question is put to him—not this time by David Deans, but by Sir George Staunton, who asks what he would think of an English living of twelve hundred pounds yearly. "What," Sir George continued, "would Mr. Butler think of as an answer, if the offer should be made to him?" Butler replies that he would not accept it, stating, at the same time, that he had no desire to enter into the various points of difference between the Churches of England and Scotland. But having chosen the latter, he was satisfied with the truth of her doctrines, and desired no change.

"What may be the value of your preferment?" said Sir George Staunton, "unless I am asking an indiscreet question."

"Probably one hundred a year, one year with another, besides my glebe and pasture ground."

"And you scruple to exchange that for twelve hundred a year, without alleging any damning difference of doctrine betwixt the two Churches of England and Scotland ?"

" I hope I have done, and am in the course of doing, my Master's work in this Highland parish," replied Butler, "and it would ill become me, *for the sake of lucre,* to leave my sheep in the wilderness. But even in the temporal view which you have taken of the matter, Sir George, this hundred pounds a year of stipend hath fed and clothed us, and left us nothing to wish for. . . . So I leave it to you, sir, to think if I were wise, not having the wish or opportunity of spending three hundred a year, to covet the possession of four times that sum."

"This is philosophy," said Sir George. "I have heard of it, but I never saw it before."

" It is common-sense," replied Butler, "which accords with philosophy and religion more frequently than pedants or zealots are apt to admit."

Moralising on "the filthy lucre of gain that men gie themselves up to," Bailie Nicol Jarvie winds up by quoting what his worthy father the deacon used to say on the subject : "The penny siller slew mair souls than the naked sword slew bodies."

In charging Timothy to mind his health, St. Paul advises him to use no longer water, but "a little wine for thy stomach's sake and thine often infirmities." In *The Monastery,* Abbot Boniface has just finished his evening meal. A lay brother removes the dishes, but leaves the wine on the table. As Father Eustace enters the apartment, the Abbot invites him to sit down and take a cup of wine—"For thy stomach's sake, brother—you know the text."

The Father, however, declines to act upon the Apostle's advice and the Abbot's invitation. "It is a dangerous one to handle alone," he says, "or at late hours. Cut off from human sympathy, the juice of the grape becomes a perilous companion of solitude, and I ever shun it."

The author of the Epistle to the Hebrews exhorts them, while running the Christian race of every-day life and duty, to "lay aside every weight and the sin which doth so easily beset us." In *The Fair Maid of Perth*, Henry Smith is told well what his besetting sins are. Catherine Glover entreats him to abjure the sins of pride and anger which most easily beset him, and fling from him those "accursed weapons to the fatal and murderous use of which thou art so easily tempted." Again she urges him to "resign utterly the manufacture of weapons of every description, and deserve the forgiveness of Heaven by renouncing all that can lead to the sin which most easily besets you." And, once more, she bids him hate in himself "the sins of vanity and wrath by which he is ever most easily beset."

In *Woodstock*, Wildrake forms the resolution of "renouncing some of the sins which most easily beset him, and especially that of intemperance, to which, like many of his wild compeers, he was too much addicted."

St. James in his Epistle teaches us to dread an unruly tongue as one of the greatest and most pernicious of evils. He shows how it needs to be watched and guarded to prevent much mischief. In the Waverley Novels we have a great many illustrations of the truth of what the Apostle says of this unruly evil—an unbridled tongue. Out of sincere and heartfelt gratitude for the assistance Edie Ochiltree had rendered to Sir Arthur Wardour and his daughter during a time of extreme peril, the latter expresses her anxiety to provide a home for their preserver. She suggests that if he would care to reside at the castle she would give orders to the servants and menials that

"They should tend the old man well."

But Edie interposes by saying that Sir Arthur and Miss Wardour can, no doubt, do much for his ease and comfort if he cares to take up his abode at the castle, but there were some things which neither a master nor a mistress could do. "Trow ye," he asks Miss Wardour, "that Sir Arthur's command could forbid the gibe o' the tongue, or the blink o' the e'e, or gaur them gie me my food wi' the look o' kindness that gaurs it digest sae weel, or that he could make them forbear a' the slights and taunts that hurt ane's spirit mair nor downright misca'ing?" And so Edie prefers his wandering independence to the gibes and taunts of the servants' tongues at Knockwinnock Castle.

In *The Heart of Midlothian,* Ratcliffe objects to being classed among murderers. "I never shed blood," he says.

"But ye sauld it, Ratten," replied Sharpitlaw. "Ye hae sauld blood mony a time. Folk kill wi' the tongue as well as wi' the hand—wi' the word as well as wi' the gully."

In numerous other instances throughout the novels we have illustrations of the mischief which can be caused by an evil tongue, and many regrets expressed that it had not been ruled in time. Mrs. Dods is sorry that she indulged in rather too plain speaking to her guest, Mr. Tyrrel; but she resolves that for the future she will guide her tongue better, for, "as the minister says, it is an unruly member—troth, I am whiles ashamed o't mysell."

St. Peter, in seeking to prove that a state of apostasy is worse than a state of ignorance, quotes, by way of illustration, this proverb—"The dog is turned to his own vomit again; and the sow that was washed to her wallowing in the mire." The latter part of this proverb is very frequently quoted by Sir Walter. In *Castle Dangerous*, the bishop advises Turnbull to adhere to the resolution he has made of giving no occasion for quarrelling while in the presence of an Englishman. "Do not be," says the prelate, "like the sow that has wallowed in the mire, and having been washed, repeats its act of pollution, and becomes again yet fouler than it was before." David Deans says to Widow Butler, with reference to the principles of her deceased husband, that "he trusts her son, who is preparing for the work of the ministry, shall not turn again, like the sow, to wallow in the mire of heretical extremes and defections, but shall have the wings of a dove, though he hath lain among the pots."

Among the names of persons incidentally mentioned in the Epistles we have Demas, Diotrephes, and Gaius, all of whom are referred to in the Waverley Novels. The preacher in *Old Mortality* brackets Lord Evandale's name with that of "an ambitious Diotrephes," and Sergeant Bothwell's with that "of a covetous and world-following Demas." The name of Gaius, whom St. Paul calls "mine host," comes in, however, for more honourable mention. At Newark, where Jeanie Deans rests for a short while on her journey to London, she asks her host what his charges are, in order that she may discharge them before setting out. But "mine host" will take nothing. "The Saracen's Head," he says, "can spare a mouthful o' meat to a stranger like o' thee." Well may Sir Walter call this kind-hearted man Jeanie's "Lincolnshire Gaius." In *Old Mortality*, we read of the widow whose husband kept the principal inn of the burgh, and who had been a Presbyterian of such strict principle and profession that he was known among his sect by the name of "Gaius, the publican."

We cannot leave these references to the Epistles without pointing out how very heartily Sir Walter enters into the spirit of the Apostle's injunction, so frequently expressed, of exercising hospitality one toward another. A warm-hearted and generous host himself, the author of *Waverley's* love of hospitality finds expression in some shape or other in almost every novel he wrote. We specially associate *The Pirate* with this apostolic injunction, for it illustrates in a most interesting manner both the general exhortation of St. Paul on this point, and that of St. Peter, who adds that hospitality is to be exercised *without grudging*. The pirate Cleveland is forgotten in the frank and generous Magnus Troil, whose house and table are free and open to mainlander and islander alike. There is neither stint nor grudging in his hospitality; but it is very different with the mean and sordid Yellowley the factor, and his sister Barbara, or Baby, as she is generally called in the novel. This close-fisted and close-hearted pair grudge not only everything in the shape and taste of meals, but even the very wood used to kindle the fire which is to cook them. Norna of the Fitful Head helps herself to refreshment from the inhospitable table of Yellowley and his sister, but not being made welcome to it, she pays for what she takes. Mordaunt Mertoun seeks shelter from the raging tempest, meat and drink and fire, a bed for the night, and a sheltie next morning to carry him home. And though Baby opens out into an unusual fit of hospitality, and gives him what he asks, we still feel how grudgingly everything is done. The smoked goose is consigned to the pot, but Mordaunt lives in Baby's memory afterwards as the youth who had "snapped up her goose as light as if it had been a sandie laverock."

It is pleasant to turn from such grudging hospitality to the groaning tables and open house of Magnus Troil; and from him, again, to other hospitable scenes and people in the Waverley Novels. In *The Surgeon's Daughter*, Dr. Gray cordially joins in his wife's hospitable request, and invites Mr. Lawford to remain and dine with them; and all the more cordial is this invitation, when it is recollected that there is to be something

R

better than usual that day to dinner—"lamb and spinage, and a veal Florentine." Sir Geoffrey Peveril's unbounded joy at the restoration of King Charles found most adequate expression in the form of a great feast at Martindale Castle, to which the whole neighbourhood was invited, and hospitality dispensed on the most liberal scale to Cavaliers and Roundheads alike. Dame Glendinning held hospitality to be a duty quite as essential as any other pressing call upon her conscience, and so we find that when her visitors arrived from the monastery, she not only waited upon them personally, but eagerly watched "every trencher as it waxed empty, and loaded it with fresh supplies ere the guest could utter a negative." Old Mr. Fairford, in *Redgauntlet*, was a scrupulous observer of the rites of hospitality, but he seemed to exercise them rather as a duty than a pleasure. Harry Bertram (Brown) greatly enjoys the genial hospitality of Dandie Dinmont at Charlieshope. On the former remarking that he fears he must resume his journey next morning, "The fient a bit o' that," exclaimed the Borderer, "I'll no part wi' ye at ony rate for a fortnight." Fergus MacIvor retrenches and economises wherever possible, in order that he may not stint the hospitality with which he so lavishly entertains his friend Waverley during his visit to Glennaquoich.

So sacred in Sir Walter's eyes is the exercise of hospitality one toward another, that he invariably lets us feel what a serious offence any one commits who neglects the apostolic injunction on this point. The charge of inhospitality is an extremely grave one. The Marquis, in

The Bride of Lammermoor, demands the meaning of the inhospitable reception which his kinsman, the Master of Ravenswood, receives at the hands of Sir William Ashton's family. What a picture of blank astonishment we get when Bailie Nicol Jarvie and party arrive at the inn of Aberfoil, and are actually refused admittance, and only get it by force. How contemptible a community the inhabitants of Bale appear, when they refuse the rites of hospitality to the Swiss Deputies, as narrated in *Anne of Geierstein*. In the *Legend of Montrose*, Sir Duncan Campbell visits Darnlinvarach, and while there he receives a message from Angus M'Aulay, to the effect that the cavalier who is to accompany him is ready and waiting, and that all is prepared for his return to Inveraray. Indignant at the affront which such a message conveyed, Sir Duncan started up, and looking towards M'Aulay exclaimed, "I little expected this. I little thought that there was a chief in the West Highlands who . . . would have bid the knight of Ardenvohr leave his castle, when the sun was declining from the meridian, and ere the second cup had been filled. But, farewell, sir, the food of a churl does not satisfy the appetite; when I next revisit Darnlinvarach, it shall be with a naked sword in one hand, and a firebrand in the other." Sir Duncan, however, was never permitted to carry out this threat. It was not to him that vengeance belonged, for he died in battle shortly after the incident here noticed.

THE REVELATION.

THE mention of Patmos, the lonely island to which St. John was banished, reminds us that, in connection with our present study, we have now entered upon the last book of the New Testament—the Revelation.

Patmos is twice mentioned in the Waverley Novels, curiously enough, so early in the series as the first and third, and in none of the others. In *Waverley*, it gives name to the Baron Bradwardine's hiding-place after the "affair" of 1745, and in *The Antiquary*, Edie Ochiltree calls the ledge of sea-surrounding rock on which he, Sir Arthur, and Miss Wardour take refuge during their perilous adventure with the rising tide, "this Patmos o' ours."

The seven-branched golden candlestick, and the seven stars, which the Apostle saw in the apocalyptic vision, are respectively used to designate the house or inn of the Cameronian, Ebenezer Cruickshanks, at Cairnvreckan, and that of Mrs. Bickerton in the Castlegate of York.

In the letter to the angel or minister of the church at Ephesus, there occurs this warning, "I will remove thy candlestick out of his place except thou repent." In Mr. Pembroke's parting exhortation to Waverley, who is preparing to set out for Dundee, there to join his regiment, the worthy clergyman remarks from his standpoint of view, that it had pleased heaven to place Scotland, "doubtless for the sins of their ancestors in 1642, in a more deplorable state of darkness than even this unhappy kingdom of England. Here, at least, although the *candlestick of the Church* of England has been in some degree *removed from its place*, it yet afforded a glimmering light. . . . But in Scotland it was utter darkness; and excepting a sorrowful, scattered, and persecuted remnant, the pulpits were everywhere abandoned to Presbyterians, and, he feared, to sectaries of every description."

In a long letter addressed to Lady Peveril, Major Bridgenorth grieves to say "that *our candlestick being about to be removed*, the land (of England) will most likely be involved in deeper darkness than ever." When the Lady's husband afterwards reads this letter, the stout old Royalist is much puzzled by the peculiar language in which it is couched. "What he means by moving of candlesticks," remarks Sir Geoffrey, "I cannot guess; unless he means to bring back the large silver candlestick which my grandsire gave to be placed in the altar at Martindale-Moultrassie, and which his crop-eared friends, like sacrilegious villains as they are, stole and melted down."

In *Woodstock*, Mr. Holdenough says to Colonel Everard when the former learned that Sir Henry Lee and his family have been allowed to return to the home of their fathers, "The paths in which you tread are dangerous, you are striving to raise the papistical candlestick which

Heaven in its justice *removed out of its place*—to bring to this hall of sorcerers those very sinners who are bewitched with them."

In *Old Mortality*, Habakkuk Mucklewrath summons Claverhouse to appear before the tribunal of God to answer for all the blood which he had shed. He then repeats the solemn invocation from Revelation sixth and tenth, " How long, O Lord, holy and true, dost thou not judge and avenge the blood of thy saints." With the last of these words on his lips the preacher fell back, and, without an attempt to save himself, was dead ere his body touched the floor.

In the vision which St. John saw of the opening of the seals, he describes in sublime and awful language the dread and terror which seized upon "the kings of the earth, the great men, the rich men, the chief captains, and the mighty men," at the opening of the sixth seal. To the mountains and to the rocks they cried, "Fall on us, and hide us . . . from the wrath of the Lamb." Sir Walter refers to this scene when he describes the astonishment and terror with which the Earl of Leicester was seized, when the incensed and indignant Queen Elizabeth burst in upon him, dragging with her the terrified Countess Amy. Waving aside the lords and ladies grouped round the Earl under an arcade, the Queen calls out in tones which alarmed and thrilled all who heard her, " Where is my Lord of Leicester ?"

Supporting with one hand the sinking form of the almost lifeless Countess, and with the fingers of the other pointing to the pale features of the unhappy lady, the Queen demands in a voice that sounded in the ears of the astonished nobleman like the last dread trumpet-call that is to summon body and spirit to the judgment-seat, "Knowest thou this woman?" "As," continues Sir Walter, "at the blast of that last trumpet, the guilty shall call upon the mountains to cover them, Leicester's inward thoughts invoked the stately arch which he had built in his pride, to burst its strong conjunction, and overwhelm him in its ruin."

In *Woodstock*, Colonel Everard says to Wildrake, who was speaking of former merry days and playhouse memories, "They were like most worldly pleasures, sweet in the mouth and bitter in digestion." There is an allusion here to the little book which the Apostle is told to take from the angel's hand and eat, adding, "It shall make thy belly bitter, but it shall be in thy mouth sweet as honey."

In this same novel, and in *Old Mortality*, with all their graphic descriptions of the religious excitement which agitated England and Scotland at the respective periods of each tale, we have a great deal of the language of the Book of Revelation introduced and quoted. Some of the characters in both novels interpret the language of this part of Scripture after their own fancies, and indulge the belief that the Second Advent of the Messiah, and the millennium, or reign of the saints upon earth, is close at hand. Thus Harrison says to Everard, "Am I not the champion chosen and commissioned to encounter and to conquer the great Dragon and the Beast which cometh out of the sea? Am I not to command the left wing, and two regiments of the centre, when the saints shall encounter with the countless legions of Gog and Magog? I tell thee that my name is written on the sea of glass mingled with fire, and that I will keep this place of Woodstock against all mortal men, and against all devils, whether in field or chamber, in the forest or in the meadow, even till the saints reign in the fulness of their glory."

Take another specimen, this time from *Old Mortality.* Old Mause Headrigg lifts up her testimony against Bothwell and all his party. "Philistines ye are, and Edomites . . . piercing serpents ye are, and allied baith in name and nature with the great Red Dragon: Revelations, twalfth chapter, third and fourth verses."

The expression "mark of the beast," which occurs several times in the Revelation, is frequently used in the Waverley Novels. As in the scriptural sense it is understood to apply to those who array themselves on the side of the enemies of the Church, so in the novels it is applied to all who are opposed to the existing government, or the established religion of the country referred to in the tale. Thus in *Redgauntlet,* the laird of that name is a Jacobite, and when Alan Fairford asks Mr. Maxwell if he knows Redgauntlet, the reply is, "You must not be angry, Mr. Fairford, that the poor persecuted nonjurors are a little upon the *qui vive,* when such clever young men as you are making inquiries. . . . Redgauntlet is, you may have heard, still under the lash of the law, *the mark of the beast* is still on his forehead, poor gentleman, and that makes us cautious." In *Peveril of the Peak*, Topham says to Dangerfield and Everett while commissioning them to go down to Derbyshire, "You must put on your Protestant spectacles, and show me where there is the shadow of a priest, or a priest's favourer." Everett replies that he "will take in hand to discover *the mark of the beast* on every one of them between sixteen and seventy as plainly as if they crossed themselves with ink instead of holy water." And in *The Fortunes of Nigel*, George Heriot waits upon King James to show him a piece of plate of such cunning and curious workmanship that he deems it advisable and respectful to submit the plate to his Majesty's inspection before offering it for sale to any of his subjects. The king asks the goldsmith where he had procured the work.

"From Italy, may it please your Majesty," replied Heriot.

"It has naething in it tending to papistrie?" said the king, looking graver than his wont.

"Surely not, please your Majesty," said Heriot; "I were not wise to bring anything to your presence that had *the mark of the beast*."

"You would be the mair beast yourself to do so," said the king; "it is weel kend that I wrestled wi' Dagon in my youth, and smote him on the ground-sill of his own temple; a gude evidence that I should be in time called, however unworthy, the Defender of the Faith."

In the pouring out of the vials described in the sixteenth chapter of the Revelation, the Apostle saw "three unclean spirits like frogs come out of the mouth of the beast, and out of the mouth of the false prophet." From this passage the Rev. Mr. Holdenough preached a sermon at Joliffe, whose violent conduct in ousting the preacher from the pulpit of Woodstock church had neither been forgiven nor forgotten. Mr. Holdenough always spoke of Joliffe in private as a "lying missionary, into whom Satan had put the spirit of delusion."

References to the woman whom St. John saw in vision sitting on seven mountains, arrayed in purple and scarlet, are of frequent occurrence in the Waverley Novels. The first occurs in the opening chapter of *The Monastery*, as

> "Yonder Harlot
> Throned on the seven hills with her cup of gold."

In *The Antiquary*, the scarlet woman is a synonym for the Roman Catholic persuasion in the incident where the maid calls at the fisherman's cottage, and relates to Maggie Mucklebackit the news of the death of the Catholic Countess of Glenallan. Speaking of the funeral, Jenny says, "It will be the grandest show ever was seen."

"Troth, hinny," answered Maggie, "if they let naebody but papists come there, it'll no be muckle o' a show in this country, for the auld harlot, as honest Mr. Blattergrowl ca's her, has few that drink o' her cup o' enchantments in this corner of our chosen lands." And in *Redgauntlet*, the hypocritical smuggler is asked if he knows Mr. Maxwell of Summertrees, to which he replies that he has no personal acquaintance with him, being, as he had heard, a papist, for the woman "that sitteth on the seven hills ceaseth not yet to pour forth the cup of her abominations in these parts."

In speaking to Colonel Everard of the trees in the park at Woodstock, General Harrison alludes to the tree of life which St. John saw in the New Jerusalem as described in the last chapter of Revelation. "The former possessors of Woodstock," says the General, "assembled in this their abode of pleasure many strange trees and plants, though they gathered not of the fruit of that tree which beareth twelve manner of fruits, or of those leaves which are for the healing of the nations."

In *Kenilworth* there is an interesting reference to the New Jerusalem, and such as are not to be allowed within her walls. Varney employs Alasco, the chemist and astrologer, to make up a poisonous draught which is to be given to the unfortunate Countess of Leicester. Foster is asked to take the cup to the lady's apartment, and when he returns to the laboratory Varney asks if "the bird has sipped."

"She has not, nor shall she, from my hands," replied Foster. "Would you have me do murder in my daughter's presence?"

The two heartless villains endeavour to reason with Foster, and convince him that the elixir will not endanger life, but he steadily refuses to have any hand in administering the draught so long as his daughter Janet remains in the house as the lady's maid and companion. "In one thing I am bound up," says Foster resolutely, "that fall back, fall edge, I will have one in this place that may pray for me, and that one shall be my daughter. I have lived ill, and the world has been too weighty with me; but she is as innocent as ever she was when on her mother's lap, and she, at least, shall have her portion in that happy city, whose walls are of pure gold, and the foundations garnished with all manner of precious stones."

The Astrploger gives *his* exposition of the vision beheld by St. John, but Foster replies that he had never heard it expounded in that way by the clergyman. "Moreover, Doctor Alasco, the Holy Writ says that the gold and the precious stones of the Holy City are in no sort for those who work abomination, or who frame lies."

"Well, my son," said the doctor, "and what is your inference from thence?"

"That those," said Foster, "who distil poisons, and administer them in secrecy, can have no portion in those unspeakable riches." ·

Our present study of the Waverley Novels draws near to its close. It has, we trust, helped the reader to see how largely and how frequently Sir Walter Scott employs the sacred narrative in the composition and construction of these famous tales and romances. Gathering together his references to the Bible, and his quotations from it, we find, after arranging them as we have done in the preceding pages, that they begin at the first chapter of Genesis; we see that they crop up out of almost every

Book onward, and we take leave of them at the last chapter of Revelation. But intimate and accurate as was Sir Walter's knowledge of the Sacred History in its letter and in its details, he was at the same time filled with the spirit of its teaching. Quietly and unostentatiously this latter point comes out in his writings, and if our readers will keep us company during one or two chapters more, we shall try to point out some of the great novelist's illustrations of the leading truths of our holy religion, his sympathy and humanity, his pictures of the family circle, and his thoughts upon death, judgment, and the life which awakens to new and glorified realities when all is over here.

SCOTT AS A RELIGIOUS TEACHER.

IF we glance over a list of modern novelists and the books which they have written, the first thing that will probably impress us is, not the extraordinary mass of work produced, but the great variety of "schools" or classes into which these novelists may be divided. Every mode of life, and almost every shade of opinion—educational, artistic, philosophical, scientific, and social—have been described in the modern novel. To none of these schools, however, does Sir Walter Scott belong. We associate his name with the *historical novel*, which he may be said to have created, and with no other. Having pointed out in the preceding chapters in what way, and to what extent, Sir Walter employs the Bible in the construction and composition of the Waverley Novels; having seen in what an interesting way he illustrates many of the more outstanding narratives and lessons of the Sacred Scriptures; it may be thought that it is our present intention to claim for the author of Waverley a place among our religious writers, or at all events, to associate his name more with the *religious novel* than with the historical. But we have no such intention. Much as Sir Walter Scott makes use of the Bible in his novels, we yet see that he does so, not for the purpose of supporting some doctrine which he is trying to teach, but simply and solely to illustrate the story he has in hand. He is describing, let us suppose, some lovely landscape or pleasant retreat; then the beauty of the primitive Eden or the joys of Paradise are quoted to heighten the effect. He is relating how the fond old King of Scotland is broken-hearted by the news of his son's death; this reminds him of the wail of lamentation by the bereaved King of Israel over the death of his much-loved Absalom. The despair of Jeanie Deans, while in the hands of the robbers, is dispelled by the consolations of religion and the thoughts of the Psalmist as he, too, when in affliction, calls upon his soul not to be disquieted, but trust in God, who is the health of his countenance and the strength of his heart. What new and fresh meaning Sir Walter throws around such scriptural texts as "Put not your trust in princes," "Hope deferred maketh the heart sick," "Vengeance is mine, saith the Lord!" and many others. How interesting is his use of the teaching and the parables of our Lord, and how practical and sensible are his illustrations of some of the apostolic injunctions!

But, notwithstanding all this wealth of Bible instruction in the Waverley Novels, we do not usually think of their author as being anything else than a romancer and a story-teller. The reason is sufficiently obvious. He makes no pretension to anything else than a romancer and a story-teller: he is not given to posing as a moral and religious teacher, but he is a great moral and religious teacher all the while. What we get of the teaching of the Bible in the Waverley Novels is got from our walk and conversation with a thoroughly true and healthy man who knows men and books well, but the meaning and teaching of the Sacred Scriptures infinitely better.

In Sir Walter's hands the Bible is always treated as the Bible—the revealed will of God, and placed above every other kind of book. In *The Fortunes of Nigel*, he makes King James say of the sacred volume that it " is indeed *principium et fons* "—the fountain and the source of religion as revealed to man. In *The Monastery*, he declares the Bible to be " the volume on which Christianity itself is founded ; " and who that has read that romance can forget what the White Lady of Avenel says in reply to Halbert Glendinning, who asks what mystery there is in the volume which she has twice recovered from those who wished the book concealed ?

> " Within that awful volume lies
> The mystery of mysteries !
> Happiest they of human race,
> To whom God has granted grace
> To read, to fear, to hope, to pray,
> To lift the latch and force the way ;
> And better had they ne'er been born,
> Who read to doubt, or read to scorn."

These lines are so often read only in connection with the story, that they are forgotten as soon as they are read ; but if we detach them from their context we shall find much in the lines worth remembering. Paraphrased, they remind us that the " awful volume " here referred to is the Bible, with its divine revelation of God manifest in the flesh. Thrice happy are they to whom the

Holy Spirit has been given to read aright the lessons of the present life; to hope and pray for the blessed realities of the future. Better had they never been born who refuse to become "as a little child," and read the Sacred Volume only to doubt its divine revelation, or scorn its awful mysteries.

We have here a kind of confession or creed on the part of Sir Walter. It comes unexpectedly, and it comes unsolicited. In all his writings he is true to this creed; his faith in the unseen and eternal is strong and unwavering—simple and child-like. God is ever in his thoughts, not the cold abstraction of Theology; not the unknown and unknowable God of Agnosticism; but the God of the Lord's Prayer—our Father in heaven, from whom His children on earth are never separated; ever near enough to hear their cry for daily bread; always present when danger, or approaching death, seems to brush aside all mortal things, and reveals the presence of Him "in whom we live, and move, and have our being." Illustrations of the fatherhood of God are so numerous in the Waverley Novels that we need only point out one or two representative instances. In *Woodstock* Colonel Everard says to Sir Henry Lee, the stout old Royalist, "I hope the time will soon come when Englishmen of all sects and denominations will be free in conscience to worship in common *the great Father*, whom they all, after their manner, call by *that affectionate name.*" In *Castle Dangerous* the Minstrel, while wishing good-night to the boy, recommends him, at the same time, to commit himself to God, "*who is the Friend and*

S

Father of us all." And Rebecca asks Ivanhoe to believe that a Jew may do service to a Christian without desiring any other reward than the blessing of the *" great Father who made both Jew and Gentile."*

By other names than the Father, God is frequently mentioned in the Waverley Novels as the great Creator, the Almighty Disposer of Events, the King of Kings, and other attributive titles.

Sir Walter encourages us to have faith in the divine government of the world. Though many things may look mis-sorted from the human point of view, he asks us to recollect that " Eternal Wisdom " has designed this world to be "a place of mixed good and evil—a place of trial at once and of suffering, where even the worst ills are checkered with something that renders them tolerable to humble and patient minds, and where the best blessings carry with them a necessary alloy of embittering depreciation." It is pleasant to note a few examples here, out of the great many to be found in the Waverley Novels, of faith and trust in God amidst much that is discouraging and apparently hopeless. In *Guy Mannering*, Harry Bertram, when a child of only five years old, is carried off by a party of smugglers. He is eventually given up for lost. In the meantime his father dies, but so strong is the faith of the boy's aunt, so certain does she feel that God's hand is about him, that she bequeathes all her property to her nephew, convinced that he will be restored to his native land in due time. When he does return it becomes necessary, of course, to produce proof that he is the heir of Ellangowan

While the law-agent sees difficulty in procuring such proof, the young heir's faithful old tutor sees none. He believes that God, who guided the boy all these years, will not leave His work imperfect. And so, eventually, all comes well.

When the Earl of Etherington, in *St. Ronan's Well*, tells Clara Mowbray that she is now in his power, she replies—

" Not so, proud man, God gave not one potsherd the power to break another, save by His Divine permission —my fate is in the will of Him without whose will even a sparrow falls not to the ground. Begone—I am strong in faith of heavenly protection ! "

In *Anne of Geierstein*, the elder Philipson is tried before that dreadful tribunal the Holy Vehme. When the worst comes to the worst, he falls back upon his last and only hope—" Then God be gracious to me, for I have no trust save in Heaven." When Halbert Glendinning meets the preacher on his way to Avenel Castle, Halbert warns him that if he goes self-invited, and without assurance of safety, he runs a great risk of losing his life. But Warden replies, "I am in God's hand ; it is on His errand that I traverse these wilds, amidst dangers of every kind ; while I am useful for my Master's service they shall not prevail against me, and when, like the barren fig-tree, I can no longer produce fruit, what imports it when or by whom the axe is laid to the root ?"

The unfortunate Countess of Leicester casts herself upon the protection of God in her sore hour of trial. " I am certain," she says to her faithful attendant, "the God I have served will not abandon me in this dreadful crisis." And another unfortunate lady commits herself to God in a time of supreme peril. Addressing the licentious Templar, Rebecca the Jewess tells him that her "resolution is anchored on the Rock of Ages. . . . I waste no more words on thee; the time that remains on earth to the daughter of Jacob must be otherwise spent— she must seek the Comforter, who may hide His face from His people, but who ever opens His ear to the cry of those who seek Him in sincerity and in truth." And when misfortune falls upon Hobbie Elliot, his grandmother comforts him with the assurance that "God can help when worldly trust is a broken reed."

Many a touching picture does Sir Walter draw of gratitude expressed to God for mercies received or dangers averted. The mention of Hobbie Elliot's name in our last extract reminds us of an interesting scene in his experience. "I am the happiest man in the world," he exclaims in the fulness of his joy when he receives back, all safe and well, his lovely bride, Grace Armstrong.

"Then, O my bairn," said his grandmother, who never lost any opportunity of teaching the lessons of religion at those moments when the heart is best open to receive them, "give praise to Him that brings smiles out of tears, and joy out of grief. . . . Was it not my word that if ye could say HIS will be done, ye might have cause to say HIS name be praised ?"

"It was—it was your word, Grannie, and I do praise HIM for His mercy, and for leaving me a good parent when my ain were gane," said honest Hobbie, taking her hand, "that pits me in mind to think of HIM baith in happiness and distress."

Not less touching are other such scenes, where the King of Scotland and his son, the Duke of Rothesay, are reconciled to each other : where Jeanie Deans learns the certainty of her sister's pardon : where Lucy Ashton sees her father rescued from what seemed a dreadful death : and where Magnus Troil is assured that all is well with his two beloved daughters—all scenes, with many more, of the deepest and sincerest gratitude to God.

Of the various attributes which we ascribe to God— such as His mercy, His goodness, and His justice—there are many illustrations to be found in Sir Walter's writings. When Harry Bertram is restored to his friends, his affectionate tutor reminds him that among other lessons which had been taught him in his childhood, there was one in particular, and that was ever " to look up to God as *the source of all that is good.*"

In *The Antiquary*, when old Elspeth hears of the death of her former mistress, the Countess of Glenallan, she exclaims, "God assoilzie her. She was a hard-hearted woman, but she's gane to account for it a', and *His mercy is infinite.*" Reuben Butler implores the mob at Edinburgh to spare the life of Porteous, their unfortunate prisoner. "In the name of *Him who is all mercy,* show mercy to this unhappy man, and do not dip your hands in his blood, nor rush into the very crime which you are desirous of avenging." Turning to the doomed man Butler thus addresses him, in the prospect of immediate death, " O turn to Him in whose eyes time and space have no existence, and to whom a few minutes are as a life-time, and a life-time as a minute."

In *Anne of Geierstein* Agnes, daughter of the murdered Albert, after shedding " oceans of blood " in avenging his death, founds the rich abbey of Königsfeldt. On making a pilgrimage to the cell of a hermit for the purpose of inducing him to take up his abode in the abbey, he listens to the proposal with horror and scorn. ·

" God," said the holy man, " will not be served with blood-guiltiness, and rejects the gifts which are obtained by violence and robbery. *The Almighty loves mercy, justice, and humanity*, and by the lovers of these only will He be worshipped."

Having already shown how largely Sir Walter makes use of the teaching of our Lord, we proceed to inquire if there is any reference to the Holy Spirit—the third person of the Trinity. We shall see that there is such reference if we take the term grace as indicating the office or work of the Holy Spirit. " For my sins," says Edie Ochiltree to the Earl of Glenallan, " *I hae had grace to repent o' them*, and to lay them where they may be better borne than by me." We have already had occasion to refer to the sermon preached by Henry Warden before the assembled household at Avenel Castle. Referring to it once more, we find the preacher stating that while self-searching and meditation can do much, it is *grace that can do all*. He concludes with an earnest exhortation to his hearers " to seek divine grace which is perfected in human weakness ;" and in *St. Ronan's Well*, Hannah Irwin confesses to the Rev. Mr. Cargill her unhappy spiritual state. "I have rejected the offer of grace," she says, "and not through ignorance, for I have sinned with my eyes open." The clergyman, however, consoles the penitent by imploring her not to despair. He reminds her that "grace is omnipotent—to doubt this is in itself a great crime."

RELIGION AND RELIGIOUS LIFE IN THE
WAVERLEY NOVELS.

IN general terms, Sir Walter defines religion as "the mother of peace." He tells us that when one of the ancestors of Edward Waverley returned home from the Holy Land, the Crusader found so much to disappoint and dishearten him that he sought in a neighbouring cloister "the peace which passeth not away." Religion may appear to be only of the common conventional type in such characters as Hobbie Elliot, who goes to consult the Black Dwarf about his lost sweetheart. "If ye could gie me but speerings o' puir Grace," says the disconsolate Hobbie, "I would consent to be your slave for life *in ony thing that didna touch my salvation.*" But religion rises into life and reality in such persons as Henry Morton, Rebecca the Jewess, and Jeanie Deans—all of whom experience the consolation and the strength of true religion in the hour of supreme and terrible peril. What a peace, too, religion brings to poor Norna of the Fitful Head. Mordaunt Mertoun seeks to turn her thoughts into other and better channels than the desire to "rule over gibbering ghosts, and howling winds, and raging torrents." "Life will again have charms," Mordaunt continues, "*and religion will have comfort for you.*" Before any change takes place, however, Norna sinks into the depths of spiritual despair, and considers herself as an outcast from divine grace. Shrouded in the occult arts and practices which she had professed to deal in, Norna's study, like that of Chaucer's physician, had been "but little in the Bible." When the change came, however, the Sacred Volume was seldom laid aside; and to the poor ignorant people who came, as formerly, to invoke her power over the elements, Norna only replied, "The winds are in the hollow of His hand." Her conversion seemed sincere; she appeared deeply to repent of her former presumptuous attempts to interfere with the course of human events; and she always expressed the bitterest compunction when any of her former pretensions were recalled to her memory.

In *The Heart of Midlothian,* Sir Walter states that it was a belief of the time and the sect to which Jeanie Deans belonged that special answers to prayer were, as the Cameronians expressed it, "borne in upon their minds" in reply to any earnest petition uttered at a time of crisis or difficulty. Sir Walter enters into no abstract point of divinity on the subject, but he says there is one thing at least which is perfectly plain, namely, "that the person who lays open his doubts and distresses in prayer, with feeling and sincerity, must necessarily, in the act of doing so, purify his mind from the dross of worldly passions and interests, and bring it into that state, when the resolutions adopted are likely to be selected rather from a sense of duty than from any inferior motive."

Then referring to the particular instance of prayer which elicited this explanation, Sir Walter adds that Jeanie Deans rose from her devotions with "her heart fortified to endure affliction and encouraged to face difficulties." In *The Abbot*, the grandmother of Roland Græme says that "the time spent in prayer is as a refreshing slumber, and the sense of doing the will of Heaven is a richer banquet than the tables of monarchs can supply." And in *Castle Dangerous*, the Minstrel thus states his opinion of prayer. "We may," he says, "without offence, intimate in our prayers the end we wish to obtain, but it is not for us, poor mortals, to point out to an all-seeing Providence the precise manner in which our petitions are to be accomplished."

From these remarks on the nature of prayer we turn to some of the instances of its exercise recorded in the novels. We have Julian Peveril, Henry Morton, Quentin Durward, and the daughters of Magnus Troil, all committing themselves to God in prayer before retiring to rest for the night. Darsie Latimer begins the day with prayer. He is wakened early by Redgauntlet, who urges him to make haste and accompany him. But Darsie replies, "I must first take the freedom to spend a few minutes alone before beginning the ordinary works of the day." In times of doubt or danger, we have the desire expressed by Dandie Dinmont that he "could mind a bit prayer" before he creeps into the smuggler's cave ; and not knowing what the effect of the medicine may be, or at least very doubtful whether or not he may recover, the Earl of Essex folds his hands and becomes absorbed

in mental devotion ere he swallows the draught prescribed by Wayland Smith. We have soldiers on the
battlefield trying to recollect the prayers of their infancy :
thus Waverley hears, among the wounded and dying
troopers, a voice in the provincial English of his native
county trying to repeat the Lord's Prayer. We have
Janet Foster praying for her unhappy mistress, and
poor Caleb Balderston retires to his room to pray for his
unfortunate master. Listen to the secret prayer of David
Deans, overheard by her who was the subject of it: "And
as for the other child Thou hast given me to be a
comfort and a stay to my old age, may her days be long
in the land, according to the promise Thou hast given to
those who shall honour father and mother—may all her
purchased and promised blessings be multiplied upon
her; keep her in the watches of the night, and in the
uprising of the morning, that all in this land may know
that Thou hast not utterly hid Thy face from those that
seek Thee in truth and in sincerity." And what a pathos
there is in this same old man's benediction as, one evening before retiring to rest, he draws his daughter to him,
kisses her forehead, and ejaculates, "The God of Israel
bless you, even with the blessings of the promise."

"And you, my dear father," exclaimed Jeanie, when
the door had closed upon the venerable old man, "may
you have purchased and promised blessings multiplied
upon you—upon *you* who walk in this world as though
ye were not of the world, and hold all that it can give
or take away but as the *midges* that the sun-blink brings
out, and the evening wind sweeps away."

With David Deans, family worship, or "the exercise," as it was called, was regularly observed, on which occasion a portion of Scripture was read, a psalm was sung, and a prayer was offered. Andrew Fairservice, too, used to assemble some of his neighbours to join him in the family exercise; and as George Heriot's dinner-party broke up, and all the guests had gone, except Mr. Windsor the clergyman, and Nigel, the worthy goldsmith addressing the latter says, "My lord, we have had our permitted hour of honest and hospitable pastime, and now I would fain delay you for another purpose, as it is our custom, when we have good Mr. Windsor's company, that he reads the prayers of the church for the evening before we separate. Your excellent father, my lord, would not have left before family worship. I hope the same from your lordship."

"With pleasure, sir," answered Nigel, "and you add in the invitation an additional obligation to those with which you have loaded me. When young men forget what is their duty, they owe deep thanks to the friend who will remind them of it."

As a general rule, all the entertainments mentioned in the Waverley Novels, such as dinner and supper parties, do not begin until a blessing has been asked on the good things spread before the company. At George Heriot's dinner-party just alluded to, the blessing of the clergyman set the guests at liberty to attack the excellent cheer set before them. And in the same novel of *Nigel*, King James, before the council breaks up, wishes his Privy Councillors a good appetite for an early supper, and specially asks one of the bishops present to "be pleased to stay and bless our meat." Captain Dalgetty thought the grace at Sir Duncan Campbell's table much too long, while David Deans on a similar occasion elsewhere censured it as being much too short.

Norna of the Fitful Head, in *The Pirate*, leaves the inhospitable roof of the close-fisted Yellowleys. The factor stands aghast, not knowing what may be the result of offending one credited with supernatural powers. His sister, however, addresses him and recalls him to a sense of duty with reference to the dinner, which is waiting. "What do ye stand glowering there for? *You* a Saunt Andrew's student!—*you* studied lair and Latin humanities, as ye ca' them, and daunted wi' the clavers of an auld randie wife! *Say your best college grace, man*, and witch or nae witch, we'll eat our dinner and defy her."

As Darsie Latimer sits down at the table of Redgauntlet, the discipline which had trained him to hear the invocation of a blessing before breaking the bread for which we are daily taught to pray, made him pause for a moment, and made his host sensible of what was wanted. With something of a sneer, Redgauntlet asked one of the two domestics sitting at the lower end of the table to say grace—"the gentleman expects one." But both domestics refused, and it was not until a young girl entered the dining-room that a blessing could be asked. At Redgauntlet's request she did so in a voice of much sweetness and with affecting simplicity of manner.

MORALITY IN THE WAVERLEY NOVELS.

In an article entitled *Fiction — Foul and Fair*,[1] Mr Ruskin states that he cannot make out from Lockhart's *farrago*, the first thing he wants to know about Sir Walter — whether or not Scott, after his weekday custom, worked at his books on Sunday mornings. Mr. Ruskin thinks not; and he then proceeds to speculate as to how Sir Walter did spend his Sundays. With this matter we have at present nothing to do; but we may point out how some of the Waverley characters spend theirs.

In various ways is the Sunday observed in the Waverley Novels. In *Rob Roy*, Sir Walter refers to a custom on the English road where those who journeyed on horseback used to halt on the Sunday morning in order that the traveller might attend divine service, and give his horse the benefit of the day of rest. This observance of the Sunday, Sir Walter adds, " is as humane to our brute labourers as profitable to ourselves." Waverley attends church in all the splendour of his new uniform previous to setting out for Scotland to join his regiment at Dundee. At Osbaldistone Hall there

[1] *Nineteenth Century,* October 1880.

was a religious service held every Sunday morning, but
the rest of the day was full of languor and weariness,
and peculiarly hard to be got over by the squire and
his fox-hunting sons. Bailie Nicol Jarvie rebukes Rob
Roy when, in the Tolbooth of Glasgow, the latter hums
over the verse of an old song. "Whisht, sir," said the
magistrate in an authoritative tone, "lilting and singing
sae near the latter end o' the Sabbath!" And when
the Bailie returns to his own house, conscience, which
he apostrophises so frequently, seems to check him for
having been transacting matters which might have been
deferred till a lawful business day. Pausing on the
threshold, and in a tone of deep contrition, Frank
Osbaldistone hears the Bailie say, "I hae my thoughts
on the Sabbath!" Then, apparently receiving inward
consolation, he turns to Frank and says in a soothed and
less troubled tone, "But there's balm in Gilead." Colonel
Mannering spends a Sunday in Edinburgh. In company
with Mr. Pleydell, the advocate, he attends divine
service in the Greyfriars' Church, where the celebrated
Dr. Erskine officiates. On the way home, Mr. Pleydell
and the Colonel discuss the sermon and the points of
difference which had split the Church of Scotland into
so many conflicting parties. The discussion, however,
seems to have little interest for the Colonel, for, being an
Episcopalian, his thoughts wandered after other and
more congenial associations.

Returning to the novel of *Rob Roy*, we find an
interesting account of a Sunday spent in Glasgow.
Frank Osbaldistone and Andrew Fairservice attend divine

service in the Cathedral. Long resident in France,
Frank had been accustomed to hear and see high mass
celebrated with all the pomp and ceremonial which the
choicest music, the richest dresses, and the most imposing
ceremonies could confer, yet, he declares, it fell short
in effect of the simplicity of the Presbyterian worship.
The devotion, in which every member of the congregation
seemed to share, appeared so superior to that which was
recited by musicians as a lesson learned by rote, that it
gave the Scotch form of worship all the advantage of
reality over acting.   The sermon of the officiating clergyman related chiefly to the abstract points of the Christian
faith—subjects grave, deep, and fathomless by mere
human reason, but for which, with equal ingenuity and
propriety, the preacher sought a key in liberal quotations
from the inspired writings.

If there be one commandment in the moral law
which Sir Walter seems to feel the meaning and the
spirit of more than any other, that commandment is the
sixth.   It declares how sacred a thing is human life; it
enjoins the protection and the preservation of it in every
possible way; and it emphasises that deed as truly
awful which would seek to break into "the tabernacle
of life," and scare away the image of God therein enshrined.   In the clearest and most positive terms Sir
Walter every now and again, in the Waverley Novels,
raises the warning words, "Thou shalt do no murder;"
and if life has been taken, as in the case of the unfortunate Morris, who was thrown into the lake at the
command of Helen Macgregor, the novelist raises his

solemn protest against the deed. "It is," says Bailie
Nicol Jarvie, who had witnessed the dreadful scene,
"a bloody and cruel murder—it is a cursed deed, and
God will avenge it in His due way and time." If, as in
the case of Waverley seeing no way out of avenging the
insult received from Balmawhapple but by arranging for
a "hostile meeting" or duel, Sir Walter seems to make
an exception to this law, and lightly or irreverently
substitute in its place the "law of honour" for the law
of God, it is well to remember that he is only describing
a practice which was common among gentlemen at the
time of the tale. Common or not common, however,
Sir Walter denounces the unlawful and sinful practice
of duelling in terms which can neither be mistaken nor
misunderstood. Thus, in *St. Ronan's Well*, Touchwood
says to Captain MacTurk with regard to duelling, "I
tell you, sir, that, besides its being forbidden both by
law and Gospel, it's an idiotical and totally absurd practice." When the Antiquary suspects that Lovel and
Hector MacIntyre have arranged to have a hostile meeting, the old gentleman affectionately warns Lovel to
take heed to his present feelings, and, as for duelling, he
characterises it as a "practice unknown to the civilised
ancients, and of all the absurdities introduced by the
Gothic tribes the most gross, impious, and cruel." Dis-
regarding this friendly admonition, Lovel and Hector
actually do meet, but they are interrupted by old Edie
Ochiltree, who thus appeals to them : "What are ye
come here for, young men ? Are ye come amongst the
most lovely works of God to break His laws ? Have ye

left the works of man, the houses and the cities that are but clay and dust, like those that built them; and are ye come here among the peaceful hills, and by the quiet waters, that will last whiles aught earthly shall endure, to destroy each other's lives, that will have but an unco short time, by the course of nature, to make up a long account at the close o't? O sirs! hae ye brothers, sisters, fathers, that hae tended ye, and mothers that hae travailed for ye, friends that hae ca'd ye like a piece o' their ain heart? and is this the way ye tak to make them childless and brotherless and friendless? Ohon! it's an ill feight whar he that wins has the warst o't. Think on't, bairns! I'm a puir man—but I'm an auld man too, and what my poverty takes awa frae the weight o' my counsel, grey hairs and a truthfu' heart should add to it twenty times." But all this impassioned and touching appeal goes for nothing. Even the seconds attached to each of the duellists recommend that the quarrel should be made up. Nothing, however, will satisfy the "law of honour" but blood, and accordingly the two young men fire at each other, one of whom falls and the other goes off like a second Cain, believing that his fellow's blood is on his head, and with something in his heart which makes it heavier than lead.

In *Peveril of the Peak* there is an instance of a gentleman refusing to fight a duel. Sir Jasper Cranbourne delivers the message of Sir Geoffrey Peveril to Major Bridgenorth, who, after reading the letter, makes this reply—"Bear back my respects to Sir Geoffrey Peveril. According to his light, his meaning may be fair toward me; but tell him that our quarrel had its rise in his own wilful agression toward me, and that, though I wish to be in charity with all mankind, I am not so wedded to his friendship as to break the laws of God, and run the risk of suffering or committing murder in order to regain it."

This reply was not made without a tear of anger and a feeling of shame; but the Major's friend, the Rev. Mr. Solsgrace, came to his assistance, and exhorted him to remember in his prayers the thanks due to Heaven, "which enabled thee to resist the strong temptation." To which Bridgenorth replies, "Reverend and dear friend, I feel that you speak the truth. Bitterer, indeed, and harder to the old Adam, is the text which ordains him to suffer shame, than that which bids him do valiantly for the truth."

Unlike too many novelists of the present day, Sir Walter steers clear as much as possible of those scenes of life which lie around, or are guarded by the seventh commandment. All the purer are the Waverley Novels in consequence. In *The Heart of Midlothian* we have the fall of Effie Deans, but her fall only brings into greater relief the most spiritually-minded and religious character which Sir Walter has ever drawn— Jeanie Deans. How precious, in Sir Walter's estimation, is purity of heart, speech, and behaviour! How delicate are his touches in the portraiture of the tender attachment which indicates the dawn or the presence of love! Rose Bradwardine writes to Waverley when the latter is on a visit to Fergus MacIvor in the Highlands.

Rose's letter originally commenced with *Dear Sir;* but these words had been carefully erased, and the monosyllable *Sir* substituted in their place. The whole letter is a model of propriety. "Forgive me," says the young lady, "if I am wrong in what I am doing, for alas! Mr. Waverley, I have no better advice than my own feelings; my dear father is gone from this place, and when he can return to my assistance and protection, God alone knows."

Alarmed and anxious about the capture of Henry Morton, Edith Bellenden writes to her uncle on the matter. But though this is the object and the subject of her letter, she says not a word about Morton until she reaches the inevitable *P.S.* of a lady correspondent, when she reveals what is uppermost in her thoughts, and states her case with the utmost modesty and propriety. On reading the letter, the gallant soldier exclaims, "'The poor lad; my old cronie's son!' And the silly wench sticks it into her *post scriptum*, as she calls it, at the tail of all this trumpery about old gowns and new romances."

Similar instances of Scott's delicacy in handling such matters are of frequent recurrence in the Waverley Novels. The scene where Catherine Glover, the Fair Maid of Perth, chooses her valentine for the year is one of the most charming little pictures which Sir Walter has ever drawn. And how skilful and healthy is his treatment of such incidents as Margaret Ramsay's visit to Nigel in the Tower of London, or the escapade of Mysie Happer's flight to Edinburgh with Sir Piercie Shafton.

A writer of such high moral tone as Sir Walter does not hesitate, when occasion requires, to paint in their true colours the disastrous consequences of impurity and unchastity. What "a pre-eminently wretched woman," to use her own words, is Norna, in *The Pirate*, as she relates the tale of her early guilt and sorrow. The memory of poor Catherine, the beautiful and devoted mistress of Julian Avenel, haunts us as we lay down *The Monastery*. On the field she seeks for him who had promised to marry her, and when she finds only his lifeless body, she dies in the excess of her grief and affection. The child of her sorrow is taken care of by Halbert Glendinning, who relates the incident to the Regent Murray. Remembering, perhaps, the associations and circumstances connected with his own birth, the Regent remarks to the Earl of Morton, who stood by his side, " What have they to answer for, Douglas, who thus abuse the sweetest gifts of affection ! "

As we follow the fortunes of Catherine's orphan child, who becomes the Roland Græme of *The Abbot*, the memory of his mother's sorrow is transfused into feelings of chastened joy and gladness as we learn that, instead of Roland being the illegitimate child of Julian Avenel and Catherine Græme, he is really the offspring of a secret but lawful marriage duly celebrated and attested by Father Philip, who lodges all the necessary attestations thereof with the Abbot of St. Mary's, under seal of the confessional, until the time arrives when everything may be made public. And having made the matter public, Sir Walter himself seems to breathe more freely, as he dismisses the handsome page, not to be known any longer as Roland Græme, but as Roland Avenel.

In his examination before the magistrate, Ratcliffe, a notorious thief, but afterwards reformed and employed as a turnkey in the Tolbooth of Edinburgh, is asked to describe his occupation. He replies by asking, in return, " What is't, again, that the aught command says ?"

" Thou shalt not steal," answered the magistrate.

" Are you sure of that ?" replied Ratcliffe. " Troth, then, my occupation and that command are sair at odds, for I read it, thou *shalt* steal, and that makes an unco difference, though there's but a wee bit word left out."

All the difference, indeed ! Andrew Fairservice, too, notwithstanding all his affected piety, has rather hazy ideas regarding the spirit of the eighth commandment— so hazy that his new master, Frank Osbaldistone, has to set him right. In their journey to Scotland, Andrew had taken one of the horses from Osbaldistone Hall without leave being asked or granted.

" How is this, sir ?" said Frank when he recognised the animal. " This is Mr. Thorncliff's mare."

" I'll no say but she may aiblin hae been his honour's in her day—but she's mine now."

" You have stolen her, you rascal."

Andrew then proceeds to explain that the squire had borrowed money from him to go to York races, and had never repaid him. " Steal the mear !" he continues, in indignant astonishment at the charge of dishonesty. " Na, na; far be the sin o' theft frae Andrew Fairservice—I have just arrested her *jurisdictionis fandandy causey.*"

Frank Osbaldistone, however, could look at the matter in no other light than simply a breach of the eighth commandment, and, accordingly, he wrote to his uncle explaining the circumstances under which the mare had been taken away, and stating the arrangements made for her being returned to Osbaldistone Hall.

So faithfully does Sir Walter describe human nature that he shows us, as the Bible shows us, the weak and imperfect side of character as well as the healthy, the strong, and the good. In literature as in daily life, in the sacred narrative as in the world of fiction, it is with something like a shock to the feelings when we hear any one deliberately state as a truth what he knows perfectly well to be a falsehood. Abraham saying of Sarah that she was his sister; Jacob deceiving his aged father; Gehazi declaring that he had not gone after Naaman; and Peter's denial of his Lord, are the Bible incidents we refer to. In the Waverley Novels there are numerous similar instances of human imperfection. Like Louis XIV., Caleb Balderstone, in *The Bride of Lammermoor*, hesitates to carry finesse the length of open falsehood; but he is quite content to deceive, if possible, without directly lying. When George Heriot visits Lord Nigel in the Tower of London, the former starts at seeing a muffled figure in the same apartment. More anxious, apparently, to prevent this figure being recognised than to keep his own affairs private, Nigel unblushingly says to Heriot, "'Tis a page of mine: you may speak freely before him. He is of France, and knows no English."

The goldsmith suspects, however, that the truth is not being told. Accordingly, he takes hold of the supposed page's cloak, and, after some gentle degree of violence, discloses to view the detected daughter of the old chronologist, Margaret Ramsay.

The scene is a painful one to all concerned. The girl is asked to explain why she is in such a questionable situation and in such a guise. "I cannot explain it further," she says, in tones of deep regret and shame, "further than that the Lady Mansel sent me here, in spite of my earnest prayers, tears, and entreaties. I was not afraid of anything, for I knew I should be protected. But I could have died then—could die now—for very shame and confusion."

While this and further explanation serves to put matters right with Margaret Ramsay, we feel that the falsehood remains with Lord Nigel, and that nothing can ever atone for any falsehood but the bitter tears and the sincere repentance of a fallen Peter.

In such exhibitions of human failings as uttering untruths, we are involuntarily led to the contemplation of the infinite beauty and the priceless worth of truth itself. The Countess Amy, in *Kenilworth*, pleads with her husband to be downright, true, and honest; urges him to forsake his deceitful policy, and return to the straight path which is at once the best and the safest. "Oh, my good Lord," she says, "make no faction in a peaceful state! There is no friend can help so well as our own candid truth and honour. Bring but these to our assistance, and you are safe amidst a whole army of the envious and the malignant. Leave these behind you, and all other defence will be fruitless."

The story of *The Heart of Midlothian* affords one of the most remarkable illustrations in English literature of obedience to the injunctions of the ninth commandment. The turning-point of the tale may be said to lie in the refusal of Jeanie Deans to perjure herself, save her sister's life, and so to render unnecessary the famous journey to London to petition for the unhappy girl's pardon. But Jeanie can see no way in which she is free to state that her sister ever communicated to her one word suggestive of her condition. For some time she remained in a state of the most agitating terror and uncertainty—afraid to communicate her thoughts freely to her father lest she should draw forth an opinion with which she could not comply. She was wrung with terror, too, on her sister's account, rendered all the more acute by reflecting that the means of saving her life lay in Jeanie's own power. But conscience prohibited her from using this power, and so she fell back upon her faith in God, and the resolution to do nothing, and say nothing, which was not strictly true.

The mind is apt to speculate upon what would have happened had Jeanie Deans borne false witness in order to save the life of her sister. It is abundantly clear that Jeanie would have been a very wretched woman all the remaining days of her life; and great as were the trials which she encountered on the long and weary walk to

London, she would rather have experienced them fifty times over, than be guilty of a breach of the ninth commandment, either in her own heart or under the awful oath prescribed by the presiding judge at Effie's trial in Edinburgh.

Traces of the large-heartedness, humanity, and sympathy which bulked so largely in Sir Walter's personal character are to be found in all his novels—plentiful as the blaeberries among the heather on his Border hills. He seems unable to paint even the worst and most dissolute characters without putting something of good into them. They draw out his sympathy even in their greatest wretchedness, for he feels they are fellow-men, and that the image of God can never be wholly blotted out of the human soul. Dirk Hatteraick, the smuggler, is redeemed from utter villainy by his one virtue of integrity to his employers. "I was always faithful," he says, "to my ship-owners—always accounted for cargo to the last stiver." Callum Beg, Fergus MacIvor's handsome but utterly unscrupulous page, has yet a tender place in his heart for his mother. On the march of the Highland army into England, Callum took the cloak which had covered the dying English soldier and concealed it among the furze on the moor, carefully marking the spot for the purpose of recognising the place on the expected return northward, when he proposed to take home the cloak as a present to his mother.

Ratcliffe, the turnkey in *The Heart of Midlothian*, is not without some good quality to balance much that is evil in his character and habits. Hardened as he is, he feels unable to witness the meeting of Jeanie Deans and her sister in the prison cell. It seems too much for him : with a gentleness that has something of reverence in it, Ratcliffe partly closes the window shutter, and, by excluding the bright sunshine, contrives to throw a veil over a scene so sad and sorrowful. And in this same novel, Staunton says to Jeanie, during the interview at Muschat's Cairn, "I am a villain steeped in guilt and wretchedness, but not wicked enough to do you any harm."

Sir Walter's kindness of heart—his love of the brotherhood—finds expression in many different ways. Great as the risk is, he makes Henry Morton not only find a shelter for Burley in one of the out-houses of Milnwood, but, at a greater risk still, he provides the fugitive with a supper. No opportunity seems to be lost of slipping a gratuity into somebody's hand, either in recognition of some service rendered, or to atone for the mortification produced by the non-acceptance of proffered attention. Edie Ochiltree characterises Isabella Wardour as one who "has aye been kind to ilka forlorn heart that came near her." And Lady Peveril tells her indulged and authoritative housekeeper to deal civilly and kindly with Deborah, the nurse, who had suddenly left the Castle, "for," added the lady, "though a light-hearted young woman, she was kind to the children."

There is a touching scene of genuine sympathy in *The Antiquary*, where Monkbarns goes to visit Saunders

Mucklebackit after Steenie's funeral. "I am glad, Saunders, that you feel able to make this exertion," says the Antiquary, as he finds the old fisherman trying to mend his boat.

"And what would you have me to do?" answered the old man gruffly, "unless I wanted to see four children starve, because ane is drowned? It's weel wi' you gentles who can sit in the house wi' handkerchers at your een when ye lose a friend, but the like o' us maun to our work again, if our hearts were beating as hard as my hammer."

Blunt as this reply was, Monkbarns took the old fisherman kindly by the arm. "Come, come," he said, "Saunders, there is no work for you this day—I'll send down Shavings, the carpenter, to mend the boat, and he may put the day's work into my account, and you had better not come out to-morrow, but stay to comfort your family under this dispensation, and the gardener will bring you some vegetables and meal from Monkbarns."

"I thank ye, Monkbarns," answered the poor fisher. "I am a plain spoken man, and hae little to say for mysell. . . . When ye laid Steenie's head in the grave,— and many thanks for the respect,—ye saw the mouls laid on an honest lad who liked you weel, though he made little phrase about it."

Melted at the recollection of his son, the old man's grief found refuge in tears. Large drops also fell from the sympathising Antiquary's face, as, with much tenderness and compassion, he gently led the sorrowing Saunders away to his bereaved and sorely-stricken home.

"Nothing," observes Sir Walter in *Kenilworth,* "nothing can so soon attract the unfortunate as real or seeming sympathy with their sorrows." And, in the same novel, he draws an affecting scene of another old man in great sorrow for the loss of a beloved daughter. Tressilian returns to Lidcote Hall after an unsuccessful expedition to recover and bring back with him Amy Robsart, who had been wiled away from home. Her father, old Sir Hugh, awakens from a state of stupor by the entrance of him whom he had fondly hoped to call his son-in-law. Sighing heavily, a slight convulsion passes over Sir Hugh's features; he opens his arms without speaking a word, and as Tressilian throws himself into them, the broken-hearted father folds him to his bosom. "There is something left to live for yet," were the first and the only words he could utter, and then he gives vent to his feelings in a paroxysm of weeping, the tears chasing each other down his sun-burnt cheeks and long white beard.

The scene was a touching one to all who witnessed it. "I never thought to have thanked God to see my master weep," said Will Badger, an old domestic, "but now I do, though I am like to weep for company."

Sir Walter's sympathy also takes the form of offering help in the way of lending money or giving credit— either of which is about as good a test of sincerity as can well be imagined. Deacon Bearcliff, in *Guy Mannering,* speaking to the hostess of the Gordon Arms on the subject of the misfortunes that have overtaken poor old Mr. Bertram and his family,—"I am sure," says the deacon, "ony sma' thing they might want frae my shop, under seven, or eight, or ten pounds, I would book them as readily for it as the first in the county." In the most delicate way possible, the Antiquary offers the loan of money to his young friend Lovel, whom he supposes in low spirits from, perhaps, the want of pecuniary help. "If—if"—making an effort—"if there be any pecuniary inconvenience—I have fifty—or a hundred guineas at your service—till—till Whitsunday—or indeed as long as you please." Dandie Dinmont is not able to let Captain Brown (Harry Bertram) leave Charlieshope without offering the loan of "a hundred or two" to help his promotion in the army. "The bit scrape o' your pen," adds the genial farmer, "would be as good to me as the siller, and ye might jist take yer ain time o' settling it." Bailie Nicol Jarvie makes a similar offer to his kinsman, Rob Roy; and when poor Lord Nigel arrives in London, he meets with a warm friend in the person of George Heriot. "I am a goldsmith," says Heriot, "and live by lending money, as well as by selling plate. I am ambitious to put an hundred pounds to be at interest in your hands till your affairs are settled." Under the impulse of genuine compassion at the sorrows of the family of David Deans, the young laird of Dumbiedykes gropes for his purse, and ejaculates, as he looks across to her whose sorrows move him most, "Jeanie, woman! Jeanie, woman! Dinna greet—it's sad wark, but siller will help it."

AMONG the happy homes of the Waverley Novels we have that of honest Dandie Dinmont, the Liddesdale farmer. As he returns home to Charlieshope from Cumberland, what joy and gladness he brings to wife and children. Regardless of the presence of a stranger whom Dandie had brought with him, his wife, nevertheless, in the tumult of her joy at her husband's return, affectionately embraces him. "Deil's in the wife," said Dandie, shaking off his wife's embrace, but gently and with a look of great affection, "deil's in ye, Ailie—d'ye no see the stranger gentleman?"

"Troth, I was sae weel pleased to see the gudeman, that——" she suddenly stopped as she observed streaks of blood both on the stranger's head and on that of her husband. "Ye've been fighting again, Dandie, wi' some o' the Bewcastle horse-coupers! Wow, man, a married man, wi' a bonny family like yours, should ken better what a father's life's worth in the warld." The tears stood in the good woman's eyes as she spoke.

Dandie, however, satisfactorily accounted for the presence of blood, and then came a scene with the children. Their father hugged them all round, distributed whistles, penny trumpets, and gingerbread; and lastly, when the excitement got beyond bearing, the farmer exclaimed to his guest, "This is a' the gudewife's fault, Captain—she will gie the bairns a' their ain way."

"Me! Lord help me!" said Ailie; "how can I help it? I have naething else to gie them, poor things!"

One of the most affecting chapters in *Waverley* is that where Sir Walter describes a brave man in sorrow. Colonel Talbot, while on duty in Scotland, receives news of the death of his infant child — the long-expected heir — and the precarious state of his wife's health. Reaching a miniature portrait of his wife to Waverley, the Colonel observes in tones which betray his mental agony, "She is a woman, my young friend, who may justify even a soldier's tears; and yet, God knows, what you see of her there, is the least of the charms which she possesses—possessed, I should perhaps say,— but God's will be done!"

Tired of his bachelor life, Bailie Nicol Jarvie promoted Mattie, his faithful housekeeper, from her wheel by the kitchen fire to the upper end of his table, in the character of Mrs. Jarvie. Some of his acquaintances in the Town Council made much merriment over the matter; "but," said the worthy magistrate, "let them say their say, I'll ne'er fash mysell, nor lose my liking for sae feckless a matter as a nine days' clash. My honest father, the deacon, had a byword,

> "Brent brow and lily skin,
> A loving heart, and a leal within,
> Is better than gowd or gentle kin."

U

When Dr. Gray, in *The Surgeon's Daughter*, lost his wife, the sunshine of his existence was gone. Every morning he missed the affectionate charges which enjoined him not to forget his own health, while labouring so hard to restore and preserve that of his patients. Every evening as he returned from his weary rounds in the country, it was with the consciousness that for him there was now no more the affectionate welcome from her who had always been so eager to relate, and so much interested in hearing, all the events of the day.

But as in daily life, so also in the Waverley Novels, there are homes where husband and wife do not seem suited to each other. The only unpleasant part of *Guy Mannering* is that where the alienation between the Colonel and his wife is related. Mrs. Mannering delighted in petty mysteries and intrigues, and yet trembled to see the indignation which such conduct excited in the mind of her husband.

Sir William Ashton and his lady, in *The Bride of Lammermoor*, don't get on well together. Much as Sir William falls in the estimation of the reader, as his schemes of political cunning and duplicity gradually unfold themselves, he falls lower still when, terrified and disconcerted by the sudden return of Lady Ashton from England, he sees no hope for his projects and schemes but the possibility of her ladyship's coach being upset, and her neck broken! She arrives at the Castle all safely, however, and the scene which follows between wife and husband is not an edifying one. Lady Ashton scatters to the wind—tears into shreds, as it were—the apostolic injunction, "Wives submit yourselves to your husbands," and prepares the way, as fast as possible, for the catastrophe which awaits her unhappy daughter, the Bride of Lammermoor.

Of all the family life, however, which Sir Walter describes so well, there is none which is done with so much loving and tender grace as that of a widower left with an only daughter. The memory of the departed mother is as sacred incense which sanctifies and sweetens the bereaved home. Beginning with the Baron Bradwardine and his daughter Rose, we get a succession of delightful portraits in almost every novel until we reach the last, and, in some respects, the most charming of them all—Simon Glover and his daughter Catherine, the Fair Maid of Perth. The love which unites father and daughter so closely and so endearingly, is the sweetest and the holiest thing which comes from Sir Walter's pen. It reaches to the heart, and awakens feelings which sometimes only find relief in tears. ·

The pictures of father and son are also an interesting study. They form some interesting illustrations of the obedience enjoined in the fifth commandment, and the promise annexed to the pious and faithful discharge of its sacred duties. Old Mr. Fairford is very anxious that his son should consent to undertake the cause of poor Peter Peebles. When Alan signifies his willingness to do so, the old man replies in great delight, " Well, well, my boy; the Lord will make your days long in the land for the honour you have done to my grey hairs.

You may find wiser advisers, Alan, but none that can wish you better."

Here and there, we find instances where the father acts with perhaps too much harshness, or, at all events, with too little sympathy. So much so that we feel, in such instances, it would have been well had they recollected and put in practice the apostolic injunction to fathers, not to provoke their children to wrath, lest they be discouraged. The novel of *Rob Roy* opens in this way. The harsh and unsympathetic conduct of old Mr. Osbaldistone, the rich and prosperous city merchant, creates a temporary estrangement between himself and his son Frank, who entertains a strong disinclination to business. Hear how Mr. Owen, the confidential clerk, pleads with Frank to remain with his father and become a partner in the great concern of Osbaldistone, Tresham, & Co. "For the love of heaven," says Owen, "look at both sides of the account. Think of what you are going to lose—a noble fortune, sir—one of the finest houses in the city. . . . Do, my dear Mr. Francis, think of the honour due to your father, that your days may be long in the land."

Filling up the spaces on the walls of the Waverley gallery, containing the pictures of father and daughter and father and son, there are numerous delightful sketches of filial devotion and duty on the part of young people to their parents. For all the wealth of India, Menie Gray, the surgeon's daughter, would not leave her father's house to get married without her father's full and free consent. Devoted to her father, Die Vernon accompanies him through all his perilous adventures in Scotland. Minna Troil says that every silver hair on her father's head is to her as precious as "the treasure of the unsunned mine." In all the grandeur of her magnificent apartments at Cumnor Hall, but in all the unhappiness of her secret marriage, the Countess Amy's heart is yearning and breaking to see her father to assure him that all is well, and that she is really a lawfully married woman, and the wedded wife of the noble Leicester. Bailie Nicol Jarvie is constantly quoting the memory of his father, and Henry Morton idolises the memory of his. So solicitous is Arthur Philipson about his father's safety, that, after the rescue of the former from the perilous precipice by Anne of Geierstein, the first request he makes is permission to go in search of his father. "The life which I owe to your assistance," says Arthur to the young lady, "can scarce be called welcome to me, unless I am permitted to hasten to my father's rescue." Cuddie Headrigg does much for his mother, old Mause: he joins the Covenanting party at her desire, and, greatly amused as we generally are at everything Cuddie says or does, we yet feel that he perceptibly falls in our estimation when he loses patience on one occasion, and speaks of his mother as an "auld jade." That expression, however, was only human nature seeking a vent in exceptional and trying circumstances; but, when the heat is off, and matters return to their normal condition, Cuddie rises once more to his former level.

THE PRINCIPLES OF GOOD AND EVIL.

IN the Waverley Novels we are constantly meeting with the two opposing principles of good and evil, or conscience and the evil one. As in Scripture, so in these works we find Satan moving to and fro, mixing himself up in the affairs of men, and ever seeking whom he may tempt or destroy. By a great many different names is he mentioned by Sir Walter—the Prince of Darkness, the old Enemy, the Arch-fiend, the Destroyer of mankind, the Author of Evil, and many others, suggestive of his nature and character. His existence is indisputable, and, as Bucklaw says, in *The Bride of Lammermoor*, "he is always at one's elbow." The preacher, in *Woodstock*, reminds Everard that the "inward tempter is ever on the watch to bring us to his lure." And in *St. Ronan's Well*, Hannah Irwin, while confessing the guilt of her past life, says to the clergyman, "The fiend, always watchful, presented a tempter at the moment when it was most dangerous."

But, persevering and constant as are Satan's temptations, we have the sacred assurance, as stated by St. James, that if we resist the devil he will flee from us. Jeanie Deans reminds Madge Wildfire, when the latter relates that while she thinks of her errors, and has the confession of them on her tongue, that "then comes the Devil and brushes my lips with his black wing, and lays his broad black loof on my mouth—for a black loof it is, Jeanie— and sweeps away a' my good thoughts, and dits up my gude words, and pits a wheen fule sangs and idle vanities in their place." Jeanie replies by recommending poor Madge to "settle your mind and make your breast clean, and you will find your heart easier. Just resist the devil, and he will flee from you, and mind that, as my worthy father tells me, there is nae devil sae deceitfu' as our ain wandering thoughts."

In *St. Ronan's Well*, there is a striking scene where Mowbray is assailed by the tempter, and where, after a fierce resistance, he flees from his victim. Maddened by his desperate fortunes and heated with wine, Mowbray threatens to take the life of his sister Clara. Grasping her by the shoulder, he flung her with great violence from him. As she rose from the floor, imploring his pity and mercy, he turned suddenly round, ran to the open window, and threw himself as far as he could, without falling out. With streaming eyes and up-lifted hands, the unhappy Clara approached her brother, and anxiously asked what it was that he appeared to be looking after so eagerly. "After the devil!" he answered fiercely; then, drawing in his head, and taking her hand, "By my soul, Clara—it is true, if ever there was truth in such a tale! He stood by me just now, and urged me to murder thee! What else could have put my hunting-knife into my thought? Ay, by God, and into my very hand at such a moment. Yonder I could almost fancy I see him fly, the wood, and the rock, and the water, gleaming back the dark-red furnace light that is shed on them by his dragon wings! By my soul! I can hardly suppose it fancy! I can hardly think but that I was under the influence of an evil spirit, under an act of fiendish possession! But, gone as he is, gone let him be—and thou, too ready implement of evil, be thou gone after him!" He drew from his pocket his right hand, which had all the time held his hunting-knife, and threw the implement into the court-yard as he spoke. With a subdued quietness and solemnity of manner, Mowbray shut the window, and led his sister by the hand to her seat, which, but for his assistance, she would not have been able to reach.

As if checkmating all the designs of Satan, and foiling him in his temptations and suggestions, we have conscience also making its presence felt, and stirring up to better things when the power of evil preferred to let matters remain as they were. Conscience is frequently on the lips of Bailie Nicol Jarvie, and seems to be his favourite exclamation of surprise. But it goes further than the lips in other cases, and asserts its tremendous power, even though it may only speak with—

> "the still
> Small voice, which is the voice of God."

·· The Laird of Dumbiedykes has lived the life of a selfish, profligate, and extortionate landlord, keeping down conscience and forbidding it to speak. But on the Laird's deathbed, conscience asserts itself and demands to be heard and listened to. This demand was made in the midst of a transport of language, so violent and profane, that both clergyman and doctor had to leave the apartment. Sinking his voice to a lower tone, he says to the attorney, who alone had the courage to remain beside the Laird, "There's ae thing—there's ae fearful thing hings about my heart, and an anker of brandy winna wash it away—The Deanses at Woodend! I sequestrated them in the dear years, and now they are to flit, they'll starve." Probably for the first time in his life, the attorney tried his hand at spiritual advice, and recommended, as an opiate to the agonised conscience of the Laird, reparation of the injuries he had done to the Deanses. But this called Mammon up to struggle with remorse, and the utmost conscience could do in the struggle, was to get the expiring sinner to charge his son to let the tenants remain "at a moderate mailing, and hae bite and sup: it will maybe be the better wi' your father whare he's gaun, lad."

Glossin, the wily and unscrupulous agent on the Ellangowan estate, sold himself to work iniquity. But conscience speaks at last, and tells him distinctly that, now he has got matters very much as he wanted, his day of reckoning is at hand. This dread voice lets him feel that his situation is perilous in the extreme, for the schemes of a life of villainy are crumbling around and above him. One night, as he sleeps, conscience awakes and presents to the vision of Glossin a strange and awful phantasmagoria—his patron, with the paleness of death on his features; the murdered

Frank Kennedy, all smashed and gory as he lay on the beach at Warroch Point; the dungeon with Dirk Hatteraick confessing the crime to a clergyman, and stating that only one man knew all about it, in addition to himself, and that man was Glo——" "No, I deny it—it was not I," cried Glossin, as, struggling in his agony to express his denial, he awoke. Then conscience and he stand face to face, and we feel how tremendous is its power, and how God-given is its authority.

But, in gentler moods and scenes than these, we meet with conscience doing its duty. It forbids the Antiquary to reprove the coachman for being late in starting from Edinburgh, because he himself was behind time in arriving at the coach-stand in the High Street. It reminds Mrs. Dods that her guests must not be supplied with more liquor, as they have already had enough, and more than enough. It tells the Duke of Rothesay that he has failed in his duty to his affectionate father, and it says to Lord Nigel that Ritchie Moniplies is perfectly right in warning him that he, Lord Nigel, is not living the life in London that he ought to be living. Chrystal Croftangry leaves his lodging in the Canongate of Edinburgh so suddenly that he does not stop to receive the change due to him on settling with his landlady. Wrapping this change in a piece of paper, conscience tells the good woman to put the money aside as it does not belong to her. Twenty years elapse, and Chrystal revisits his former lodging in the Canongate, and makes himself known to old Janet, his Highland landlady. After a warm welcome, Janet-goes in search of a little parcel, which, being opened, is found to contain fifteen shillings, the change she had so conscientiously treasured all these twenty years! "Here they are," said Janet in honest triumph, "just the same I was holding out to ye when ye ran as if ye had been fey. Shanet has had siller, and Shanet has wanted siller, many a time since that—and the gauger has come, and the factor has come, and the butcher, and baker—Cot bless us—just like to tear poor auld Shanet to pieces; but she took good care of Mr. Croftangry's fifteen shillings." Truly, this is a striking instance of the power of conscience.

DEATH AND THE FUTURE LIFE.

THE subject of death, with its solemn associations of judgment and the future life, seems to be much in the mind, and often in the thoughts, of the men and women whom we meet in the pages of the Waverley Novels. As Henry Morton proceeds up the ravine which leads to the lonely cottage of Bessie Maclure, the widow, the brawling brook at his feet turns his thoughts upon the course of human life and its ultimate absorption in the great ocean of eternity. Thoughts of a similar import seem to be in the thoughts of Sir George Staunton as he and the Rev. Mr. Butler are being rowed up the Gareloch to the manse of the latter. Sir George looks upon death as merely the consummation of human existence; but the clergyman looks "across the flood," and, true to the commission he bears as a minister of the Gospel, he declares that "death is to us change, not consummation, and the commencement of a new existence, corresponding in character to the deeds which we have done in the body."

The Black Priest, in *Anne of Geierstein*, reminds us not only of the certainty of death, but of the possibility of its approach at any moment; and from the most unexpected quarter. " Death," he says, " waits upon life as surely as night upon day, or the shadow upon the sunbeam, though we know not from whence it is to come upon us." And in the following lines, prefixed to the twenty-fifth chapter of *The Fortunes of Nigel*, we have an intimation of how suddenly death may come and remove us for ever from all our cherished earthly associations and possessions—

> " Death finds us 'mid our playthings—snatches us,
> As a cross nurse might do a wayward child,
> From all our toys and baubles. His rough call
> Unlooses all our favourite ties on earth;
> And well if they are such as may be answered
> In yonder world, where all is judged of truly."

Well, indeed; "the readiness is all," as Hamlet says.

How solicitous for the immortal welfare of the soul, is Catherine Glover when the atheistic apothecary, Dwining, speaks of the probably near approach of his death, and his soon being in "the place where all mysteries shall be cleared."

"Old man," said Catherine, "if thou be indeed so near the day of thy deserved doom, other thoughts were far wholesomer than the vain-glorious ravings of a vain philosophy. Ask to see a holy man."

Equally solicitous is Harry Bertram, in *Guy Mannering*, as he looks upon the dying Meg Merrilies. "Is there no clergyman near," he anxiously asks, "to assist this unhappy woman's devotions?" When the clergyman is brought, he seeks to administer consolation and comfort, but the patient seems to mind him not. When all is over, Bertram takes the clergyman's hands and asks if he has any hope in her death.

"My dear sir," says the good man, "I trust this poor woman had remaining sense to feel and join in the import of my prayers.　To Him who can alone weigh our crimes and errors against our efforts towards virtue, we consign her with awe, but not without hope."

Perhaps the saddest death described by Sir Walter is that of the Bohemian juggler and fortune-teller in *Quentin Durward*.　Deeply interested in his welfare, and anxious to get the poor man into a proper frame of mind in the prospect of immediate execution, Durward speaks to him of his immortal soul.

"Name not that word again," said Hayraddin, his countenance assuming a dreadful expression; "there is— there can be—there shall be—no such thing!　It is a dream of priestcraft!"

"Unhappy—most unhappy being!　Think better!— let me speed for a priest. . . .　What canst thou expect, dying in such opinions, and impenitent?"

In vain, however, does Quentin Durward reason and plead with the unhappy man, who died in the hope and expectation that his humanity would dissolve into the general mass of nature, and be no more.

But we turn from such deaths as those of the atheistic apothecary and the materialistic Bohemian to others full of hope, and anticipation of a better world when all is over here.　Feeling his end approaching, David Deans expressed his gratitude to God for all the blessings and mercies he had received and enjoyed.　He prayed earnestly for his affectionate daughter and family, and in a pathetic petition, too well understood by those who knew the circumstances, "he besought the Shepherd of souls, while gathering His flock, not to forget the little one that had strayed from the fold, and even then might be in the hands of the ravening wolf." In the full spirit of charity with all men, the aged saint, about an hour after pouring out these last earthly prayers, peacefully "slept in the Lord."

In the following incidents we get, expressed in the simplest possible way, Sir Walter's trust and belief in the reality of a future state. Queen Margaret, in *Anne of Geierstein*, speaks of her departed husband as having exchanged the state of "a suffering saint upon earth for that of a glorified saint in heaven." The clergyman comforts the Highland widow's son under sentence of military execution, and reminds him that he will soon exchange his "short and miserable existence here, for a life in which you will experience neither sorrow nor pain."

Widow MacCandlish, in *Guy Mannering*, speaks of her husband having been called to a better place: so does Dame Glendinning of her husband; and Bailie Nicol Jarvie thinks of his deceased father, not as dead or lost to him, but in a state of happiness elsewhere.

What strength and consolation does Ephraim Macbriar, the preacher in *Old Mortality*, find in his hope of another and a better world, during the awful tortures to which he was subjected before the Scottish Privy Council at Edinburgh! In answer to the Lord President, who asks if the martyr has anything to say, Macbriar replies, "I forgive you, my Lords, for what you have appointed and I have sustained. And why should I not? You send me to a happy exchange—to the company of angels, and the spirits of the just, for that of frail dust and ashes; ye send me from darkness into day; from mortality to immortality; and, in a word, from earth to heaven! If the thanks, therefore, and pardon of a dying man can do you good, take them at my hand, and may your last moments be as happy as mine."

With a countenance all radiant from joy and gladness, the martyr was taken to the place of execution where, within an hour after receiving sentence of death, he died in the "sure and certain hope of the resurrection to eternal life through our Lord Jesus Christ."

Our present study is finished. During its entire course we have followed Sir Walter, not as a novelist, but for the purpose of seeing in what way he uses the sacred Scriptures in the composition of his world-famous tales and romances. The wealth of Scripture illustration and teaching, which he employs so happily, and in such rich abundance, is, no doubt, the outcome and the result of the strictly religious education which Sir Walter, as a child, received from his affectionate parents. This lay at the bottom of all his education, and coloured, more or less, all that he ever wrote. The old ballads, songs, and legends which he afterwards read and collected so eagerly, reappeared in the *Border Minstrelsy* and the *Lay of the Last Minstrel:* the recollection of a tour in the Highlands blossomed and bore fruit in *The Lady of the Lake* and *Waverley:* the repetition of some marvellous tale or affecting incident suggested the remaining volumes of the series. But, underlying all these ballads, songs, legends, recollections, tales, and incidents, were the earlier lessons, · scenes, and incidents of Bible history, which, in some form or other, crop out in every novel of the Waverley series. In some form or other, too, Scott's moral and religious character impresses itself upon all his writings; and if we have learned anything at all in this new study of the Waverley Novels, we have surely learned to feel how true are Mr. Lockhart's words when he says that Sir Walter's "works teach the practical lessons of morality and Christianity in the most captivating form—unobtrusively and unaffectedly."

INDEX

Printed by R. & R. CLARK, *Edinburgh.*